THE SON OF MONTE-CRISTO

ALEXANDRE DUMAS

THE SON OF MONTE-CRISTO

VOLUME TWO

Fredonia Books
Amsterdam, The Netherlands

The Son of Monte-Cristo
Volume Two

by
Alexandre Dumas

ISBN 1-58963-212-5

Reprinted from the 1902 edition

Fredonia Books
Amsterdam, The Netherlands
http://www.fredoniabooks.com

CONTENTS

THE SON OF MONTE-CRISTO

CHAPTER I

FANFARO'S ADVENTURES

SPERO, the son of Monte-Cristo, was peacefully sleeping in another room, while, gathered around the table in the dining-room of Fanfaro's house, were Monte-Cristo, Miss Clary, Madame Caraman, Coucou, and Albert de Morcerf, ready to listen to the story of Fanfaro's adventures, which, as narrated at the close of the preceding volume, he was about to begin.

The following is Fanfaro's narrative:

It was about the middle of December, 1813, that a solitary horseman was pursuing the road which leads through the Black Forest from Breisach to Freiburg. The rider was a man in the prime of life. He wore a long brown overcoat, reaching to his knees, and shoes fastened with steel buckles. His powdered hair was combed back and tied with a black band, while his head was covered with a cap that had a projecting peak. The evening came, and darkness spread over the valley: the Black Forest had not received its name in vain. A few miles from Freiburg there stands a lonely hill, named the Emperor's Chair. Dark masses of basalt form the steps of this natural throne; tall evergreens stretch their branches protectingly over the hill. A fresh mountain air is cast about by the big trees, and the north wind is in eternal battle with this giant, which it bends but can never break.

Pierre Labarre, the solitary horseman, was the confidential servant of the Marquis de Fougereuse, and the darker the road became the more uncomfortable he felt. He continually spurred on his horse, but the tired animal at every stride struck against tree roots which lined the narrow path.

"Quick, Margotte," said Pierre to the animal, "you know how anxiously we are awaited, and besides we are the bearers of good news."

The animal appeared to understand the words, began to trot again at a smart pace, and for a time all went well.

Darker and darker grew the night, the storm raged fiercer and fiercer, and the roar of the distant river sounded like the tolling of church-bells.

Pierre had now reached a hill, upon which century-old lindens stretched their leafless branches toward heaven; the road parted at this point, and the rider suddenly reined in his horse. One of the paths led to Breisach, the other to Gundebfingen. Pierre rose in the stirrups and cautiously glanced about, but then he shook his head and muttered:

"Curious, I can discover nothing, and yet I thought I heard the clatter of a horse's hoofs."

He mechanically put his hand in his breast-pocket and nodded his head in a satisfied way.

"The portfolio is still in the right place," he whispered. "Forward, Margotte—we must get under shelter."

But just as the steed was about to start, the rider again heard the sound of a horse's hoofs on the frozen ground, and in a twinkling a horse bounded past Pierre like the wind. It was the second rider who had rushed past the servant at such a rapid gait.

Pierre was not superstitious, yet he felt his heart move quickly when the horseman galloped past him, and old legends about spectres rose up in his mind. Perhaps the rider was the wild huntsman of whom he had heard so much, or what was more likely, it was no spectre, but a robber. This last possibility frightened Pierre very much. He bent down and took a pistol out of the saddle-bag. He cocked the trigger and continued on his way, while he muttered to himself:

"Courage, old boy; if it should come to the worst you will kill your man."

Pierre rode on unembarrassed, and had reached a road which would bring him to Freiburg in less than half an hour. Suddenly a report was heard, and Pierre uttered a hollow groan. A bullet had struck his breast.

Bending with pain over his horse's neck he looked about. The bushes parted and a man enveloped in a long cloak sprung forth and rushed upon the servant. The moment he put his hand on the horse's rein, Pierre raised himself and in an angry voice exclaimed:

"Not so quickly, bandits!"

At the same moment he aimed his pistol and fired. The bandit uttered a moan and recoiled. But he did not sink to the ground as Pierre had expected. He disappeared in the darkness. A second shot fired after him struck in the nearest tree, and Pierre swore roundly.

"Confound the Black Forest," he growled as he rode

along; "if I had not fortunately had my leather portfolio in my breast-pocket, I would be a dead man now! The scoundrel must have eyes like an owl: he aimed as well as if he had been on a rifle range. Hurry along, Margotte, or else a second highwayman may come and conclude what the other began."

The horse trotted along, and Pierre heard anew the gallop of a second animal. The bandit evidently desired to keep his identity unknown.

"Curious," muttered Pierre, "I did not see his face, but his voice seemed familiar."

CHAPTER II

THE GOLDEN SUN

M R. SCHWAN, the host of the Golden Sun at Sainte-Ame, a market town in the Vosges, was very busy. Although the month of February was not an inviting one, three travellers had arrived that morning at the Golden Sun, and six more were expected.

Schwan had that morning made an onslaught on his chicken coop, and, while his servants were robbing the murdered hens of their feathers, the host walked to the door of the inn and looked at the sky.

A loud laugh, which shook the windows of the inn, made Schwan turn round hurriedly: at the same moment two muscular arms were placed upon his shoulders, and a resounding kiss was pressed upon his brown cheek.

"What is the meaning of this?" stammered the host, trying in vain to shake off the arms which held him. "The devil take me, but these arms must belong to my old friend Firejaws," exclaimed Schwan, now laughing; and hardly had he spoken the words than the possessor of the arms, a giant seven feet tall, cheerfully said:

"Well guessed, Father Schwan. Firejaws in *propria persona*."

While the host was cordially welcoming the new arrival, several servants hurried from the kitchen, and soon a bottle of wine and two glasses stood upon the cleanly scoured inn table.

"Make yourself at home, my boy," said Schwan, gayly, as he filled the glasses.

The giant, whose figure was draped in a fantastical costume, grinned broadly, and did justice to the host's invitation. The sharply curved nose and the large mouth with dazzling teeth, the full blond hair, and the broad, muscular shoulders, were on a colossal scale. The tight-fitting coat of the athlete was dark red, the trousers were of black velvet, and richly embroidered shirt-sleeves made up the wonderful appearance of the man.

"Father Schwan, I must embrace you once more," said the giant after a pause, as he stretched out his arms.

"Go ahead, but do not crush me," laughed the host.

"Are you glad to see me again?"

"I should say so. How are you getting along?"

"Splendidly, as usual; my breast is as firm still as if it were made of iron," replied the giant, striking a powerful blow upon his breast.

"Has business been good?"

"Oh, I am satisfied."

"Where are your people?"

"On their way here. The coach was too slow for me, so I left them behind and went on in advance."

"Well, and—your wife?" asked the host, hesitatingly.

The giant closed his eyes and was silent; Schwan looked down at his feet, and after a pause continued:

"Things don't go as they should, I suppose?"

"Let me tell you something," replied the giant, firmly;

"if it is just the same to you, I would rather not talk on that subject."

"Ah, really? Poor fellow! Yes, these women!'

"Not so quickly, cousin—my deceased wife was a model of a woman."

"True; when she died I knew you would never find another one to equal her."

"My little Caillette is just like her."

"Undoubtedly. When I saw the little one last, about six years ago, she was as pretty as a picture."

"She is seventeen now, and still very handsome."

"What are the relations between your wife and you?"

"They couldn't be better; Rolla cannot bear the little one."

The host nodded.

"Girdel," he said, softly, "when you told me that day that you were going to marry the 'Cannon Queen,' I was frightened. The woman's look displeased me. Does she treat Caillette badly?"

"She dare not touch a hair of the child's head," hissed the giant, "or—"

"Do not get angry; but tell me rather whether Bobichel is still with you?"

"Of course."

"And Robeckal?"

"His time is about up."

"That would be no harm; and the little one?"

"The little one?" laughed Girdel. "Well, he is about six feet."

"You do not say so! Is he still so useful?"

"Cousin," said the giant, slowly, "Fanfaro is a treasure! Do you know, he is of a different breed from us; no, do not contradict me, I know what I am speaking about. I am an athlete; I have arms like logs and hands like claws, therefore it is no wonder that I perform difficult exercises; but Fanfaro is tender and fine; he has arms and hands like a girl, and skin like velvet, yet he can stand more than I can. He can down two of me, yet he is soft and shrewd, and has a heart of gold."

"Then you love him as much as you used to do?" laughed the host, in a satisfied way.

"Much more if it is possible; I—"

The giant stopped short, and when Schwan followed the direction of his eye, he saw that the wagon which carried the fortune of Cesar Girdel had rolled into the courtyard.

Upon four high wheels a large open box swung to and fro; on its four sides were various colored posts, which served to carry the curtains, which shut out the interior of the box from the eyes of the curious world. The red and white curtains were now cast aside, and one could see a mass of iron poles, rags, weights, empty barrels, hoops with and without purple silk paper, the use of which was not clear to profane eyes.

The driver was dressed in yellow woollen cloth, and could at once be seen to be a clown; he wore a high pasteboard cap adorned with bells, and while he swung the whip with his right hand he held a trumpet in his left, which he occasionally put to his lips and blew a blast loud enough to wake the very stones. The man's face was terribly thin, his nose was long and straight, and small dark eyes sparkled maliciously from under his bushy eyebrows.

Behind Bobichel, for this was the clown's name, Caillette, the giant's daughter, was seated. Her father had not overpraised his daughter: the tender, rosy face of the young girl had wonderfully refined features; deep blue soulful eyes lay half hidden under long, dark eyelashes, and gold-blond locks fell over her white neck. Caillette appeared to be enjoying herself, for her silvery laugh sounded continually, while she was conversing with Bobichel.

At the rear of the wagon upon a heap of bedding sat a woman whose dimensions were fabulous. She was about forty-five years of age; her face looked as if it had been chopped with an axe; the small eyes almost disappeared beneath the puffed cheeks, and the broad breast as well as the thick, red arms and claw-like hands were repulsive in the extreme. Bushy hair of a dirty yellow color hung in a confused mass over the shoulders of the virago, and her blue cloth jacket and woollen dress were full of grease spots.

Robeckal walked beside the wagon. He was of small stature, but nervous and muscular. The small face lighted up by shrewd eyes had a yellowish color; the long, thin arms would have done honor to a gorilla, and the elasticity of his bones was monkeyish in the extreme. He wore a suit of faded blue velvet, reddish brown hair only half covered his head, and a mocking laugh lurked about the corners of his lips while he was softly speaking to Rolla.

Bobichel now jumped from the wagon. Girdel hurried from the house and cordially exclaimed:

"Welcome, children; you have remained out long and are not hungry, are you?"

"I could eat pebblestones," replied Bobichel, laughing. "Ah, there is Schwan too. Well, old boy, how have you been getting along?"

While the host and the clown were holding a conversation, Girdel went to the wagon and stretched out his arms.

"Jump, daughter," he laughingly said.

Caillette did not hesitate long; she rose on her pretty toes and swung herself over the edge of the wagon into her father's arms. The latter kissed her heartily on both cheeks, and then placed her on the ground. He then glanced around, and anxiously asked:

"Where is Fanfaro?"

"Here, Papa Firejaws," came cheerfully from the interior of the wagon, and at the same moment a dark head appeared in sight above a large box. The head was followed by a beautifully formed body, and placing his hand lightly on the edge of the wagon, Fanfaro swung gracefully to the ground.

"Madcap, can't you stop turning?" scolded Girdel, laughingly; "go into the house and get your breakfast!"

Caillette, Fanfaro, and Bobichel went away; Girdel turned to his wife and pleasantly said:

"Rolla, I will now help you down."

Rolla looked at him sharply, and then said in a rough, rasping voice:

"Didn't I call you, Robeckal? Come and help me down!"

Robeckal, who had been observing the chickens in the courtyard, slowly approached the wagon.

"What do you want?" he asked.

"Help me down," repeated Rolla.

Girdel remained perfectly calm, but a careful observer might have noticed the veins on his forehead swell. He measured Rolla and Robeckal with a peculiar look, and before his look Rolla's eyes fell.

"Robeckal, are you coming?" cried the virago, impatiently.

"What do you wish here?" asked Girdel, coolly, as Robeckal turned to Rolla.

"What do I wish here?" replied Robeckal; "Madame Girdel has done me the honor to call me, and—"

"And you are thinking rather long about it," interrupted Rolla, gruffly.

"I am here," growled Robeckal, laying his hand upon the edge of the wagon.

"No further!" commanded Girdel, in a threatening voice.

"Ha! who is going to prevent me?"

"I, wretch!" thundered Firejaws, in whose eyes a warning glance shone.

"Bah! you are getting angry about nothing," said Robeckal, mockingly, placing his other hand on the edge of the wagon.

"Strike him, Robeckal!" cried Rolla, urgingly.

Robeckel raised his right hand, but at the same moment the athlete stretched him on the ground with a blow of his fist; he could thank his stars that Girdel had not struck him with his full force, or else Robeckal would never have got up again. With a cry of rage he sprung up and threw himself upon the giant, who waited calmly for him with his arms quietly folded over his breast; a sword shone in Robeckal's hand, and how it happened neither he nor Rolla knew, but immediately after he lay on top of the wagon, close to the Cannon Queen.

"Enough of your rascality, Robeckal," said the voice of him who had thrown the angry man upon the wagon.

"I thought the wretched boy would come between us again," hissed Rolla; and without waiting for any further help she sprung from the wagon and rushed upon Fanfaro, for he it was who had come to Girdel's assistance.

"Back, Rolla!" exclaimed Firejaws, hoarsely, as he laid his iron fist upon his wife's shoulder. Schwan came to the door and cordially said:

"Where are your comrades? The soup is waiting."

Robeckal hurriedly glided from the wagon, and approaching close to Rolla, he whispered a few words in her ear.

"Let me go, Girdel," said the giantess. "Who would take such a stupid joke in earnest? Come, I am hungry."

Firejaws looked at his wife in amazement. Her face, which had been purple with anger, was now overspread by a broad grin, and shrugging his shoulders, Girdel walked toward the house. Fanfaro followed, and Robeckal and Rolla remained alone.

"We must make an end of it, Rolla," grumbled Robeckal.

"I am satisfied. The sooner the better!"

"Good. I shall do it to-night. See that you take a little walk afterward on the country road. I will meet you there and tell you my plan."

"Do so. Let us go to dinner now, I am hungry."

When Rolla and Robeckal entered the dining-room, Girdel, Caillette, Bobichel, and Fanfaro were already sitting at table, and Schwan was just bringing in a hot, steaming dish.

CHAPTER III

OLD AND NEW ACQUAINTANCES

WHILE the hungry guests were eating, the door at the back of the large dining-room was very softly opened. None of the strangers observed this, but the host, whose eyes were all over, went toward the door, at the threshold of which stood a man about forty years of age. The man was small and lean, and wore a brown overcoat trimmed with fur; the coat was cut out at the bosom and allowed a yellow vest and sky-blue tie to be seen. Trousers of dark-blue cloth reached to the knee, and his riding-boots, with spurs, completed the wonderfully made toilet.

The man's face had a disagreeable expression. He had deep squinting eyes, a large mouth, a broad nose, and long, bony fingers.

When the host approached the stranger he bowed and respectfully asked:

"How can I serve you, sir?"

The stranger did not reply; his gaze was directed toward the table and the guests, and the host, who had observed his look, again repeated the question.

The stranger walked into the middle of the room, and, seating himself at a table, said:

"Bring me a glass of brandy."

"I thought—I believed—" began the host.

"Do as I told you. I am expecting some one. Get a good dinner ready, and as soon as—the other one arrives, you can serve it."

"It shall be attended to," nodded Schwan, who thought the man was the steward of some big lord.

Just as the host was about to leave the room, the door was opened again and two more travellers entered. The first comer threw a look at the new arrivals, and a frown crossed his ugly face.

The last two who entered were entirely dissimilar. One of them, to judge from his upright bearing, must have formerly been a soldier. He was dressed plainly in civilian's clothes, and his bushy white mustache gave his face a threatening look; the deep blue eyes, however, served to soften the features. The other man was evidently a carman; he wore a blue linen blouse, leathern shoes, knee-breeches and a large round hat. When the host praised his kitchen to the new-comers, his words fell on fertile ground, for when he asked the first guest whether he would like to have some ham and eggs, the proposition was at once accepted.

"Where shall I serve the gentlemen?"

For a moment there was deep silence. The guests had just perceived the first comer and did not seem to be impressed by his appearance. Nevertheless, the man who looked like a soldier decided that they should be served at one of the side tables. When he said this Girdel looked up, and his features showed that the new-comers were not strangers to him. The man in the brown overcoat laughed mockingly when he perceived that the two strangers chose a table as far away from his as possible. He looked fixedly at them, and when Schwan brought him the brandy he had ordered, he filled his glass and emptied it at one gulp. He then took some newspapers out of his pocket and began to read, holding the pages in such a way as to conceal his face.

The host now brought the ham and eggs. As he placed them on the table, the carman hastily asked:

"How far is it, sir, from here to Remiremont?"

"To Remiremont? Ah, I see the gentlemen do not belong to the vicinity. To Remiremont is about two hours."

"So much the better; we can get there then in the course of the afternoon."

"That is a question," remarked Schwan.

"How so? What do you mean?"

"The road is very bad," he replied.

"That won't be so very dangerous."

"Oh, but the floods!"

"What's the matter with the floods?" said the old soldier.

"The enormous rainfall of the last few weeks has swollen all the mountain lakes," said the host, vivaciously, "and the road to Remiremont is under water, so that it would be impossible for you to pass."

"That would be bad," exclaimed the carman, excitedly.

"It would be dangerous," remarked the old soldier.

"Oh, yes, sir; last year two travellers were drowned between Sainte-Ame and Remiremont; to tell the truth, the gentlemen looked like you!"

"Thanks for the compliment!"

"The gentlemen probably had no guide," said the carman.

"No."

"Well, we shall take a guide along; can you get one for us?"

"To-morrow, but not to-day."

"Why not?"

"Because my people are busy; but to-morrow it can be done."

In the meantime, the acrobats had finished their meal. Girdel arose, and, drawing close to the travellers, said:

"If the gentlemen desire, they can go with us to-morrow to Remiremont."

"Oh, that is a good idea," said the host gleefully; "accept, gentlemen. If Girdel conducts you, you can risk it without any fear."

In spite of the uncommon appearance of the athlete, the strangers did not hesitate to accept Girdel's offer; they exchanged glances, and the soldier said:

"Accepted, sir. We are strangers here, and would have surely lost ourselves. When do you expect to go?"

"To-morrow morning. To-night we give a performance here, and with the dawn of day we start for Remiremont."

"Good. Can I invite you now to join us in a glass of wine?"

Girdel protested more politely than earnestly; Schwan brought a bottle and glasses, and the giant sat down by the strangers.

While this was going on, the first comer appeared to be deeply immersed in the paper, though he had not lost a word of the conversation, and as Firejaws took a seat near the strangers, he began again to laugh mockingly.

Robeckal and Rolla now left the dining-room, while Fanfaro, Caillette and Bobichel still remained seated; a minute later Robeckal returned, and drawing near to Girdel, softly said to him:

"Master."

"Well?"

"Do you need me?"

"What for?"

"To erect the booth?"

"No, Fanfaro and Bobichel will attend to it."

"Then good-by for the present."

Robeckal left. Hardly had the door closed behind him than the man in the brown overcoat stopped reading his paper and left the room too.

"One word, friend," he said to Robeckal.

"Quick, what does it concern?"

"Twenty francs for you, if you answer me properly."

"Go ahead."

"What is this Firejaws?"

"Athlete, acrobat, wrestler—anything you please."

"What is his right name?"

"Girdel, Cesar Girdel."

"Do you know the men with whom he just spoke?"

"No."

"You hate Girdel?"

"Who told you so, and what is it your business?"

"Ah, a great deal. If you hate him we can make a common thing of it. You belong to his troupe?"

"Yes, for the present."

"Bah, long enough to earn a few gold pieces."

"What is asked of me for that?"

"You? Not much. You shall have an opportunity to pay back the athlete everything you owe him in the way of hate, and besides you will be well rewarded."

Robeckal shrugged his shoulders.

"Humbug," he said, indifferently.

"No, I mean it seriously."

"I should like it to be done," replied Robeckal, dryly.

"Here are twenty francs in advance."

Robeckal stretched out his hand for the gold piece, let it fall into his pocket, and disappeared without a word.

"You have come too late, my friend," he laughed to himself. "Girdel will be a dead man before the morrow comes, as sure as my name is Robeckal."

In the meantime Girdel continued to converse with the two gentlemen; Schwan went here and there, and Fanfaro, Caillette and Bobichel were waiting for the athlete's orders for the evening performance.

"How goes it?" asked the carman, now softly.

"Good," replied Girdel, in the same tone.

"The peasants are prepared?"

"Yes. The seed is ripe. They are only waiting for the order to begin to sow.

"We must speak about this matter at greater length, but not here. Did you notice the man who was reading the paper over there a little while ago?"

"Yes; he did not look as if he could instil confidence into any one; I think he must be a lackey."

"He could be a spy too; when can we speak to one another undisturbed?"

"This evening after the performance, either in your room or in mine."

"Let it be in yours; we can wait until the others sleep; let your door remain open, Girdel."

"I will not fail to do so."

"Then it is settled; keep mum. No one must know of our presence here."

"Not even Fanfaro?"

"No, not for any price."

"But you do not distrust him? He is a splendid fellow—"

"So much the better for him; nevertheless, he must not know anything. I can tell you the reason; we wish to speak about him; we desire to intrust certain things with him."

"You couldn't find a better person."

"I believe it. Good-by, now, until to-night."

"*Au revoir!*"

"Sir," said the carman, now aloud, "we accept your proposal with thanks, and hope to reach Remiremont to-morrow with your help."

"You shall."

Girdel turned now to Fanfaro, and gayly cried:

"To work, my son; we must dazzle the inhabitants of Sainte-Ame! Cousin Schwan, have we got permission to give our performance? You are the acting mayor."

"I am," replied Schwan; "hand in your petition; here is some stamped paper."

"Fanfaro, write what is necessary," ordered Girdel; "you know I'm not much in that line."

"If you are not a man of the pen, you are a man of the heart," laughed Fanfaro, as he quickly wrote a few lines on the paper.

"Flatterer," scolded Girdel. "Forward, Bobichel; bring me the work-box; the people will find out to-night that they will see something."

CHAPTER IV

BROTHER AND SISTER

HALF an hour later the inhabitants of Sainte-Ame crowded about the open place in front of the Golden Sun. They seldom had an opportunity of seeing anything like this, for very few travelling shows ever visited the small Lorraine village; and with almost childish joy the spectators gazed at Bobichel, Fanfaro, and Girdel, who were engaged in erecting the booth. The work went on briskly. The posts which had been run into the ground were covered with many-colored cloths, and a hurriedly arranged wooden roof protected the interior of the tent from the weather. Four wooden stairs led to the right of the entrance, where the box-office was; this latter was made of a primitive wooden table, on which was a faded velvet cover embroidered with golden arabesques and cabalistic signs. All the outer walls of the booth were covered with yellow bills, upon which could be read that "Signor Fire-jaws" would lift with his teeth red-hot irons of fabulous weight, swallow burning lead, and perform the most startling acrobatic tricks. Rolla, the Cannon Queen, would catch cannon balls shot from a gun, and do other tricks; at the same time the bill said she would eat pigeons alive, and with their feathers on. Caillette, the "daughter of the

air," as she was called, would send the spectators into ec-
stasies by her performance on the tight rope, and sing
songs. Robeckal, the "descendant of the old Moorish
kings," would swallow swords, eat glass, shave kegs with
his teeth; and Fanfaro would perform on the trapeze, give
his magic acts, and daze the public with his extraordinary
productions. A pyramid, formed of all the members of the
troupe, at the top of which Caillette shone with a rose in
her hand, stood at the bottom of the bills in red colors, and
was gazed upon by the peasants in open-mouthed wonder.
The hammering which went on in the interior of the booth
sounded to them like music, and they could hardly await
the night, which was to bring them so many magnificent
things.

Girdel walked up and down in a dignified way and
the crowd respectfully made way for him, while the
giant, in stentorian tones, gave the orders to Fanfaro
and Bobichel.

Bobichel's name was not on the bills; he was to surprise the public as a clown, and therefore his name was
never mentioned. He generally amused the spectators
in a comical way, and always made them laugh; even
now, when he had finished his work, he mingled with
the peasants and delighted them with his jokes.

Fanfaro and Caillette were still engaged constructing
the booth. The young man arranged the wooden seats
and the giant's daughter hung the colored curtains,
which covered the bare walls, putting here and there
artificial flowers on them. Sometimes Caillette would
pause in her work, to look at Fanfaro with her deep
blue eyes.

Fanfaro was now done with the seats and began to

fasten two trapezes. They hung to a centre log by iron hooks, and were about twelve feet from the ground and about as far distant from each other.

Fanfaro lightly swung upon the centre log and hammered in the iron hooks with powerful blows.

The wonderfully fine-shaped body was seen to advantage in this position, and a sculptor would have enthusiastically observed the classical outlines of the young man, whose dark tights fitted him like a glove.

Fanfaro's hands and feet were as small as those of a woman, but, as Girdel had said, his muscles and veins were as hard as iron.

The iron hooks were fast now, and the young man swung himself upon a plank; he then glided down one trapeze, and with a quick movement grasped the other.

Like an arrow the slim body shot through the air, and then Fanfaro sprung lightly to the ground, while the trapeze flew back.

At the very moment the young man let go of the trapeze a faint scream was heard, and Caillette, deadly pale, stood next to Fanfaro.

"How you frightened me, you wicked fellow," said the young girl, drawing a deep breath.

"Were you really frightened, Caillette? I thought you would have got used to my exercises long ago."

"I ought to be so," pouted Caillette, pressing her hands to her fast-beating heart, "but every time I see you fly, fear seizes hold of me and I unconsciously cry aloud. Oh, Fanfaro, if an accident should happen to you—I would not survive it."

"Little sister, you are needlessly alarming yourself."

Caillette held down her pretty little head and the hot blood rushed to her velvety cheeks, while her hands nervously clutched each other.

"Caillette, what ails you?" asked Fanfaro.

"Oh—tell me, Fanfaro, why do you always call me 'little sister'?"

"Does the expression displease you, mademoiselle?" laughingly said the young man; "is it the word 'little,' or the word 'sister'?"

"I did not say the expression displeased me."

"Should I call you my big sister?"

"Why do you call me sister at all?"

A cloud spread over the young man's face.

"Did we not grow up together like brother and sister?" he asked; "you were six years old when your father took the deserted boy to his home."

"But you are not my brother," persisted Caillette.

"Perhaps not in the sense commonly associated with the term, but yet I love you like a brother. Doesn't this explanation please you?"

"Yes and no. I wished—"

"What would you wish?"

"I had rather not say it," whispered Caillette, and hastily throwing her arms about Fanfaro she kissed him heartily.

Fanfaro did not return the kiss; on the contrary he turned away and worked at the trapeze cord. He divined what was going on in Caillette, as many words hastily spoken had told the young man that the young girl loved him not as the sister loves the brother, but with a more passionate love. Caillette was still unaware of it, but every day, every hour could explain her feel-

ings to her, and Fanfaro feared that moment, for he—
did not love her.

How was this possible? He could hardly account for
it himself. Caillette was so charming, and yet he could
not think of the lovely creature as his wife; and as an
honest man it did not enter his mind to deceive the
young girl as to his feelings.

"Caillette," he said, now trying to appear cheerful,
"we must hurry up with our preparations, or the performance will begin before we are done."

Caillette nodded, and taking her artificial flowers
again in her hand, she began to separate them. At the
same time the door opened and Firejaws appeared in
company with two ladies. Fanfaro and Caillette glanced
at the unexpected guests and heard the elderly lady
say:

"Irene, what new caprice is it that brings you here,
and what will the countess say if she hears of it?"

"Madame Ursula, spare your curtain lectures," laughed
the young lady; "and if you cannot do so, you are free
to return to the castle."

"God forbid," exclaimed Madame Ursula in affright.

She was a perfect type of the governess, with long
thin features, pointed nose, small lips, gray locks, and
spectacles. She wore a hat which fell to her neck, and a
long colored shawl hung over her shoulders.

The appearance of the young lady compared very
favorably with that of the duenna. A dark-blue riding
costume sat tightly on a magnificent form; a brown
velvet hat with a long white feather sat coquettishly on
her dark locks; fresh red lips, sparkling black eyes, a
classically formed nose, and finely curved lips completed

her charming appearance. The young lady appeared to be about eighteen or nineteen years old; a proud smile hovered about her lips and the dark eyes looked curiously about.

Fanfaro and Caillette paused at their work, and now the young girl exclaimed in a clear bell-like voice:

"Monsieur Girdel, would it be possible for me to secure a few places for this evening, that is, some that are hid from the rest of the spectators?"

"H'm—that would be difficult," said Girdel, looking about.

"Of course I shall pay extra for the seats," continued the young lady.

"We have only one price for the front rows," said Firejaws, simply; "they cost twenty sous and the rear seats ten sous."

The governess sighed sorrowfully; Irene took an elegant purse from her pocket and pressed it in Girdel's hand.

"Take the money," she said, "and do what I say."

"I will try to get you the seats you desire, mademoiselle," he said politely, "but only for the usual price. Fanfaro," he said, turning to the young man, "can't we possibly fix up a box?"

Fanfaro drew near, and the young lady with open wonder gazed at the beautiful youth.

"What's the trouble, Papa Girdel?" he said.

Before the giant could speak Irene said:

"I do not ask very much. I would like to look at the performance, but naturally would not like to sit with the crowd. You know, peasants and such common people—"

"H'm!" growled Girdel.

"It is impossible," said Fanfaro, coolly.

"Impossible?" repeated the young lady in amazement.

"But, Fanfaro," interrupted Girdel, "I should think we could do it. A few boards, a carpet, and the thing is done."

"Perhaps, but I shall not touch a finger to it."

"You refuse?" exclaimed Irene. "Why, if I may ask?"

"Bravo, Fanfaro!" whispered Caillette, softly.

"Will you answer my question, monsieur —— I do not know your name?" said Irene, impatiently.

"I am called Fanfaro," remarked the young man.

"Well then, Monsieur Fanfaro," began Irene, with a mocking laugh, "why do you refuse to lend your master a helping hand?"

"His master?" replied Girdel, with flaming eyes; "excuse me, mademoiselle, but you have been incorrectly informed."

"Come, Papa Girdel," laughed Fanfaro, "I will tell the young lady my reasons, and I think you will approve of them. The public of 'peasants,' and such 'common people,' who are so repulsive to you, mademoiselle, that you do not desire to touch them with the seam of your dress, admire us and provide us with our sustenance. The hands which applaud us are coarse, I cannot deny it; but in spite of this, we regard their applause just as highly as that given to us by people whose hands are incased in fine kid gloves. To give you an especial box, mademoiselle, would be an insult to the peasants, and why should we do such a thing? Am I right or not?"

While Fanfaro was speaking, Irene looked steadily at

his handsome face. The governess muttered something about impertinence. When the young man looked up, Irene softly said:

"That was a sharp lesson."

"No; I merely told you my opinion."

"Good. Now let me give you my answer; I will come this evening!"

"I thought so," replied Fanfaro simply.

CHAPTER V

MASTER AND SERVANT

WHEN the young lady and her governess left the booth and wended their way along the country road, the peasants respectfully made way for them and even Bobichel paused in his tricks. Irene held her little head sidewise as she walked through the crowd, while the governess marched with proudly uplifted head.

"Thank God," said Madame Ursula, "there is the carriage."

An elegant equipage came in sight, and a groom led a beautiful racer by the bridle.

"Step in, Madame Ursula," said Irene, laughing, as she vaulted into the saddle.

"But you promised me——"

"To be at the castle the same time as you," added the young lady. "And I shall keep my promise. Forward, Almanser!"

The horse flew along like an arrow, and Madame Ursula, sighing, got into the carriage, which started off in the same direction.

"Who is the handsome lady?" asked Bobichel.

"The richest heiress in Alsace and Lorraine, Mademoiselle de Salves," was the answer.

"Ah, she suits me," said the clown.

"Bah, she is as proud as a peacock," growled an old peasant.

"It is all the same to me," said a second peasant; "she is going to be married to a gentleman in Paris, and there she fits better."

A heavy mail-coach, which halted at the Golden Sun, interrupted the conversation. Mr. Schwan ran to the door to receive the travellers, and at the same moment the man in the brown overcoat appeared at the threshold of the door. Hardly had he seen the mail-coach than he hurried to open the door, and in a cringing voice said:

"Welcome, Monsieur le Marquis; my letter arrived, then, opportunely?"

The occupant of the coach nodded, and leaning on the other's arm, he got out. It was the Marquis of Fougereuse. He looked like a man prematurely old, whose bent back and wrinkled features made him look like a man of seventy, while in reality he was hardly fifty.

In the marquis's company was a servant named Simon, who, in the course of years, had advanced from the post of valet to that of steward.

"What does the gentleman desire?" asked the host, politely.

"Let the dinner be served in my room," ordered Simon; and, giving the marquis a nod, he strode to the upper story in advance of him.

The door which Simon opened showed an elegantly furnished room according to Schwan's ideas, yet the marquis appeared to pay no attention to his surroundings, for he hardly gazed around, and in a state of exhaustion sank into a chair. Simon stood at the window and looked out, while the host hurriedly set the table; when this was finished, Simon winked to Schwan and softly said:

"Leave the room now, and do not enter it until I call for you."

"If the gentlemen wish anything—"

"I know, I know," interrupted Simon, impatiently. "Listen to what I say. You would do well to keep silent about the purpose of my master's visit here. In case any one asks you, simply say you know nothing."

"Neither I do," remarked Schwan.

"So much the better, then you do not need to tell a lie; I advise you in your own interest not to say anything."

The host went away and growled on the stairs:

"Confound big people and their servants. I prefer guests like Girdel and his troupe."

As soon as the door had closed behind Schwan, Simon approached the marquis.

"We are alone, master," he said timidly.

"Then speak; have you discovered Pierre Labarre's residence?"

"Yes, master."

"But you have not gone to see him yet?"

"No, I kept within your orders."

"You were right. I must daze the old scoundrel through my sudden appearance; I hope to get the secret from him."

"Is everything better now, master?" asked Simon, after a pause.

"Better? What are you thinking of?" exclaimed the marquis, angrily. "Every one has conspired against me, and ruin is near at hand."

"But the protection of his majesty—"

"Bah! the protection of the king is useless, if the cabinet hate me. Besides, I have had the misfortune to anger Madame de Foucheres, and since then everything has gone wrong."

"The king cannot have forgotten what you did for him," said Simon.

"A few weeks ago I was driven to the wall by my creditors, and I went to the king and stated my case to him. Do you know what his answer was? 'Monsieur,' he said, earnestly, 'a Fougereuse should not demean himself by begging,' and with that he gave me a draft for eighty thousand francs! What are eighty thousand francs for a man in my position? A drop of water on a hot stove."

Simon nodded.

"But the vicomte," he observed; "his majesty showers favors upon him—"

"I am much obliged for the favors! Yes, my son is spoken of, but in what a way! The vicomte gambles, the vicomte is always in a scrape, the vicomte is the hero of the worst adventures—and kind friends never fail to tell me all about it! I hope his marriage will put a stop to all this business. Have you heard anything further of the De Salves ladies?"

"Not much, but enough. The estate of the young heiress is the largest for miles about, and she herself is a beauty of the first class."

"So much the better. Think of it, four millions! Oh, if this should be lost to us!"

"That will hardly be the case, Monsieur le Marquis; the marriage has been decided upon."

"Certainly, certainly, but then—if the old countess

should find out about our pecuniary embarrassments all would be lost. But no, I will not despair; Pierre Labarre must talk, and then—"

"Suppose he won't? Old people are sometimes obstinate."

"Have no fear, Simon, my methods have subdued many wills."

"Yes, yes, you are right, sir," laughed Simon.

"I can rely on you, then?"

"Perfectly so, sir. If it were necessary I would pick it up with ten Pierres!"

"You will find me grateful," said the marquis. "If Pierre Labarre gives the fortune to the Fougereuse and the vicomte becomes the husband of the countess, we will be saved."

"I know that you have brilliant prospects, my lord," replied Simon, "and I hope to win your confidence. The last few weeks I had an opportunity to do a favor to the family of my honored master."

"Really? You arouse my curiosity."

"My lord, Monsieur Franchet honored me with his confidence."

The marquis looked in amazement at his steward; Franchet was the superintendent of police. Recommended by the Duke of Montmorency, he was an especial favorite of the Society of Jesus. The Jesuits had spun their nets over the whole of France, and the secret orders emanated from the Rue de Vaugirard. Franchet had the reins of the police department in his hands, and used his power for the furtherance of the Jesuits' plans. The amazement which seized the marquis when he heard that his steward was the confidant of Franchet, was only natural; that

Simon would make a good spy, Fougereuse knew very well.

"Go on," he softly said, when Simon paused.

"Thanks to the superintendent's confidence in me," said Simon, "I am able to secure a much more influential position at court for Monsieur le Marquis than he has at present."

"And how are you going to perform the miracle?" asked the marquis, sceptically.

"By allowing Monsieur le Marquis to take part in my projects for the good of the monarchy."

"Speak more clearly," ordered the marquis, briefly.

"Directly."

Simon went close to his master, and whispered:

"There exists a dangerous conspiracy against the state. People wish to overturn the government and depose the king."

"Folly! that has been often desired."

"But this time it is serious. A republican society—"

"Do not speak to me about republicans!" exclaimed Fougereuse, angrily.

"Let me finish, Monsieur le Marquis. My news is authentic. The attempt will perhaps be made in a few weeks, and then it will be a question of *sauve qui peut!* Through a wonderful chain of circumstances the plans of the secret society came into my hands. I could go to the king now and name him all the conspirators who threaten his life, but what would be my reward? With a servant little ado is made. His information is taken, its truth secretly looked into and he is given a small sum of money with a letter saying that he must have been deceived. If the Marquis of Fougereuse, on the other hand, should come, he is immediately master of the situation. The matter is investigated, the king calls him his savior, and his fortune is made."

The marquis sprung up in excitement.

"And you are in a position to give me the plans of this society? You know who the conspirators are?" he exclaimed, with sparkling eyes.

"Yes, my lord."

"You would allow me to reap the profit of your discovery?"

"Yes, my lord; I am in the first place a faithful servant."

"Simon, let us stop this talk with turned down cards. What do you wish in return?"

"Nothing, my lord; I depend upon your generosity."

"You shall not have cause to regret it," said the marquis, drawing a deep breath. "Should I succeed in securing an influential position at court, you shall be the first to profit by it."

"Thanks, my lord. I know I can count on your word. To come back to Pierre Labarre, I think we should hunt him up as soon as possible."

"I am ready; where does he live?"

"At Vagney, about three hours distant."

"It is now three o'clock," said the marquis, pulling out his watch. "If we start now, we will be able to return to-night."

"Then I shall order horses at once!"

Simon went away, and the marquis remained behind thinking. No matter where he looked, the past, present and future were alike blue to him.

The old marquis had died in 1817, and the vicomte

had immediately set about to have the death of his
brother, which had taken place at Leigoutte in 1814,
confirmed.   Both the wife and the children of Jules
Fougere had disappeared since that catastrophe, and
so the Vicomte of Talizac, now Marquis of Fougereuse,
claimed possession of his father's estate.

But, strange to say, the legacy was far less than the
vicomte and Madeleine had expected, and, as they both
had contracted big debts on the strength of it, nothing
was left to them but to sell a portion of the grounds.

Had the marquis and his wife not lived so extrava-
gantly they would not have tumbled from one difficulty
into the other, but the desire to cut a figure in the
Faubourg St. Germain consumed vast sums, and what
the parents left over, the son gambled away and dissipated.

Petted and spoiled by his mother, the Vicomte de
Talizac was a fast youth before he had attained his
fifteenth year.   No greater pleasure could be given his
mother than to tell her, that her son was the leader of
the *jeunesse dorée.*   He understood how to let the money
fly, and when the marquis, alarmed at his son's ex-
travagance, reproached his wife, the latter cut him short
by saying:

"Once for all, Jean, my son was not made to save;
he is the heir of the Fougereuse, and must keep up his
position."

"But in this way we shall soon be beggars," complained the marquis.

"Is that my fault?" asked Madame Madeleine,
sharply.   "What good is it that you—put your brother
out of the way?   His portion of the fortune is kept

from you, and if you do not force Pierre Labarre to speak you will have to go without it."

"Then you think Pierre Labarre knows where the major part of my father's fortune is?" asked the marquis.

"Certainly. He and no one else has it in safe keeping, and if you do not hurry up, the old man might die, and we can look on."

The marquis sighed. This was not the first time Madeleine provoked him against Pierre Labarre, but the old man had disappeared since the death of his master, and it required a long time before Simon, the worthy assistant of the marquis, found out his residence.

In the meantime the position of the Fougereuses was getting worse and worse. At court murmurs were heard about swindling speculations with which the marquis's name was connected, and the vicomte did his best to drag the proud old name in the dust. A rescue was at hand, in a marriage of the vicomte with the young Countess of Salves, but this rescue rested on a weak footing, as a new escapade of "The Talizac Buckle," as the heir of the Fougereuse was mockingly called, might destroy the planned union.

Talizac was the hero of all the scandals of Paris; he sought and found his companions in very peculiar regions, and several duels he had fought had made his name, if not celebrated, at least disreputable.

This was the position of the marquis's affairs when Simon found Pierre Labarre; the marquis was determined not to return to Paris without first having settled the affair, and as Simon now returned to the room with the host, his master exclaimed:

"Are the horses ready?"

"No, my lord; the Cure has overflowed in consequence

of the heavy rains, and the road from here to Vagney is impassable.''

"Can we not reach Vagney by any other way?"

"No, my lord."

"Bah! the peasants exaggerate the danger so as to get increased prices for their services. Have you tried to get horses?"

"Yes, my lord; but unfortunately no one in the village except the host owns any."

"Then buy the host's horses."

"He refuses to give me the animals. An acrobat who came here this morning, and who owns two horses, refused to sell them to me."

"That looks almost like a conspiracy!" exclaimed the marquis.

"I think so too, and if I am permitted an advice—"

"Speak freely; what do you mean?"

"That the best thing we can do is to start at once on foot. If we hurry, we can reach Vagney this evening, and the rest will take care of itself."

"You are right," replied the marquis; "let us go."

Schwan was frightened when he heard of their intention, but the marquis remained determined, and the two were soon on the road.

"If no accident happens," growled the host to himself, "the Cure is a treacherous sheet of water; I wish they were already back again."

CHAPTER VI

THE PERFORMANCE

WHILE the marquis and Simon were starting on their journey, Robeckal and Rolla had met on the country road as appointed, and in a long whispered conversation had made their plans. They both hated Girdel, Caillette, Fanfaro and Bobichel, and their idea was to kill both Girdel and Fanfaro that very evening. Caillette could be attended to afterward, and Bobichel was of no importance. Rolla loved Robeckal, as far as it was possible for a person like her to love any one, and desired to possess him. Robeckal, on his side, thought it would not be a bad idea to possess Girdel's business along with its stock, with which he ungallantly reckoned Rolla and Caillette. Caillette especially he admired, but he was smart enough not to say a word to Rolla.

"Enter, ladies and gentlemen, enter," exclaimed Bobichel, as he stood at the box-office and cordially greeted the crowds of people.

"I wonder whether she will come?" muttered Caillette to herself.

"Everything is ready," whispered Robeckal to Rolla; the Cannon Queen nodded and threw dark scowls at Girdel and Fanfaro.

The quick gallop of a horse was now heard, and the next minute Irene de Salves stepped into the booth.

"Really, she has come," muttered Caillette in a daze, as she pressed her hand to her heart and looked searchingly at Fanfaro.

The latter looked neither to the right nor left. He was busy arranging Girdel's weights and iron poles, and Caillette, calmed by the sight, turned around.

When Irene took her seat a murmur ran through the crowded house. The Salves had always occupied an influential position in the country; the great estate of the family insured them power and influence at court, and they were closely attached to the monarchy.

Irene's grandfather, the old Count of Salves, had been guillotined in 1793; his son had served under Napoleon, and was killed in Russia when his daughter had hardly reached her third year. The count's loss struck the countess to the heart; she retired to her castle in the neighborhood of Remiremont and attended to the education of her child.

Irene grew up, and when she often showed an obstinacy and wildness strange in a girl, her mother would say, with tears in her eyes:

"Thank God, she is the picture of her father."

That nothing was done under the circumstances to curb Irene's impetuosity is easily understood. Every caprice of the young heiress was satisfied, and so it came about that the precocious child ruled the castle. She thought with money anything could be done, and more than once it happened that the young girl while hunting trod down the peasants' fields, consoling herself with the thought:

"Mamma gives these people money, and therefore it is all right."

When Irene was about fifteen years old her mother became dangerously ill, and remained several months in bed. She never recovered the use of her limbs, and day after day she remained in her arm-chair, only living in the sight of her daughter. When Irene entered the room the poor mother thought the sun was rising, and she never grew tired of looking in her daughter's clear eyes and listening to her silvery voice. The most singular contradictions reigned in Irene's soul; she could have cried bitterly one minute, and laughed aloud the next; for hours at a time she would sit dreaming at the window, and look out at the autumnal forest scenery, then spring up, hurry out, jump into the saddle and bound over hill and valley. Sometimes she would chase a beggar from the door, the next day overload him with presents; she spent nights at the bedside of a sick village child, and carried an old woman at the risk of her life, from a burning house; in short, she was an original.

A few months before, the lawyer who administered the countess's fortune had appeared at the castle and had locked himself up with her mother. When he left the castle the next day, the young lady was informed that she was to be married off, and received the news with the greatest unconcern. She did not know her future husband, the Vicomte de Talizac, but thought she would be able to get along with him. That she would have to leave her castle and her woods displeased her; she had never had the slightest longing for Paris, and the crowded streets of the capital were intolerable to her; but seeing that it must be she did not complain.

It was a wild caprice which had induced the young girl

to attend Girdel's performance; Fanfaro's lecture had angered her at first, but later on, when she thought about it, she had to confess that he was right. She was now looking expectantly at the young man, who was engaged with Bobichel in lighting the few lamps, and when he drew near to her, she whispered to him:

"Monsieur Fanfaro, are you satisfied with me?"

Fanfaro looked at her in amazement, but a cordial smile flew over his lips, and Irene felt that she could stand many more insults if she could see him smile oftener.

Madame Ursula, who sat next to her pupil, moved up and down uneasily in her chair. Irene did not possess the least *savoir vivre.* How could she think of addressing the young acrobat? and now—no, it surpassed everything—he bent over her and whispered a few words in her ear. The governess saw Irene blush, then let her head fall and nod. What could he have said to her?

Caillette, too, had noticed the young lady address Fanfaro, and she became violently jealous.

What business had the rich heiress with the young man, whom she was accustomed to look upon as her own property?

For Caillette, as well as Madame Ursula, it was fortunate that they had not heard Fanfaro's words, and yet it was only good advice which the young man had given Irene.

"Mademoiselle, try to secure the love of those who surround you," he had earnestly said. And Irene had, at first impatiently and with astonishment, finally guiltily, listened to him. Really, when she thought with what indifference her coming and going in the village was looked upon, and with what hesitation she was greeted, she began to think

Fanfaro was right; the young man had been gone long, and yet his words still sounded in her ears. Yes, she would try to secure love.

In the meantime the performance had begun. Girdel played with his weights, Rolla swallowed stones and pigeons, Robeckal knives and swords, and Caillette danced charmingly on the tight-rope. During all these different productions, Fanfaro was continually assisting the performers; he handed Girdel the weights and took them from him; he accompanied Robeckal's sword exercise with hollow beats on a tambourine; he played the violin while Caillette danced on the rope, and acted as Bobichel's foil in his comic acts. Fanfaro himself was not to appear before the second part; for the conclusion of the first part a climax was to be given in which Girdel would perform a piece in which he had everywhere appeared with thunders of applause; the necessary apparatus was being prepared.

This apparatus consisted of a plank supported by two logs which stood upright in the centre of the circus. In the centre of the plank was a windlass, from which hung an iron chain with a large hook.

Fanfaro rolled an empty barrel under the plank and filled it with irons and stones weighing about three thousand pounds. Thereupon the barrel was nailed up and the chain wound about it; strong iron rings, through which the chain was pulled, prevented it from slipping off.

Girdel now walked up. He wore a costume made of black tights, and a chin-band from which an iron hook hung. He bowed to the spectators, seized the barrel with his chin hook and laid himself upon his back. Fanfaro stood next to his foster-father, and from time to time blew a blast with his trumpet. At every tone the heavy cask rose a few inches in the air, and breathlessly the crowd looked at Girdel's performance. The cask had now reached a height on a level with Girdel; the spectators cheered, but suddenly an ominous breaking was heard, and while a cry of horror ran through the crowd, Fanfaro, quick as thought, sprung upon the cask and caught it in his arms.

What had happened? Girdel lay motionless on the ground. Fanfaro let the heavy cask glide gently to the floor and then stood pale as death near the athlete. The chain had broken, and had it not been for Fanfaro's timely assistance Girdel would have been crushed to pieces by the heavy barrel.

The violent shock had thrown Girdel some distance away. For a moment all were too frightened to stir, but soon spectators from all parts of the house came running up and loud cries were heard.

Caillette had thrown herself sobbing at her father's feet; Bobichel and Fanfaro busied themselves trying to raise the fallen man from the ground, and Rolla uttered loud, roaring cries which no doubt were intended to express her grief. Robeckal alone was not to be seen.

"Oh, Fanfaro, is he dead?" sobbed Caillette.

Fanfaro was silent and bent anxiously over Girdel; Rolla, on the other hand, looked angrily at the young man and hissed in his ear:

"Do not touch him. I will restore him myself."

Instead of giving the virago an answer, Fanfaro looked sharply at her. The wretched woman trembled and recoiled, while the young man, putting his ear to Girdel's breast, exclaimed:

"Thank God, he lives!"

Caillette uttered a low moan and became unconscious; two soft hands were laid tenderly on her shoulders, and when the tight-rope dancer opened her eyes, she looked in Irene's face, who was bending anxiously over her.

Girdel still remained motionless; the young countess handed Fanfaro an elegantly carved bottle filled with smelling-salts, but even this was of no avail.

"Wait, I know what will help him!" exclaimed Bobichel, suddenly, and hurrying out he returned with a bottle of strong brandy.

With the point of a knife Fanfaro opened Girdel's tightly compressed lips; the clown poured a few drops of the liquid down his throat, and in a few moments Girdel slowly opened his eyes and a deep sigh came from his breast. When Bobichel put the bottle to his mouth again, he drank a deep draught.

"Hurrah, he is rescued!" exclaimed the clown, as he wiped the tears from his eyes. He then walked to Rolla and mockingly whispered: "This time you reckoned without your host."

Rolla shuddered, and a look flew from Bobichel to Fanfaro.

Robeckal now thought it proper to appear and come from behind a post. He said in a whining voice:

"Thank God that our brave master lives. I dreaded the worst."

Schwan, who was crying like a child, threw a sharp look at Robeckal, and Fanfaro now said:

"Is there no physician in the neighborhood?"

"No, there is no physician in Sainte-Ame, and Vagney is several miles distant."

"No matter, I shall go to Vagney.'

"Impossible, the floods have destroyed all the roads; you risk your life, Fanfaro," said Schwan.

"And if that is so, I am only doing my duty," replied the young man. "I owe it to my foster-father that I did not die of cold and starvation."

"You are an honest fellow. Take one of my horses and ride around the hill. It is certainly an out-of-the-way road, but it is safe. Do not spare the horse; it is old, but when driven hard it still does its duty."

"Monsieur Fanfaro," said Irene, advancing, "take my riding horse; it flies like the wind, and will carry you to Vagney in a short time."

"She is foolish," complained Madame Ursula, while Fanfaro accepted Irene's offer without hesitating; "the riding horse is an English thoroughbred and cost two thousand francs."

No one paid any attention to her. Fanfaro swung himself into the saddle, and, throwing a cloak over his shoulders, he cordially said:

"Mademoiselle, I thank you."

"Don't mention it; I am following your advice," laughed Irene.

CHAPTER VII

PIERRE LABARRE

THE marquis and his steward had likewise hurried along the road to Vagney. They were often forced to halt to find the right direction, as the overflowing Cure had flooded the road at different points, but yet they reached the hill on which the city rests before night.

"The danger is behind us now," said Simon.

A quarter of an hour later they stopped before a small solitary house. Simon shook the knocker, and then they both waited impatiently to get in.

For a short time all was still, and Simon was about to strike again, when a window was opened and a voice asked:

"Who is there?"

The two men exchanged quick glances; Pierre Labarre was at home, and, as it seemed, alone.

"I am the Marquis of Fougereuse," said the marquis, finally.

No sooner had the words been spoken than the window was closed. The bolt of the house door was shoved back in a few moments and a lean old man appeared on the threshold.

Ten years had passed since Pierre Labarre rode alone through the Black Forest, and saved himself from the bullet of the then Vicomte de Talizac by his portfolio. Pierre's hair had grown gray now, but his eyes looked as fearlessly on the world as if he had been thirty.

"Come in, vicomte," said the old man, earnestly.

The marquis and Simon followed Pierre into a small, plainly furnished room; the only decoration was a black piece of mourning almost covering one of the walls. While the old man turned up the small lamp, Simon, without being noticed, closed the door. Pierre pointed to a straw chair and calmly said:

"Monsieur le Vicomte, will you please take a seat?"

The marquis angrily said:

"Pierre Labarre, it surprises me that in the nine years which have passed since the death of my father, the Marquis of Fougereuse, you should have forgotten what a servant's duties are! Since seven years I bear the title of my father; why do you persist in calling me Monsieur le Vicomte?"

Pierre Labarre stroked the white hair from his forehead with his long bony hand and slowly said:

"I know only one Marquis of Fougereuse."

"And who should bear this title if not I?" cried the marquis, angrily.

"The son of the man who was murdered at Leigoutte in the year 1805," replied Pierre.

"Murdered?" exclaimed the marquis, mockingly: "that man fell fighting against the legitimate masters of the country."

"Your brother, Monsieur le Vicomte, was the victim

of a well-laid plan; those persons who were interested in his death made their preparations with wonderful foresight."

The marquis frothed with anger, and it did not require very much more until he would have had the old man by the throat. He restrained himself, though; what good would it do him if he strangled Pierre before he knew the secret?

"Let us not discuss that matter," he hastily said; "other matters have brought me here—"

As Pierre remained silent, the marquis continued:

"I know perfectly well that that affair disturbed you. As the old servitor of my father you naturally were attached to the dead man. Yet, who could avert the catastrophe? The father, the mother and the two children were all slain at the same hour by the Cossacks, and—"

"You are mistaken, vicomte," interrupted Pierre, sharply; "the father fell in a struggle with paid assassins, the mother was burned to death, but the children escaped."

"You are fooling, old man," exclaimed the marquis, growing pale; "Jules's two children are dead."

The old man crossed his arms over his breast, and, looking steadily at the marquis, he firmly said:

"Monsieur le Vicomte, the children live."

The marquis could no longer restrain himself.

"You know where they are?" he excitedly exclaimed.

"No, vicomte, but it cheers me to hear from your words that you yourself do not believe the children are dead."

The marquis bit his lips. He had betrayed himself. Simon shrugged his shoulders and thought in his heart that the marquis was not the proper person to intrust with diplomatic missions for the Society of Jesus.

"Monsieur le Marquis," he hurriedly said, "what is the use of these long discussions? Put the question which concerns you most to the obstinate old man, and if he does not answer, I will make him speak."

"You are right," nodded the marquis; and turning to Pierre again he threateningly said:

"Listen, Pierre Labarre; I will tell you the object of my visit. It is a question of the honor of the Fougereuse."

A sarcastic laugh played about the old man's lips, and half muttering to himself, he repeated:

"The honor of the Fougereuse—I am really curious to know what I shall hear."

The marquis trembled, and, casting a timid look at Simon, he said:

"Simon, leave us to ourselves."

"What, Monsieur le Marquis?" asked Simon in amazement.

"You should leave us alone," repeated the marquis, adding in a whisper: "Go, I have my reasons."

"But, Monsieur le Marquis!"

"Do not say anything; go!"

Simon went growlingly away, and opening the door he had so carefully locked, he strode into the hall; taking care, however, to overhear the conversation.

As soon as the nobleman was alone with Pierre, his demeanor changed. He approached close to the old man, took his hand and cordially shook it. Pierre looked at the marquis in amazement, and quickly withdrawing his hand, he dryly said:

"To business, vicomte."

"Pierre," the marquis began, in a voice he tried to render as soft and moving as possible, "you were the confidant of my father; you knew all his secrets, and were aware that he did not love me. Do not interrupt me—I know my conduct was not such as he had a right to expect from a son. Pierre, I was not wicked, I was weak and could not withstand any temptation, and my father often had cause to be dissatisfied with me. Pierre, what I am telling you no human ear has ever heard; I look upon you as my father confessor and implore you not to judge too harshly."

Pierre held his eyes down, and even the marquis paused—he did not look up.

"Pierre, have you no mercy?" exclaimed the nobleman, in a trembling voice.

"Speak further, my lord," said Pierre; "I am listening."

The marquis felt like stamping with his foot. He saw, however, that he had to control himself.

"If you let me implore hopelessly to-day, Pierre," he whispered, gritting his teeth, "the name of Fougereuse will be eternally dishonored."

"The name of Fougereuse?" asked Pierre, with faint malice; "thank God, my lord, that it is not in your power to stain it; you are only the Vicomte de Talizac."

The marquis stamped his foot angrily when he heard the old man's cutting words; it almost surpassed his strength to continue the conversation to an end, and yet it must be if he wished to gain his point.

"I see, I must explain myself more clearly," he said after a pause. "Pierre, I am standing on the brink of a precipice. My fortune and my influence are gone; neither my wife nor my son imagines how I am situated, but if help does not come soon—"

"Well, what will happen?" asked Pierre, indifferently.

"Then I will not be able to keep my coat of arms, which dates from the Crusades, clean and spotless."

"I do not understand you, vicomte. Is it only a question of your fortune?"

"No, Pierre, it is a question of the honor of the Fougereuse. Oh, God! You do not desire to understand me; you want me to disclose my shame. Listen then," continued the marquis, placing his lips to the old man's ears: "to rescue myself from going under, I committed an act of despair, and if assistance does not come to me, the name of the Fougereuse will be exposed to the world, with the brand of the forger upon it."

The old man's face showed no traces of surprise. He kept silent for a moment, and then asked in cold tones:

"Monsieur le Vicomte, what do you wish of me?"

"I will tell you," said the marquis, hastily, while a gleam of hope strayed over his pale face; "I know that my father, to have the major part of his fortune go to his eldest son, made a will and gave it to you—"

"Go on," said Pierre, as the marquis paused.

"The will contains many clauses," continued the nobleman. "My father hid a portion of his wealth, and in his last will named the spot where it lies buried, providing that it should be given to his eldest son or his descendants! Pierre, Jules is dead, his children have disappeared, and therefore nothing hinders you from giving up this wealth. It must be at least two millions. Can you hesitate to give me the money which will save the name of Fougereuse from shame and exposure?"

The marquis hesitated; Pierre rose slowly and, turning to a side wall, grasped the mourning cloth and shoved it aside.

The nobleman wonderingly observed the old man, who now took a lamp and solemnly said:

"Vicomte, look here!"

The marquis approached the wall, and in the dim light of the lamp he saw a tavern sign, upon which a few letters could be seen. The sign had evidently been burned.

"Monsieur le Vicomte, do you know what that is?" asked Pierre, threateningly.

"No," replied the marquis.

"Then I will tell you, vicomte," replied Pierre. "The inscription on this sign once read, 'To the Welfare of France.' Do you still wish me to give you the will and the fortune?"

"I do not understand you," stammered the nobleman, in a trembling voice.

"Really, vicomte, you have a short memory, but I, the old servant of your father, am able to refresh it! This sign hung over the door of the tavern at Leigoutte; your brother, the rightful heir of Fougereuse, was the landlord and the bravest man for miles around. In the year 1805 Jules Fougere, as he called himself, fell. The world said Cossacks had murdered him. I, though, vicomte, I cry it aloud in your ear—his murderer was—you!"

"Silence, miserable lackey!" exclaimed the marquis, enraged, "you lie!"

"No, Cain, the miserable lackey does not lie," replied Pierre, calmly; "he even knows more! In the year 1807 the old Marquis of Fougereuse died; in his last hours his son, the Vicomte of Talizac, sneaked into the chamber of death and, sinking on his knees beside the bedside of the dying man, implored his father to make him his sole heir. The marquis hardly had strength enough to breathe, but his eyes looked threateningly at the scoundrel who dared to imbitter his last hours, and with his last gasp he hurled at the kneeling man these words: 'May you be eternally damned, miserable fratricide!'

"The vicomte, as if pursued by the furies, escaped; the dying man gave one more gasp and then passed away, and I, who was behind the curtains, a witness of this terrible scene—I shall so far forget myself as to deliver to the man who did not spare his father the inheritance of his brother? No, vicomte, Pierre Labarre knows his duty, and if to-morrow the name of the Fougereuse should be trampled in the dust and the present bearer of the name be placed in the pillory as a forger and swindler, then I will stand up and say:

"'He is not a Fougereuse, he is only a Talizac. He murdered the heir, and let no honest man ever touch his blood-stained hand!' Get out of here, Vicomte Talizac, my house has no room for murderers!"

Pale as death, with quaking knees, the marquis leaned against the wall. When Pierre was silent he hissed in a low voice:

"Then you refuse to help me?"

"Yes, a thousand times, yes."

"You persist in keeping the fortune of the Fougereuse for Jules's son, who has been dead a long time?"

"I keep the fortune for the living."

"And if he were dead, nevertheless?"

Pierre suddenly looked up—suppose the murderer were to prove his assertion?

"Would you, if Jules's son were really dead, acknowledge me as the heir?"

"I cannot tell."

"For the last time, will you speak?"

"No; the will and fortune belong to the Marquis of Fougereuse, Jules's son."

"Enough; the will is here in your house; the rest will take care of itself."

Hereupon the marquis gave a penetrating whistle, and when Simon appeared his master said to him:

"Take hold of this scoundrel!"

"Bravo! force is the only thing," cried Simon, as he rushed upon the old man. But he had reckoned without his host; with a shove Pierre Labarre threw the audacious rascal to the ground, and the next minute the heavy old table lay between him and his enemies. Thereupon the old man took a pistol from the wall, and, cocking the trigger, cried:

"Vicomte Talizac, we still have an old score to settle! Years ago you attempted to kill me in the Black Forest; take care you do not arouse my anger again."

The vicomte, who had no weapon, recoiled: Simon, however, seized a pocket-pistol from his breast, and mockingly replied: "Oh, two can play at that game!"

He pressed his hand to the trigger, but Pierre Labarre put his pistol down, and contemptuously said:

"Bah! for the lackey the dog will do. Catch him, Sultan!"

As he said these words he opened a side door; a large Vosges dog, whose glowing eyes and crispy hair made him look like a wolf, sprang upon Simon, and, clutching him by the throat, threw him to the ground.

"Help, my lord marquis!" cried the steward.

"Let go, Sultan," commanded Pierre.

The dog shook his opponent once more and then let him loose.

"Get out of here, miscreants!" exclaimed Pierre now, with threatening voice, as he opened the door, "and never dare to come into my house again."

The wretches ran as if pursued by the Furies. Pierre caressed the dog and then laughed softly; he was rid of his guests.

CHAPTER VIII

A MEETING

FANFARO had urged Irene's horse on at great speed, and while it flew along like a bird, the most stormy feelings raged in his heart.

The gaze of the pretty girl haunted him; he heard her gentle voice and tried in vain to shake off these thoughts. What was he, that he should indulge in such wild fancies? A foundling, the adopted son of an acrobat, who had picked him up upon the way, and yet—

Further and further horse and rider flew; before Fanfaro's eyes stood Girdel's pale, motionless face, and he thought he could hear Caillette's bitter sobs. No, he must bring help or else go under, and ceaselessly, like lightning, he pushed on toward the city.

The marquis and Simon ran breathlessly along. Their only thought was to get far from the neighborhood of the old man and his wolf-hound. Neither of the two spoke a word. The stormy, roaring Cure was forgotten, the danger to life was forgotten; on, on they went, like deer pursued by a pack of bloodthirsty hounds, and neither of them paid any attention to the ominous noise of the overflowing mountain streams.

Suddenly Simon paused and seized the marquis's arm.

"Listen," he whispered, tremblingly, "what is that?"

A thunderous noise, ceaseless, rolling, and crashing, reached their ears from all sides; from all sides frothy, bubbling masses of water dashed themselves against the rocks, and now—now an immense rock fell crashing in the flood, which overflowed into the wide plain like a storm-whipped sea.

Despair seized the men; before, behind, and around them roared and foamed the turbulent waters; they turned to the right, where a huge rock, which still projected above the waves, assured them safety, but just then the marquis struck his foot against a stone—he tumbled and fell with a half-smothered cry for help, "Help—I am sinking!" into the dark depths.

Simon did not think of lending his master a helping hand; he sprang from rock to rock, from stone to stone, and soon reached a high point which protected him from the oncoming waters.

The marquis had been borne a short distance along by the raging waters, until he succeeded in clambering upon a branch of an evergreen tree. The flood still rolled along above his body, but with superhuman strength he managed to keep his head above water and despairingly cry, "Help, Simon! Rescue me!"

Suddenly it seemed to the half-unconscious man as if he heard a human voice calling to him from above:

"Courage—keep up."

With the remainder of his strength the marquis gazed in the direction from which it came, and recognized a human form which seemed to be hanging in the air.

"Attention, I will soon be with you," cried the voice, now coming nearer.

The marquis saw the form spring, climb, and then the water spurted up and the marquis lost consciousness.

Fanfaro, for naturally he was the rescuer, who appeared at the hour of the greatest need, now stood up to his knees in water, and had just stretched his hand out toward the marquis, when the latter, with a groan, let go of the tree branch, and the next minute he was borne along by the turbulent waters.

Fanfaro uttered a slight cry, but he did not hesitate a moment. Plunging into the seething waves, he parted them with muscular strokes, and succeeded in grasping the drowning man. Throwing his left arm about him, he swam to the rocky projection upon which the evergreen tree stood. Inch by inch he climbed toward the pathway which was upon the top of the hill. Perspiration dripped from his forehead, and his wind threatened to give out, but Fanfaro went on, and finally stood on top. Putting the marquis softly on the ground, Fanfaro took out a small pocket-lantern which he always carried with him. With great trouble he lighted the wet wick, and then let the rays fall full on the pale face of the motionless man. Seized by an indescribable emotion, the young man leaned over the marquis. Did he suspect that the man whom he had rescued from the stormy waters, at the risk of his life, was the brother of the man who had taken mercy on the helpless orphan, and was at the same time his father? The marquis now opened his eyes, heaved a deep sigh, and looked wildly around him.

"Where am I?" he faintly stammered. "The water—ah!"

"You are saved," said Fanfaro, gently.

The sound of the voice caused all the blood to rush to the marquis's heart.

"Did you save me?"

"Yes."

"Who are you?"

"My name is Fanfaro, and I am a member of Girdel's troupe, which is at present in Sainte-Ame. Can you raise yourself?"

With the young man's assistance, the marquis raised himself up, but uttered a cry of pain when he put his feet on the ground.

"Are you wounded?" asked Fanfaro, anxiously.

"No, I do not think so; the water knocked me against trees and stones, and my limbs hurt me from that."

"That will soon pass away. Now put your arm about my neck and trust yourself to me; I will bring you to a place of safety."

The marquis put his arms tightly about the young man's neck, and the latter strode along the narrow pathway which led to the heights.

Soon the road became broader, the neighing of a horse was heard, and drawing a deep breath the young man stood still.

"Now we are safe," he said, consolingly; "I will take you on the back of my horse, and in less than a quarter of an hour we will be in Sainte-Ame. I rode from there to Vagney, to get a physician for my foster-father, Girdel, who injured himself, but unfortunately he was not at home, and so I had to return alone. Get up, the road is straight ahead, and the mountains now lie between us and the water."

In the meantime Fanfaro had helped the marquis on the back of the horse, and now he raised his lantern to untie the knot of the rope with which he had bound the animal to a tree. The light of the lamp fell full upon his face, and the marquis uttered a slight cry; his rescuer resembled in a startling way the old Marquis of Fougereuse.

Had he Jules's son before him?

A satanic idea flashed through the brain of the noble rogue, and when Fanfaro, after putting out his lantern, attempted to get on the horse's back, the marquis pressed heavily against the horse's flank and they were both off like the wind in the direction of the village.

Fanfaro, who only thought that the horse had run away with the marquis, cried in vain to the rider, and so he had to foot the distance, muttering as he went:

"If the poor fellow only doesn't get hurt; he is still feeble, and the horse needs a competent rider."

CHAPTER IX

THE GRATITUDE OF A NOBLEMAN

FANFARO was hardly a hundred feet away from Sainte-Ame, when Girdel opened his eyes and looked about him.

"What, my little Caillette is weeping!" he muttered, half-laughing. "Child, you probably thought I was dead?"

"Oh, God be praised and thanked!" cried Caillette, springing up and falling upon her father's neck.

Bobichel almost sprung to the ceiling, and Schwan, between laughing and crying, exclaimed:

"What a fright you gave us, old boy. The poor fellow rode away in the night to get a physician, and—"

"A physician? For me?" laughed Girdel. "Thank God, we are not so far gone."

"But you were unconscious more than half an hour; we became frightened, and Fanfaro rode to Vagney."

"He rode? On our old mare, perhaps? If he only returns," said Girdel, anxiously. "The water must be dangerous about Vagney."

"He has a good horse; the Countess of Salves gave Fanfaro her thoroughbred," said Bobichel.

"Ah! that is different. Now, children, let me alone. Cousin Schwan, send me the two men whom I am to bring to Remiremont to-morrow; I must speak to them."

Caillette, Bobichel, Schwan and Rolla went away. In the dark corridor a figure passed by Rolla, and a hoarse voice said:

"Well?"

"All for nothing," growled Rolla; "he lives, and is as healthy as a fish in the water."

"You don't say so," hissed Robeckal.

"It was your own fault," continued the virago. "A good stab in the right place, and all is over; but you have no courage."

"Silence, woman!" growled Robeckal. "I have attended to that in another way; he shall not trouble us long. Tell me, does he ever receive any letters?"

"A great pile," said Rolla.

"And you cannot tell me their contents?"

"No; I never read them."

This discretion had good grounds. Rolla could not read, but she did not wish to admit it to him. Whether Robeckal suspected how things were, we do not know; anyhow, he did not pursue the subject any further, but said:

"Schwan brought two men to Girdel a little while ago; come with me to the upper story; we can listen at the door there and find out what they say."

When Robeckal and Rolla, after listening nearly two hours, slipped downstairs they had heard all that Girdel and the two gentlemen had said. They knew Fanfaro had been deputed to take important papers to Paris and give them to a certain person who had been designated;

Girdel had guaranteed that Fanfaro would fill the mission promptly.

When Robeckal returned to the inn, Simon rushed in pale and trembling. He could hardly reply to the landlord's hurried questions; the words, "In the water—the flood—dead—my poor master!" came from his trembling lips, and immediately afterward he sank to the floor unconscious.

While Schwan was busy with him, the sound of a horse's hoofs was heard.

"Thank God, here comes Fanfaro!" exclaimed Bobichel and Caillette, simultaneously, and they both rushed to the door.

Who can describe their astonishment when they saw the marquis, dripping with water and half frozen, get down from the horse and enter the room?

"Where is Fanfaro?" asked Bobichel, anxiously.

"He will soon be here," replied the marquis; "the horse ran away with me, and I could not hold him."

"Then the brave fellow is not injured?" asked Schwan, vivaciously.

"God forbid; quick, give me a glass of brandy and lead me to Girdel; I must speak to him at once."

While the host went to get the brandy, Simon and the marquis exchanged looks; the next minute Schwan returned and the nobleman drank a large glass of brandy at a gulp.

"Ah, that warms," he said, smacking his lips, "and now let us look for Girdel."

As soon as the marquis left the room, Robeckal drew near to the steward and whispered:

"Follow me, I must speak to you."

They both went into the hall and held a conversation in low tones.

Suddenly a cry of joy reached their ears, and the next minute they saw Bobichel, who, in his anxiety about Fanfaro, had hurried along the road, enter the house with the young man.

"There he is," whispered Robeckal, "God knows how it is, but neither fire nor water seems to have the slightest effect on him."

"We will get rid of him, never fear," said Simon, wickedly.

From the upper story loud cries were heard. Rolla danced with a brandy bottle in her hand, and Girdel was asking himself how he ever could have made such a low woman his wife.

A knock was now heard on his door; Girdel cried, "Come in," in powerful tones, and a man, a stranger to him, crossed the threshold.

"Have I the honor of addressing Monsieur Girdel?" the stranger politely asked.

"At your service; that is my name."

"I am the Marquis of Fougereuse, and would like to have an interview with you."

"Take a seat, my lord marquis, and speak," said Girdel, looking expectantly at his visitor.

"I will not delay you long, Monsieur Girdel," the marquis began; "I know you have met with a misfortune—"

"Oh, it was not serious," said the athlete.

"Monsieur Girdel," continued the nobleman, "about one hour ago I was in peril of my life, and one of your men rescued me at the risk of his."

"You don't say so? How did it happen?" cried Girdel.

"I was in danger of drowning in the Cure; a young man seized me from out of the turbulent waters and carried me in his arms to a place of safety."

"Ah, I understand, the young man of whom you spoke—"

"Was your son, Fanfaro!"

"I thought so," said the athlete; "if Fanfaro is alone only one second, he generally finds time to save somebody. Where is the boy now?"

"He will be here soon. He asked me to get on the back of the horse with him. I got up first, and hardly had the fiery steed felt some one on his back than he flew away like an arrow. I was too feeble to check the horse, and so my rescuer was forced to follow on foot."

"Fanfaro doesn't care for that; he walks miles at a time without getting tired, and in less than fifteen minutes he will be here."

"Then it is the right time for me to ask you a few questions which I do not wish him to hear. You are probably aware what my position at court is?"

"Candidly, no; the atmosphere of the court has never agreed with me."

"Then let me tell you that my position is a very influential one, and consequently it would be easy for me to do something for you and your—son."

The marquis pronounced the word "son" in a peculiar way, but Girdel shook his head.

"I wish Fanfaro was my son," he sighed; "I know of no better luck."

"If the young man is not your son," said the marquis,

"then he would need my assistance the more. His parents are, perhaps, poor people, and my fortune—"

"Fanfaro has no parents any more, my lord marquis."

"Poor young man!" said the nobleman, pityingly; "but what am I saying?" he interrupted himself with well-played anger. "Fanfaro has no doubt found a second father in you; I would like to wager that you were a friend of his parents, and have bestowed your friendship upon the son."

"You are mistaken, my lord; I found Fanfaro on the road."

"Impossible! What singular things one hears! Where did you find the boy?"

"Ah! that is an old story, but if it interests you I will relate it to you: One cold winter day, I rode with my wagon—in which was, besides my stock, my family and some members of my troupe—over a snow-covered plain in the Vosges, when I suddenly heard loud trumpet tones. At first I did not pay any attention to them. It was in the year 1814, and such things were not uncommon then. However, the tones were repeated, and I hurried in the direction form whence they proceeded. I shall never forget the sight which met me. A boy about ten years of age lay unconscious over a dead trumpeter, and his small hands were nervously clutched about the trumpet. It was plain that he had blown the notes I had heard and then fallen to the ground in a faint. I took the poor little fellow in my arms; all around lay the bodies of many French soldiers, and the terrors of the neighborhood had no doubt been too much for the little rogue. We covered him in the wagon with warm cloaks, and because the poor fellow had blown such fanfares upon the trumpet, we had called him Fanfaro.''

"Didn't he have any name?" asked the marquis, nervously.

"That, my dear sir, wasn't so easy to find out. Hardly had we taken the boy to us than he got the brain-fever, and for weeks lay on the brink of the grave. When he at length recovered, he had lost his memory entirely, and only after months did he regain it. At last he could remember the name of the village where he had formerly lived—"

"What was the name of this village?" interrupted the marquis, hurriedly.

"Leigoutte, my lord."

The nobleman had almost uttered a cry, but he restrained himself in time, and Girdel did not notice his guest's terrible excitement.

"His name, too, and those of his parents and sister, we found out after a time," continued Girdel; "his father's name was Jules, his mother's Louise, his sister's Louison, and his own Jacques. On the strength of his information I went to Leigoutte, but found out very little. The village had been set on fire by the Cossacks and destroyed. Of the inhabitants only a few women and children had been rescued, and the only positive thing I heard was that Jacques's mother had been burned to death in a neighboring farmhouse. The men of Leigoutte had made a stand against the Cossacks, but had been fairly blown into the air by them. I returned home dissatisfied. Fanfaro remained with us; he learned our tricks, and we love him very much. Where he managed to procure the knowledge he has is a riddle to me; he never went to a regular school, and yet he knows a great deal. He is a genius, my lord marquis, and a treasure for our troupe."

Cold drops of perspiration stood on the nobleman's forehead. No, there was no longer any doubt: Fanfaro was his brother's son!

"Have you never been able to find out his family name?" he asked, after a pause.

"No; the Cossacks set fire to the City Hall at Weissenbach and all the records there were destroyed. An old shepherd said he had once been told that Jules was the scion of an old noble family. Anything positive on this point, I could not find out—I—"

At this point the door was hastily opened and Fanfaro entered. He rushed upon Girdel and enthusiastically cried:

"Thank God, Papa Girdel, that you are well again."

"You rascal, you," laughed Girdel, looking proudly at the young man. "You have found time again to rescue some one."

"Monsieur Fanfaro," said the marquis now, "permit me once more to thank you for what you have done for me. I can never repay you."

"Don't mention it, sir," replied Fanfaro, modestly, "I have only done my duty."

"Well I hope if you should ever need me you will let me know. The Marquis of Fougereuse is grateful."

When the marquis went downstairs shortly afterward, he found Simon awaiting him.

"Simon," he said, hurriedly, "do you know who Fanfaro is?"

"No, my lord."

"He is the son of my brother, Jules de Fougereuse."

"Really?" exclaimed Simon, joyfully, "that would be splendid."

"Listen to my plan; the young man must die, but under such circumstances as to have his identity proved, so that Pierre Labarre can be forced to break his silence. You understand me, Simon?"

"Perfectly so, my lord; and I can tell you now that I already know the means and way to do the job. A little while ago a man, whom I can trust, informed me that Fanfaro is going to play a part in the conspiracy against the government which I have already spoken to you about."

"So much the better; but can he be captured in such a way that there will be no outlet for him?"

"I hope so."

"Who gave you this information?" asked the marquis, after Simon had told him all that Robeckal had overheard.

"A man called Robeckal; he is a member of Girdel's troupe."

"Good."

The marquis took out a note-book, wrote a few lines, and then said:

"Here, take this note, Simon, and accompany Robeckal at once to Remiremont. There you will go to the Count of Vernac, the police superintendent, and give him the note. The count is a faithful supporter of the monarchy, and will no doubt accede to my request to send some policemen here this very night to arrest Girdel and Fanfaro. The rest I shall see to."

"My lord, I congratulate you," said Simon, respectfully.

CHAPTER X

ESCAPED

BEFORE Robeckal had gone with Simon, he had hurried to Rolla and told her that he was going to Remiremont now to get some policemen.

"Our score will be settled now on one board," he said, with a wink.

The fat woman had looked at him with swimming eyes, and in a maudlin voice replied:

"That—is—right—all—must—suffer—Caillette—also!"

"Certainly, Caillette, too," replied Robeckal, inwardly vowing to follow his own ideas with respect to this last, and then he hurried after the steward.

Caillette and Rolla slept in the same room; when the young girl entered it she saw the Cannon Queen sitting in an intoxicated condition at the table surrounded by empty bottles. The horrible woman greeted the young girl with a coarse laugh, and as Caillette paid no attention to her, Rolla placed her arms upon the table, and threateningly exclaimed:

"Don't put on such airs, you tight-rope princess; what will you do when they take your Fanfaro away?"

"Take Fanfaro away? What do you mean?" asked Caillette, frightened, overcoming her repulsion, and looking at Rolla.

"Ha! ha! ha! Now the pigeon thaws—yes, there is nothing like love," mocked the drunken woman. "Ah, the policemen won't let themselves be waited for; Robeckal and the others will look out for that."

Caillette, horror-stricken, listened to the virago's words. Was she right, and were her father and Fanfaro in danger?

"I am going to sleep now," said Rolla, "and when I wake up Fanfaro and Girdel will have been taken care of."

Leaning back heavily in the chair, the woman closed her eyes. Caillette waited until loud snoring told her Rolla was fast asleep, and then she silently slipped out of the room, locked it from the outside, and tremblingly hurried to wake her father.

As she reached Girdel's door, a dark form, which had been crouching near the threshold, arose.

"Who's there?" asked Caillette softly.

"I, little Caillette," replied Bobichel's voice. "I am watching, because I do not trust Robeckal."

"Oh, Bobichel, there is danger. I must waken father at once."

"What is the matter?"

"Go, wake father and tell him I must speak to him; do not lose a minute," urged Caillette.

The clown did not ask any more questions. He hurried to wake Girdel and Fanfaro, and then called Caillette. The young girl hastily told what she had heard. At first Girdel shook his head doubtingly, but he soon became pensive, and when Caillette finally said Rolla even muttered in her sleep about an important conspiracy and papers, he could no longer doubt.

"What shall we do?" he asked, turning to Fanfaro.

"Fly," said the young man quickly. "We owe our lives and our strength to the fatherland and the good cause; to stay here would be to put them both rashly at stake. Let us pray to God that it even now may not be too late."

"So be it, let us fly. We can leave the wagon go, and take only the horses. Is Robeckal at home?" asked Girdel, suddenly turning to Bobichel.

"No, master, he has gone."

"Then forward," said the athlete firmly. "I will take Caillette on my horse and you two, Fanfaro and Bobichel, mount the second animal."

"No, master, that won't do," remarked the clown, "you alone are almost too heavy for a horse; Fanfaro must take Caillette upon his and I shall go on foot. Do not say otherwise. My limbs can stand a great deal, and I won't lose sight of you. Where are we going?"

"We must reach Paris as soon as possible," said Fanfaro. "Shall we wake the landlord?"

"Not for any money," said Girdel; "we would only bring him into trouble.

"You are right," replied Fanfaro; "we must not open the house door either, we must go by way of the window."

"That won't be very difficult for such veterans as we are," laughed Girdel. "Bobichel, get down at once and saddle the horses. You will find the saddles in the large box in the wagon. But one minute—what will become of my wife?"

The others remained silent, only Fanfaro said:

"Her present condition is such that we cannot take

her along; and, besides, there is no danger in store for her.''

Girdel scratched his head in embarrassment.

''I will look after her,'' he finally said, and hurried out.

In about two minutes he returned.

''She is sleeping like a log,'' he said; ''we must leave her here. Schwan will take care of her.''

In the meantime Bobichel had tied the bedclothes, opened the window, and fastened the clothes to the window hinges. He then whispered jovially: ''Good-evening, ladies and gentlemen,'' and let himself slide down the improvised rope. Caillette followed the clown, then came Girdel, and finally Fanfaro.

''Let the clothes hang,'' ordered Girdel.

They all crept softly to the stable and in about five minutes were on the street.

Bobichel ran alongside Girdel. Suddenly he stopped and hurriedly said:

''I hear the sound of horses' hoofs; we escaped just in time.''

The noise Bobichel heard really came from the policemen, who had hurried from Remiremont to Sainte-Ame and were now surrounding the Golden Sun. Robeckal and Simon were smart enough to keep in the background. The brigadier, a veteran soldier, knocked loudly at the house-door, and soon the host appeared and asked what was the matter.

''Open in the name of the king,'' cried the brigadier impatiently.

''Policemen, oh my God!'' groaned Schwan, more dead than alive. ''There must be a mistake here.''

"Haven't arrested any one yet who didn't say the same thing," growled the brigadier. "Quick, open the door and deliver up the malefactors."

"Whom shall I deliver?" asked Schwan, terror-stricken.

"Two acrobats, named Girdel and Fanfaro," was the answer.

"Girdel and Fanfaro? Oh, Mr. Brigadier, you are mistaken. What are they accused of?"

"Treason! They are members of a secret organization, which is directed against the monarchy."

"Impossible; it cannot be!" groaned Schwan.

"I will conduct the gentlemen," said Robeckal, coming forward.

"Scoundrel!" muttered the host, while Robeckal preceded the policemen up the stairs, and pointed to Girdel's room.

"Open!" cried the brigadier, knocking at the door with the hilt of his sword.

As no answer came, he burst open the door, and then uttered an oath.

"Confound them—they have fled!" exclaimed Robeckal.

"Yes, the nest is empty," said the brigadier; "look, there at the window, the bed-sheets are still hanging with which they made their escape."

"You are right," growled Robeckal; "but they cannot be very far off yet."

"No; quick—to horse!" cried the brigadier to his men; and while they got into the saddle, Robeckal looked in the stables and discovered the loss of the two horses. The tracks were soon found, and the pursuers, with Robeckal at the head, quickly gained the forest. But here something singular happened. The brigadier's horse stumbled and fell, the horse of the second policeman met with the same accident, and before the end of two seconds two more horses, together with their riders, lay on the ground. All four raged and cried in a horrible manner; one of them had broken a leg, the brigadier's sword had run into his left side, and two horses were so badly hurt that they had to be killed on the spot.

"The devil take them!" cried Robeckal, who was looking about with his lantern to discover the cause of these accidents, "the scoundrels have drawn a net of thin cords from one tree to the other."

"Yes, the scoundrels happened to be smarter than other people," came a mocking voice from the branch of an oak-tree, and looking up, Robeckal saw the clown, who, with the quickness of an ape, had now slid down the tree and disappeared in the bush.

"Villain!" exclaimed Robeckal, angrily, and taking a gun from one of the policemen he fired a shot at Bobichel.

Did the shot take effect?

CHAPTER XI

IN PARIS

ON THE 29th of February, 1824, a great crowd of laughing, noisy people wandered up and down the streets of the French capital, for it was the last Sunday of the carnival; the boulevards in the neighborhood of the Palais-Royal especially being packed with promenaders of both sexes.

An elegant carriage drawn by two thoroughbreds halted at the edge of the pavement, and three young men got out. They had cigars in their mouths, which at that time was something extraordinary; white satin masks hid their faces, and dark (so-called) Venetian mantles, with many colored bands on their shoulders, covered their forms.

The young men answered the jokes and guys of the crowd in a jolly manner, and then took seats in the Cafe de la Rotonde. Darkness came on, the lights gleamed, and one of the young men said, sorrowfully:

"The carnival is coming to an end; it's a great pity—we had such fun."

"Fernando, are you getting melancholy?" laughed the second young man.

"Fernando is right," remarked the third; "the last day of the carnival is so dull and spiritless that one can plainly see it is nearing the end. For more than two hours we have been strolling about the boulevards, but have not met with one adventure. Everywhere the stereotyped faces and masks; the same jokes as last year; even the coffee and the cake look stale to me. Arthur, don't you agree with me?"

"You demand too much," cried Arthur, indifferently; "we still have the night before us, and it would not be good if we could not find something to make the hours fly. As a last resort we could get up a scandal."

"Hush! that smells of treason. The dear mob now-adays is not so easy to lead, and the police might take a hand in the fight," warned Fernando.

"So much the better; the scandal would be complete then. The police are naturally on our side, and our motto—'after us the deluge'—has always brought us luck."

The young men laughed loudly. They were evidently in good humor. The one whom his companions called Arthur was the son of the Count of Montferrand, who made a name for himself in the House of Deputies on account of his great speech in favor of the murderers of Marshal Brune; the second, Gaston de Ferrette, was related to the first families of the kingdom; he had accompanied the Duke of Angoulême to Spain, and was known as an expert fencer. He was hardly twenty years of age, but had already come out victorious in several duels.

The third young man was a foreigner, but having the very best recommendations he was soon at home in the capital. His name was Fernando de Velletri, and he was by birth an Italian of the old nobility; he was received in all the palaces of the Faubourg St. Germain, and was acquainted with everything that went on in the great world.

"Where is Frederic?" asked Arthur now.

"Really, he seems to have forgotten us," replied Fernando, "I cannot understand what delays him so long."

"Stop!" exclaimed Gaston de Ferrette. "Come to think of it, I understand that he was going to accompany the Countess of Salves to some ceremony at Notre Dame."

"Poor fellow!"

"He is not to be pitied. The Countess of Salves is a charming girl."

"Bah, she is going to become his wife."

"So much the more reason that he should love her before the marriage; afterward, it isn't considered good form to have such feelings."

"He loves her, then?"

"I am very grateful to you, gentlemen; even in my absence you occupy yourselves with my affairs," said a clear, sharp voice now.

"Frederic, at last; where have you been?"

"Oh, I have been standing over five minutes behind you, and heard your conversation."

"Has it insulted you?" asked Gaston, laughing.

Frederic did not answer immediately; he let his gaze fall pityingly over his companion, and Gaston hastily said:

"Really, Frederic, your splendor throws us in the shade; look at him, he has no mask, and is dressed after the latest fashion."

The costume of the last comer was, indeed, much more elegant than those of the other young men. A long overcoat, made of fine brown cloth, sat tightly about the body and reached to the knees; the sleeves, wide at the shoulder, narrowed down toward the wrists and formed cuffs, which fell over the gloved hand. A white satin handkerchief peeped out coquettishly from the left breast pocket. White trousers, of the finest cloth, reached to the soles of his shoes, which were pointed and spurred. A tall, silk hat, with an almost invisible brim, covered his head.

Frederic allowed himself to be admired by his friends, and then said:

"Take my advice and put off your masks at once, and dress yourselves as becomes young noblemen; let the mob run around with masks on."

"Frederic is right," said Gaston, "let us hurry to do so."

"I shall await you here and bring you then to Robert; or better still, you can meet me at the Cafe Valois."

The three masks left, and the Vicomte Talizac, for he was the last comer, remained alone.

His external appearance was very unsympathetic. The sharply-cut face had a disagreeable expression, the squinting eyes and rolling look were likewise repulsive, and if his back was not as much bent as usual, it was due to the art of Bernard, the tailor of the dandies.

The Cafe de Valois, toward which the vicomte was now going, was generally the meeting-place of old soldiers, and the dandies called it mockingly the cafe of the grayheads. Rumor had it that it was really the meeting-place of republicans, and it was a matter of surprise why Delevan, the head of the police department, never took any notice of these rumors.

When the vicomte entered the gallery of the cafe, he looked observingly about him, and then approached a group of young men who all wore plain black clothing and whose manners were somewhat military.

The young men moved backward at both sides when the vicomte approached them. Not one of them gazed at the dandy. The latter, however, stepped up to one of them, and laying his hand lightly upon his shoulder, said:

"Sir, can I see you for a moment?"

The person addressed, a man about twenty-five years of age with classically formed features, turned hurriedly around; seeing the vicomte, he said in a cold voice:

"I am at your service, sir."

The vicomte walked toward the street and the man followed. On a deserted corner they both stopped, and the vicomte began:

"Monsieur, first I must ask you to tell me your name; I am the Vicomte de Talizac."

"I know it," replied the young man coldly.

"So much the better; as soon as I know who you are I will be able to tell whether I should speak to you as an equal or punish you as a lackey."

The young man grew pale but he replied with indomitable courage:

"I don't know what we two could ever have in common."

"Sir!" exclaimed Talizac angrily, "in a month I shall lead the Countess de Salves to the altar; therefore it will not surprise you if I stigmatize your conduct as outrageous. You rode to-day at noon past the De Salves palace, and threw a bouquet over the wall and into the garden."

"Well, what else?"

"You have probably good reasons not to give your name, the name of an adventurer, but in spite of all I must inform you that in case you repeat the scene I shall be obliged to punish you. I—"

The vicomte was unable to proceed; the iron fist of the young man was laid upon his shoulder, and so powerful was the pressure of his hand that the vicomte was hardly able to keep himself on his feet. The young man gave a whistle, upon which signal the friends who had followed him hurried up. When they were near by, Talizac's opponent said:

"Vicomte, before I provoke a scene, I wish to lay the matter before my friends; have patience for a moment. Gentlemen," he said, turning to his companions, "this man insulted me. Shall I fight a duel with him? It is the Vicomte de Talizac."

"The Vicomte de Talizac?" replied one of the men addressed, who wore the cross of the Legion of Honor. "With a Talizac one does not fight duels."

The vicomte uttered a hoarse cry of rage, and turned under the iron fist which was still pressed on his shoulder and held him tight; the young man gave him a look which made his cowardly heart quake, and earnestly said:

"Vicomte, we only fight with people we honor. If you do not understand my words, ask your father the meaning of them; he can give you the necessary explanations. Perhaps a day may come when I myself may not refuse to oppose you, and then you may kill me if you are able to do so! I have told you now what you ought to know, and now go and look up your dissipated companions, and take your presence out of the society of respectable people.''

Wild with rage, his features horribly distorted, unable to utter a word, the Vicomte de Talizac put his hand in his pocket, and threw a pack of cards at his opponent's face. The young man was about to rush upon the nobleman, but one of his companions seized his arm and whispered:

"Don't be too hasty, you must not put your life and liberty at stake just now—you are not your own master;'' saying which, he pointed to three masked faces who had just approached the group.

The young man shook his head affirmatively, and Talizac took advantage of this to disappear. He had hardly gone a few steps, when an arm was thrown under his own and a laughing voice exclaimed:

"You are punctual, vicomte; your friends can vouch for that.''

The vicomte kept silent, and Fernando, lowering his voice, continued:

"What was the difficulty between you and the young man? You wanted to kill him. Are you acquainted with him?''

"No, I hardly know him; you overheard us?''

"Excuse me, my dear fellow; your opponent spoke so loudly that we were not obliged to exert ourselves to hear his estimate of you. Anyhow I only heard the conclusion of the affair; you will no doubt take pleasure in relating the commencement to me!''

The words, and the tone in which they had been said, wounded Talizac's self-love, and he sharply replied:

"If it pleases me, Signor Velletri!''

The Italian laughed, and then said, in an indifferent tone:

"My dear vicomte, in the position in which you find yourself, it would be madness for me to imagine that you intend to insult me, and therefore I do not consider your words as spoken."

"What do you mean, signor?"

"Oh, nothing, except that yesterday was the day of presentation for a certain paper, which you, in a fit of abstraction, no doubt, signed with another name than your own!"

The vicomte grew pale, and he mechanically clinched his fist.

"How—do—you—know—this?" he finally stammered.

The Italian drew an elegant portfolio from his pocket, and took a piece of stamped paper from it.

"Here is the *corpus delicti,*" he said, laughing.

"But how did it get into your hands?"

"Oh, in a very simple way: I bought and paid for it."

"You, signor? For what purpose?"

"Could it not be for the purpose of doing you a service?"

The vicomte shrugged his shoulders; he had no faith in his fellow-men.

"You are right," said Fernando, replying to the dumb protest, "I will be truthful with you. I would not want the Vicomte de Talızac to go under, because my fate is closely attached to his, and because the vicomte's father, the Marquis de Fougereuse, has done great service for the cause I serve. Therefore if I earnestly ask you not to commit such follies any more, you will thank me for it

and acknowledge that this small reciprocation is worth
the favor I am showing you."

"Then you will return the paper to me?" cried the
vicomte, stretching out his hand for it.

"No, the paper does not belong to me."

"But you just said—"

"That I bought it, certainly. I paid the price for it
only because I received the amount from several friends."

"And these friends—"

"Are the defenders and supporters of the monarchy;
they will not harm you."

Talizac became pensive.

"Let us not speak about the matter," continued Fernando; "I only wished to show you that I have a right
to ask your confidence, and I believe you will no longer
look upon it as idle curiosity if I ask you what business
you had with that man."

The Italian's words confirmed to Talizac the opinion
of the world that Velletri was a tool of the Jesuits.
However, he had done him a great service, and he no
longer hesitated to inform Velletri of the occurrence.

"I accompanied the Countess de Salves and her
daughter to a party at Tivoli," he began, as he walked
slowly along with his companion, "and we were enjoying
ourselves, when suddenly loud cries were heard and the
crowd rushed wildly toward the exits. The platform
where dancing was indulged in gave way, and the young
countess, in affright, let go of my arm and ran into the
middle of the crowd. I hurried after her, but could not
catch up with her; she was now in the neighborhood of
the scene of the accident, and, horror-stricken, I saw a
huge plank which hung directly over her head get loose

and tumble down. I cried aloud; the plank would crush her to death. At the right minute I saw a man grasp the plank and hold it in the air. How he did it I have never been able to tell; the plank weighed at least several hundred pounds, but he balanced it as if it had been a feather. The young countess had fainted away. When I finally reached her, the young man held her in his arms, and from the way in which she looked at him when she opened her eyes, I at once concluded that that wasn't the first time she had seen him. The old countess thanked him with tears in her eyes; I asked him for his name, for I had to find out first if it were proper for me to speak with him. He gave me no answer, but disappeared in the crowd. The only reward he took was a ribbon which the lady wore on her bosom and which he captured. The ribbon had no intrinsic value, but yet I thought it my duty to inform Irene about it. Do you know what answer she gave me?"

"No," replied Velletri, calmly.

"None at all. She turned her back to me."

"Impossible," observed the Italian, laughing; "well, I suspect that the knight without fear or reproach followed up the thing?"

"He did; he permits himself to ride past the Salves's palace every day, throws flowers over the wall, and I really believe the young countess picks up the flowers and waits at the window until he appears. Should I stand this?"

"No," replied Velletri, laughing; "you must, under all circumstances, get rid of this gallant. For your consolation, I can tell you it is not a difficult job."

"Then you know the man? I sent my servant after

him, but could not find out anything further than that he visits the Cafe Valois every day at this hour, and that is the reason I went there to-day.''

''Without having been able to accomplish your object. My dear vicomte, I place my experience at your service. The man is no rival, cannot be any; and if the young countess has built any air-castles in her romantic brain, I can give you the means to crumble them to pieces.'

''And the means?''

''Simply tell her the name of her admirer.''

''Yes; but he didn't mention his name to me.''

''That does not surprise me. He was formerly an acrobat, and his name is Fanfaro.''

The vicomte laughed boisterously. Fanfaro, a former acrobat, ran after young, noble ladies—it was too comical!

''So that is why the young man did not wish to fight me,'' he finally cried; ''it doesn't surprise me any more, and is cowardly too.''

The Italian, who had witnessed the scene in which Fanfaro had refused to cross weapons with a Talizac, laughed maliciously.

''The companions of the former acrobat are, no doubt, ignorant of whom they are dealing with?'' asked Talizac.

''On the contrary, they know him well.''

''I don't understand it! They speak to him, shake hands with him; it is extraordinary.''

The vicomte's stupidity excited the Italian's pity, but he did not allow his feelings to be perceived, and said:

''I think we have discussed this Fanfaro long enough. Let us not forget that we are still in the Carnival, and that we must hurry if we still wish to seek some distraction; forget the fatal scene of a short while ago.''

The vicomte had forgotten long ago that he and his father had been stigmatized as dishonorable rogues, and in great good humor he accompanied his companion toward the Rue Vivienne.

They had not gone far when the vicomte paused and nudged his friend.

Leaning against the balustrade of a house, a young girl, whose features were illuminated by the rays of a street lamp, sang in a clear voice to the accompaniment of a guitar. A large crowd of passers-by had assembled around the singer, who was a perfect vision of beauty.

Chestnut brown hair framed a finely cut face, and deep black eyes looked innocently from underneath long eye-lashes. The fingers which played on the instrument were long and tapering, and every movement of the body was the personification of grace.

When the song was finished loud applause was heard. Ths young songstress bowed at all sides, and a flush of pleasure lighted up the charming face. Every one put a penny on the instrument. When the vicomte's turn came, he threw forty francs on the guitar, and approached close to the songstress.

"You are alone to-day?" he boldly asked.

The young girl trembled from head to foot and walked on. The vicomte gazed after her, and the Italian laugh-ingly observed:

"The 'Marquise' is very strict to-day."

Thereupon he bent down and picked something up from the ground.

"Here, vicomte, is your money; the little one threw it away."

The vicomte uttered a cry of rage.

"The impertinent hussy!" he hissed.

"The affair has been going on in this way for the last two months," said the Italian, dryly; "and you could have known long ago, vicomte, that the 'Marquise' spurns your attentions."

"Fernando, I really believe you play the spy upon me!" exclaimed Talizac; "have a care, my patience has its limits."

"You are too tragical," replied Velletri, shrugging his shoulders; "instead of pursuing the little one with platonic declarations, you ought to try to break her spirit."

"Velletri, you are right," replied Talizac; "yes, I will revenge myself upon Fanfaro and possess this girl. What am I peer of France for?"

"Bravo, vicomte, you please me now—let us go to dinner, and then—"

"But the 'Marquise'?"

"Have patience. You will be satisfied with me."

CHAPTER XII

THE "MARQUISE."

MARDI-GRAS had come and folly reigned supreme at Paris. Opposite the Café Turque, which had already at that time a European reputation, stood a small poverty-stricken house. It was No. 48 Boulevard du Temple, and was inhabited by poor people.

In a small but cleanly room on the fifth story a young girl stood before a mirror arranging her toilet. The "Marquise," for it was she, looked curiously out of place in her humble surroundings.

A dark, tightly fitting dress showed her form to perfection, and the dark rose in her hair was no redder than the fresh lips of the young girl. The little singer gave a last glance in the mirror, smoothed back a rebellious curl, and seized her guitar to tune it.

A low moan came from a neighboring room. The street-singer immediately opened the curtained door and slipped into the room from which a cry now came.

"Louison—little Louison!"

"The poor thing—she has woke up," sighed the girl as she approached the small bed which stood in the equally small space.

"Mamma, how goes it?" she asked.

The form which lay on the bed looked almost in-

human.   The cadaverous face was half burned and the
bloodshot eyes, destitute of eyebrows, could not stand
the least ray of light.   The hands were horribly burned,
and her laugh exposed her toothless gums.

"Thirst, Louison," stammered the woman, pulling her
long gray hair over her eyes.

"There, mamma, drink," said Louison, bending tenderly over the poor woman.

The woman drank eagerly the glass of milk offered,
and then muttered softly to herself.

"It is so warm, I am burning, everywhere there are
flames."

The poor woman was crazy, and no one would have
ever recognized in her, Louise, the wife of the landlord
Jules Fougeres.

The reader will have guessed long since that Louison,
the street-singer, was none other than Fanfaro's lost sister.   The young girl, however, did not know that the
poor woman she so tenderly nursed was her mother.

Louison had once lost herself in the woods, and in her
blind fear had run farther and farther until she finally
reached an exit.   As she stood in a field sobbing bitterly,
a man approached her and asked her who she was and
where she had come from.   The child, exhausted by the
excitement of the last few days, could not give a clear
answer, and so the man took her on his arm and brought
her to his wife, who was waiting for him in a thicket.
The man and his wife carried on a terrible trade; they
hovered about battlefields to seek prey, and more than
one wounded man had been despatched by them if his
purse or his watch attracted the robbers' attention.   Nevertheless, these "Hyenas of the battlefield" were good

and kind to the lost child; they treated her just like their own children, of whom they had three, and at the end of the war, in consequence of the good crop they had secured on the battlefield, they were possessed of sufficient competence to buy a little place in Normandy.

Louison grew up. An old musician, who discovered that she had a magnificent voice, took pride in teaching the child how to sing, and when on Sundays she would sing in the choir, he would enthusiastically exclaim, "Little Louison will be a good songstress some day, her voice sounds far above the others."

An epidemic came to the village soon after, and at the end of two days her foster-parents were carried away, and Louison was once more alone in the world.

The nuns of the neighboring convent took the child, taught it what they knew themselves, and a few years passed peacefully for Louison.

A thirst to see the world took hold of her; the convent walls stifled her, and she implored the nuns to let her wander again. Naturally her request was refused, and so Louison tried to help herself.

One dark, stormy night she clambered over the garden wall, and when the nuns came to wake her next morning for early mass, they found her bed empty and the room vacant.

Singing and begging, the child wandered through Normandy. In many farmhouses she was kept a week as a guest, and one old woman even presented her with a guitar, which a stranger had left behind.

The proverb "all roads lead to Rome" would be more true in many cases if it said they lead to Paris; and thus it was with Louison. After a long and difficult journey she reached the capital, the El Dorado of street singers from Savoy; and, with the sanguine temperament of youth, the fifteen-year-old girl no longer doubted that she would support herself honestly.

In a miserable quarter of the great city, in the midst of people as poor as herself, Louison found a habitation. The wondrous beauty of the girl soon attracted attention, and when she sang songs on some street-corner she never failed to reap a harvest. At the end of four weeks she had her special public, and could now carry out a project she had long thought of. She went to the inspector of the quarter and begged him to name her some poor, sickly old woman whom she could provide for.

"I do not wish to be alone," she said, as the inspector looked at her in amazement, "and it seems to me that my life would have an aim if I could care for some one."

Petitions of this kind are quickly disposed of, and on the next day Louison received an order to go to another house in the same quarter and visit an old mad woman whose face had been terribly disfigured by fire.

Louison did not hesitate a moment to take the woman, whose appearance was so repulsive, to her home. When she asked the crazy woman, who gazed at her, "Mother, do you wish to go with me?" the deserted woman nodded, and from that day on she was sheltered.

Who could tell but that Louison's voice recalled to that clouded memory the recollection of happier days? Anyhow the maniac was tender and obedient to the young girl, and a daughter could not have nursed and cared for the poor old woman better than Louison did.

The sobriquet of the "Marquise" had been given to

Louison by the people of the quarter. She was so different from her companions; she looked refined and aristocratic, although her clothes were of the cheapest material, and no one would have dared to say an unkind or bold word to the young girl.

As the old woman handed the empty glass back to the girl, Louison cheerfully said:

"Mother, I must go out; promise me that you will be good during my absence."

"Good," repeated the maniac.

"Then you can put on your new cap to-morrow."

"The one with the ribbons?"

"Yes."

"Oh, then I will be good."

The poor thing clapped her hands, but suddenly she uttered a cry of pain.

"Ah!—my head—it is burning!"

Louison, with heavenly patience, caressed her gray hair and calmed her.

"Ah! where is the box?" the maniac complained after a while.

"To-morrow I will bring it to you," said the songstress, who knew the whims of the sick woman.

"Do not forget it," said the old woman; "in that box is luck. Oh, where did I put it?"

She continued to mutter softly to herself. Louison allowed her to do so, and slipped into the other room. It was time for her to go about her business. This being Mardi-Gras, she expected to reap a rich harvest. As she was about to open the door, she suddenly paused; she thought she heard a voice, and listened. A knock now sounded at the door, and Louison asked:

"Who is there?"

"A friend," came back in a loud voice.

"Your name?"

"You do not know me."

"Tell me your name."

"Robeckal; please admit me."

The young girl did not open at once; an indefinable fear seized her. Suppose the vicomte, who had followed her all over, had at last found out where she lived?

"Well, are you going to open?" cried Robeckal, becoming impatient.

Hesitatingly Louison pushed back the bolt, and with a sigh of relief she saw Robeckal's face; no, that was not the vicomte.

"H'm, mademoiselle, you thought perhaps that I was a beggar?" asked Robeckal, mockingly.

"Please tell me quickly what you want," cried Louison, hurriedly. "I must go out, and have no time to lose."

"You might offer me a chair, anyway," growled Robeckal, looking steadily at the handsome girl.

"I told you before I am in a hurry," replied Louison, coldly; "therefore please do not delay me unnecessarily."

Robeckal saw that the best thing he could do would be to come to the point at once, and grinning maliciously, he said:

"Mademoiselle, would you like to earn some money?"

"That depends—go on."

"Let me first speak about myself. I am an extra waiter. Do you know what that is?"

"Yes, you assist in saloons on Sundays and holidays."

"Right. For the past three days I have been at The Golden Calf, just in the street above."

"Ah, by Monsieur Aube?"

"Yes. The landlord would like to treat his guests to-day to some special amusement, and so he said to me last night, 'Robeckal, do you know of anything new and piquant!'

" 'The "Marquise," master,' I replied.

" 'But will she come?'

" 'H'm, we must ask her. How much do you intend to spend?'

" 'Twenty francs.'

" 'Good,' I said, 'I will ask her,' and here I am."

Louison had allowed Robeckal to finish. The man displeased her, but his offer was worth considering. Twenty francs! For the young girl the sum was a small fortune, and her heart ceased to beat when she thought of the many little comforts she could provide her *protégée* with it.

"Did not Monsieur Aube give you a letter for me?" she asked, still hesitating.

"No, mademoiselle. Do you mistrust me?"

"I did not say that, but I cannot decide so hastily. I will be at the Golden Calf in a little while, and give the gentleman my answer."

"Mademoiselle, tell me at once that you don't care to go, and I will get the man without arms, who will do just as well. He won't refuse, I warrant you."

With these words, Robeckal took out a card and pointed to two addresses thereon. The first was Louison's address, the second that of a street-singer who was well known to the young girl. Louison no longer doubted.

"I shall come," she said firmly; "when shall I make my appearance?"

"At eight o'clock."

"And when will I be done?"

A peculiar smile, unnoticed by Louison, played about Robeckal's lips.

"I really do not know," he finally replied, "but it will be between ten and eleven. With such good pay a minute more or less won't make much difference."

"No, but it must not be later than midnight."

"On no account, mademoiselle; if you are afraid, why, I will see you home," Robeckal gallantly cried.

"Good—tell Monsieur Aube I shall be punctual."

"Done. I suppose, mademoiselle, you will not forget to give me a portion of the twenty francs? I was the one, you know, who brought it about."

"With pleasure."

"Then good-by until this evening."

Robeckal hurried down the five flights of stairs. In front of the house a man enveloped in a wide mantle walked up and down.

When he saw Robeckal, he anxiously asked:

"Well?"

"It is settled."

"Really? Will she come?"

"Certainly."

The man in the cloak, who was no other than Fernando de Velletri, let some gold pieces slip into Robeckal's hand.

"If everything goes all right, you will get five hundred francs more," he cried.

"It is as good as if I had the money already in my

pocket. Besides, the racket is rather cheap, for the little one is a picture."

"So much the better," laughed the Italian.

While the worthy pair were discussing their plans, Louison went as usual to the boulevards and sang her pretty songs.

In the Golden Calf, Monsieur Aube's restaurant, things were very lively. The guests fairly swarmed in. The landlord ran busily to and fro, now in the kitchen turning over the roast, then again giving orders to the waiters, pulling a tablecloth here, uncorking a bottle there, and then again greeting new guests. On days like this the place was too narrow, and it always made Aube angry that he could not use the first story. The house belonged to an old man, who had until recently lived on the first floor, but since then new tenants had moved in, who were a thorn in the saloon-keeper's side. He had tried his best to get rid of them, advanced the rent, implored, chicaned, but all in vain. They stayed.

If they had only been tenants one could be proud of; but no! The family consisted of an athlete who called himself Firejaws; his daughter Caillette, a tight-rope dancer, a clown called Mario, and a young acrobat, Fanfaro. Every day the troupe performed on the Place du Chateau d'Eau, and, besides this, people visited the house under the pretence of taking lessons from Fanfaro in parlor magic.

These visitors, strange to say, looked very respectable; most of them appeared to be old soldiers. They certainly had no need to learn magic.

The large hall was filled to the last seat, and the waiters ran here and there with dishes, when an elegant

equipage drove up and immediately afterward the stentorian voice of the landlord cried:

"Jean, the gentlemen who have ordered room No. 11
have arrived. Conduct them upstairs."

The gentlemen were the Vicomte de Talizac, Arthur
de Montferrand and Fernando de Velletri. Jean led them
to the room and began to set the table.

"Tell me, Frederic," began Arthur, as he threw himself lazily in a chair, "how you got the idea of inviting us
to this hole for dinner?"

The waiter threw an angry look at Arthur, who had
dared to call the Golden Calf a hole.

"My dear Arthur," said the vicomte, coldly, "have
patience yet a while. It is not my fashion to speak about
my affairs in the presence of servants."

Jean hastily drew back, and only the thought of losing
his tip prevailed upon him to serve his customers.

"Now we are alone," said Arthur, "and we'll finally
find out all about it—"

"I must beg your pardon once more," interrupted the
vicomte, "but before dessert I never bother about serious
affairs."

"Ah, it is serious then," remarked Arthur. He knew
that Talizac was often short and feared that he was about
to ask for a loan. The young men dined with good appetite, and as the waiter placed the dessert upon the
table, the vicomte threw a glass filled with red wine
against the wall and exclaimed:

"Champagne, bring champagne!"

"Well, I must say that you end the Carnival in a
worthy way," laughed Velletri.

"Bah! I must drown my troubles in champagne," replied the vicomte, shrugging his shoulders. "I tell you, my friends, I had a conversation with my father to-day which made me wild."

"Ah, it was about your marriage, no doubt!" said the Italian.

"Yes. The marquis wants me to go to the altar in fourteen days. That would be a fine thing."

"But I thought the marriage was a good one for both sides; the fortune of the Salves—"

"Oh, bother with the fortune!" interrupted the vicomte.

"And, besides, the young countess is very beautiful," continued Arthur.

"Beautiful?" repeated the vicomte, mockingly; "not that I can see. She puts on airs, as if the whole world lay at her feet, and poses as such a virtuous being. And yet I really believe she is no better than other people; I—"

"Frederic," interrupted Velletri, warningly; he feared that the vicomte would inform young Montferrand what had occurred between his bride and the acrobat.

"Well," said Arthur, hastily, "I hope that when Irene de Salves becomes your bride you will be more pleasant to her."

"Really, Arthur, you have such antediluvian notions," laughed the vicomte; "formerly we said that marriage was the grave of love; but if there has been no love beforehand, it follows that the grave will remain empty. No, my friends, if I am bound by marriage ties, I authorize you both to hunt on my ground, and it will give me pleasure if you score a success. Who knows? The countess is, perhaps, less prudish than she seems."

"Perhaps I shall make use of the permission," laughed Arthur, carelessly.

"I wish you joy. I haven't the stuff of a jealous husband in me, and the freedom I ask for myself I grant to others!"

"That is unselfish," said the Italian; "not every one is so liberal with his wife."

"Bah! the wife of a friend is decidedly more piquant than one's own, and who knows but that I may revenge myself later on. I—"

At this moment a clear, fresh girlish voice was heard coming from downstairs, and the first verse of a ballad by Romagnesi was delightfully phrased. The young men listened attentively to the simple song, and when at the end of the same a storm of applause followed, Arthur clapped his hands too.

"What a pity," he said, "that one cannot hear this nightingale nearer."

"Why should not that be possible?" cried the vicomte, springing up as if electrified.

Fernando grew frightened. This idea might disturb his plan.

"What is there in a street-singer?" he contemptuously asked.

Talizac, however, who was under the influence of the champagne he had drunk, did not understand the hint, and angrily exclaimed:

"Now she shall just come upstairs; first she must sing to us, and then—"

"And then?" repeated Arthur curiously.

"Ah, it is merely a little surprise we arranged for the little one," observed Velletri, with a cynical laugh.

"What! a surprise?"

"Yes."

"And she does not suspect anything?"

"Nothing."

"Well, I am curious to see the little one; let us call Aube, he can show his singer to us."

"Gentlemen, no folly," warned Velletri, "we are not in the Palais Royal here, and in some things the mob does not see any fun."

"I will attend to the people downstairs," said Arthur, while the vicomte rang loudly.

When the waiter came he received the order to send the landlord up, and in less than five minutes the latter came and bowed respectfully to the guests who had drunk so much champagne.

"Monsieur Aube," began the vicomte, "who is the little bird that sings so beautifully downstairs?"

"A young, modest, and very respectable girl, gentlemen."

The young men burst into loud laughter.

"A saint, then?" exclaimed Arthur.

"Really, gentlemen, she is very virtuous and respectable."

"So much the better," said the young men to Aube. "We would like to take a good look at the little one. Send her up to us so that she can sing a few songs for us, and at the same time put a few more bottles on the ice."

Monsieur Aube did not know what to do.

"What are you waiting for?" asked the vicomte, in a maudlin voice.

"Gentlemen, the little one is so pure," said the landlord, earnestly.

"Are we going to ruin her?" exclaimed Talızac, with a laugh. "She shall sing, and we will pay her well for it. She shall get a hundred francs; is that enough?"

The landlord considered. He knew Louison was poor, and he said to himself he had no right to prevent the pretty girl from earning so much money. Moreover, she was not called "The Marquise" for nothing, and Velletri's mien reassured the host. So he came to the conclusion that there was no danger to be feared for his *protégée.* Even if the other two were drunk, the Italian was sober; and so the host finally said:

"I will send the little one."

As the landlord entered the hall, Louison was just going about and collecting. The crop was a rich one, and with sparkling eyes the songstress returned to her place, to give a few more songs, when Aube drew her into a corner.

"Louison," he softly said, "I have got a good business to propose to you."

"What is it, Father Aube?"

The landlord, somewhat embarrassed, stammeringly answered:

"If you desire you can make one hundred francs in fifteen minutes."

"So much? You are joking?"

"Not at all; you sing two or three songs, and the money is earned."

"Where shall I sing?"

"Here in my house, on the first story."

At this minute the hall-door opened and loud laughter came from above. Louison looked anxiously at the host and asked:

"Who wants to hear me?"

"Some guests, Louison; high-toned guests."

"Are they ladies and gentlemen, or only gentlemen?"

"Gentlemen, jolly young gentlemen."

"And if I go up will you stay in the neighborhood?"

"Certainly; this house is my house, and you are under my protection."

Louison considered. One hundred francs was a treasure with which she could do wonders. A comfortable chair could be bought for the invalid, wine and other strengthening things kept in the house, and—

"I agree," she said, picking up her guitar; "when shall I go up?"

"Directly, Louison, I will accompany you."

"H'm, what does that mean?" exclaimed a solid-looking citizen as he saw Louison go up the stairs; "is the performance over?"

"No," said Aube to his guests, "Louison will sing more later on. Have a little patience."

When the landlord and the young girl entered the room of the young men, Aube was agreeably surprised at seeing that the vicomte had disappeared. He was perfectly calm now. It had been the vicomte of whom Aube had been afraid, and with a light heart he left the apartment.

"'Marquise,' will you be so kind as to sing us a song?" asked Arthur, politely.

Louison's modesty began to have a good influence on him, and he already regretted having assisted Talizac in his plan.

Louison tuned her instrument and then began to sing a pretty little air. Montferrand and Velletri listened attentively, and when she had ended they both asked her in the most polite way imaginable to sing another song. Louison did not wait to be coaxed; she began a simple ballad and sang it with melting sweetness. Suddenly she uttered a loud scream and let her guitar fall. Frederic de Talizac stood before her.

"Continue your song, my pretty child," giggled the vicomte; "I hope I have not frightened you?"

As he said this he tried to put his arm around Louison's waist.

She recoiled as if stung by a rattlesnake.

"I will not sing any more," she said firmly; "let me go."

"Nonsense, my little pigeon, you remain here," said the vicomte huskily, placing himself in front of the door, "and for each note you sing I will give you a kiss."

The poor child was paralyzed with fear. She threw an agonizing look upon the drunken man's companions, and when she saw them both sit there so calm and indifferent, her eyes sparkled with anger.

"Miserable cowards!" she contemptuously exclaimed. "Will you permit a drunken scoundrel to insult a defenceless girl?"

Arthur sprang up. A flash of shame was on his classically formed features, and turning to Talizac he hastily said:

"She is right, vicomte; are you not ashamed?"

"Are you speaking to me?" laughed Talizac, mockingly. "I really believe you wish to be the Don Quixote of this virtuous Dulcinea del Toboso! No, my friend, we did not bet that way; the girl must be mine, and I should like to see the man who will oppose me. '

He grasped Louison's arm; the young girl cried aloud for help, and the next minute the vicomte tumbled back struck by a powerful blow of the fist. Montferrand had come to the street-singer's rescue.

The vicomte roared like a wild bull, and, seizing a knife from the table, rushed upon Arthur. The two men struggled with one another. The table fell over; and while Louison unsuccessfully tried to separate the combatants, Velletri looked coolly at the fray.

"Help! murder!" cried Louison in desperation. She did not think of escape. She hoped Aube would make his appearance.

The landlord had really hastened up at the first cry, but at the head of the stairs Robeckal had held him tight and uttered a peculiar whistle. Two powerful men came in answer to the signal, and seizing the host in their arms, they bore him to a small room where the brooms were kept. Aube imagined his house had been entered by burglars. He threw himself with all his force against the door, he cried for help, and soon a few guests who had been sitting in the restaurant came to his assistance and rescued him.

"Follow me, gentlemen," cried the landlord, angrily. "It is a dastardly conspiracy! Upstairs there they are driving a poor, innocent girl to despair. Help me to rescue her. It's the 'Marquise.' Oh, heavens! her cries have ceased, she must be dead!"

Twenty men, in company with the landlord, rushed into the young men's rooms. Louison was no longer there, and in the centre Montferrand and the vicomte were still fighting with one another. Montferrand had already taken the knife away from the drunken man, when the vicomte angrily rushed at Arthur and hit him in the neck. A stream of blood gushed from the wound, and with a low moan the wounded man sank to the ground.

Before he could rise to his feet again, Velletri had seized the vicomte by the arm, and in spite of his resistance dragged him down the stairs. When Aube looked around for them, they had already left and not a trace of Louison could be found.

"Merciful God!" he despairingly cried, "where is the poor child? I promised her I would protect her, and now—"

"The scoundrels have abducted her!" exclaimed Arthur, who had in the meantime recovered. "It was, a shrewdly planned piece of business."

"Abducted her? Impossible!" cried the landlord, looking at Arthur in amazement. "Who are the men?"

A crowd of guests had gathered about Arthur and the landlord, and while a barber tried to stanch the still bleeding wound, Montferrand bitterly said:

"One of the scoundrels bears a noble old name. Shame over the nobility of France that it tolerates a Talizac and Fougereuse in its ranks."

"Who speaks of Talizac and Fougereuse?" cried a fresh voice, and a very handsome man approached Monsieur Aube.

"Ah, Monsieur Fanfaro," said the landlord vivaciously, "Heaven sends you at the right time. Forget all the troubles and the cares I have caused you; I will never say another word against athletes and acrobats, but help us!"

"What has happened?" asked Fanfaro in astonishment. "I just came home and found every one in the restaurant excited. I asked, but no one knew anything, so I hurried here. Tell me what I can do for you; I am ready."

"May God reward you, Monsieur Fanfaro; oh, if it is only not too late."

"Monsieur Aube," asked Fanfaro, politely, "what is the matter?"

"A young girl—it will bring me to my grave when I think that such a thing should happen in my house—I—"

"Landlord," interrupted Arthur, "let me tell the story to the gentleman.

"Unfortunately," continued Montferrand, turning to Fanfaro, "I am mixed up in the affair myself. I let myself be persuaded by the Vicomte de Talizac—"

"I thought so," growled Fanfaro.

"And his friend Velletri to accompany them here—"

"Velletri? The Italian spy? The tool of the Jesuits, who treacherously betrayed his own countrymen, the Carbonari?" asked Fanfaro, contemptuously.

"Really, you are telling me something new," replied Arthur, "but it served me right. Why wasn't I more particular in the choice of my companions! Well, this worthy pair have abducted a young girl, a street-singer."

"The scoundrels! Where have they carried the poor child to?"

"God alone knows! I only heard here about the plan, but the scoundrels did not inform me where they intended to bring the poor child," replied Arthur, feeling ashamed at having had even the slightest connection with the affair, and inwardly vowing never again to have anything to do with the scoundrels who bear noble names.

"But the girl, no doubt, has relatives, parents or friends, who will follow her traces?"

"No," replied Aube, "she is an orphan, and is called the 'Marquise.'"

"Why has she received that sobriquet?"

"I do not know. She is a very respectable girl."

"Where does she live?"

"Not far from here, No. 42 Boulevard du Temple, fifth story. Robeckal, an extra waiter, who, as I have since found out, is a cunning scoundrel, had engaged her for to-night."

"If Robeckal had a hand in the affair then it can only be a scoundrelly one!" exclaimed Fanfaro, with a frown.

"Do you know him?"

"Unfortunately, yes; tell me what more do you know?"

"Not much. The 'Marquise' lives with an old, poor crazy woman, who lost her reason and the use of her limbs at a fire. The young girl, whose name is Louison—"

"Louison?" cried Fanfaro, in affright.

"Yes; why, what is the matter with you?"

"Nothing; tell me how old is the girl?"

"About sixteen."

"My God, that would just be right; but no, it cannot be."

"Monsieur Fanfaro," said Montferrand, gently, "can I do anything for you, you seem to be in trouble?"

"Oh, I have a horrible suspicion, I cannot explain it to you now, but the age and the name agree. Ah, that infamous Talizac! again and again he crosses my path; but if I catch him now, I will stamp upon him like a worm!"

"Do you intend to follow the robbers?"

"Certainly, I must rescue the girl."

"Monsieur Fanfaro," said Montferrand, "do with me what you will, I will help you!"

CHAPTER XIII

THE PURSUIT

FANFARO looked gratefully at the young nobleman and then said:

"Please tell me your name, so that I may know whom I am under obligations to?"

"My name is Arthur de Montferrand," said the nobleman, handing his card to the young man, whose profession he knew, with the same politeness as if he were a peer of France.

Fanfaro bowed and then hurriedly said:

"Let us not lose any more time; I—"

Loud knocking at the house-door and the murmur of several voices, which came from below, made the young man pause. The planting of muskets on the pavement was now heard and a coarse voice cried:

"Open in the name of the law!"

Fanfaro trembled.

"The police!" exclaimed Aube, breathing more freely; "perhaps the robbers have already been captured."

Fanfaro laid his hand upon Aube's shoulder.

"Monsieur Aube," he said bitterly, "the police to-day do not bother about such trivial affairs. The minions of Louis XVIII. hunt different game."

"Open," came louder than before, "or we shall burst in the door."

"My God! my God! what a day this is," complained Aube, sinking helplessly on a chair; "what do the police want in my house?"

"Monsieur Aube, they seek conspirators, heroes of freedom and justice," said Fanfaro earnestly.

"How so? What do you mean?" asked Aube, opening wide his eyes and looking at the young man.

"I am one of the men the police are looking for," exclaimed Fanfaro coolly.

"You!" exclaimed Montferrand in terror, "then you are lost."

"Not yet," laughed Fanfaro. "Monsieur Aube, hurry and open the door and try to detain the people. That is all that is necessary. Good-by for the present, and do not forget to hunt for the girl; with the aid of God we will find her."

He ran out, and the nobleman and the landlord heard him bound up the stairs. Aube now began to push back the iron bolt of the street door, and when it opened several policemen and an inspector entered.

"I must say, Monsieur Aube," cried the inspector angrily, "you took a long time to obey his majesty's order."

"But at this time of night," stammered Aube. "What are you looking for, inspector?"

"Ask rather whom I am looking for?" retorted the inspector.

His gaze fell on Arthur, who did not look very attractive with his bloody clothes and torn shirt.

"Who is this tramp?" asked the inspector roughly.

"The tramp will have you thrown out if you are impertinent. My name is Arthur de Montferrand, and I am the son of the Marquis of Montferrand."

The inspector opened his eyes wide with astonishment. How could such a mistake happen to him? The son of the Marquis of Montferrand. The inspector would have preferred just now to hide himself in a corner. He stammered apology upon apology, and then in an embarrassed way muttered:

"I have got a painful mission. I am to look for a 'suspect' in this house."

"A 'suspect'?" whispered Aube, anxiously.

"Yes; conspirators who threaten the sacred person of the king."

"And you are looking for these people in my house?" asked Aube, apparently overwhelmed at the intelligence.

"Yes, they are said to live here; two acrobats, named Girdel and Fanfaro."

"Inspector, I am inconsolable; but I will not oppose you; do your duty," said Aube, with the mien of a man who gives a kingdom away.

Arthur and the landlord exchanged knowing looks as the inspector strode toward the door. Fanfaro must be in safety by this time.

"The house is surrounded," said the inspector, as he went away, "and I think we shall have little to do."

Montferrand trembled. Suppose Fanfaro had been captured! The policemen went to the upper story, which had been pointed out to them by the landlord as the residence of Girdel and Fanfaro.

"Open, in the name of the law!" thundered a voice,

which shook the house; and then followed, hardly less loud, the angry exclamation:

"By Jupiter, the nest is empty; the birds have flown!"

At this moment a voice cried from the street:

"Inspector, they are escaping over the roofs."

It was Simon, the worthy steward of the Marquis of Fougereuse, who assisted the police to-day. He had stationed himself, with several officers, in front of the house, and had noticed two shadows gliding over the roofs.

"Forward, men," cried the inspector. "We must catch them, dead or alive."

In a moment, Simon had bounded up the stairs and now stood near the official at the skylight.

"How slanting that roof is!" growled the inspector. "One misstep and you lie in the street."

He carefully climbed out; Simon followed, and then they both looked around for the escaped conspirators.

"There they are!" exclaimed the steward, hastily. "Look, they have reached the edge of the roof and are going to swing themselves over to the neighboring roof! They are fools; the distance must be at least ten feet. They will either fall down and smash their heads on the pavement, or else fall into our hands."

Simon had seen aright. Girdel and Fanfaro were at the edge of the roof, and now the young man bent down and swung something his pursuers could not make out.

"Surrender!" cried the inspector, holding himself on a chimney.

Fanfaro now rose upright. He made a jump and the next minute he was on the neighboring roof.

The inspector and Simon uttered a cry of rage, and redoubled it when they saw Fanfaro busying himself tying a stout rope to an iron hook which he connected with another hook on the roof he had just left.

Girdel now clambered to the edge of the roof, grasped the rope with both hands, and began to work his way across to Fanfaro.

"Quick, a knife!" cried the inspector.

Simon handed him his pocket-knife and the policeman began to saw the rope through. Luckily for Girdel, the work went very slow, for the knife was as dull as the rope was thick, and Simon, who only now began to remember that Girdel must not be killed at any price, loudly exclaimed:

"Stop, inspector, are you out of your senses?"

The policeman was no longer able to heed the warning. The knife had done its duty, the rope was cut!

Girdel did not fall to the pavement though. At the decisive moment Fanfaro bent far over the roof, and with superhuman strength held on to the rope on which Girdel was, at the same time crying to him:

"Attention, the rope is cut, take your teeth."

Girdel understood at once, and his mighty jaws held the rope firmly.

Fanfaro had bent far forward to hinder Girdel from being dashed against the wall, and kept in that position, until the athlete could work himself with his hands and teeth to the edge of the roof.

The roof was at length reached. Fanfaro swung his arms about Girdel, and the next minute they both disappeared behind a tall chimney!

"Papa Girdel, we have nothing to fear now," said Fanfaro, laughing; but soon he thought of Louison, and he sighed heavily.

"What is the matter with you, my boy?" asked Girdel, in amazement.

"I will tell you some other time. Let us try to reach the street first, for our pursuers will surely try to get into the house and begin the hunt anew."

The athlete saw he was right, and they both began their perilous flight over the roofs. For a time everything went right, but suddenly Fanfaro paused and said:

"We are at a street corner."

"That is a fatal surprise," growled Girdel; "what shall we do now?"

"We must try to reach a roof-pipe and glide down."

"That is easier said than done. Where will you find a roof-pipe able to sustain my weight?'

Fanfaro looked at Girdel in amazement. He had not thought of that.

"Then let us try to find a skylight and get into some house," he said, after a pause.

"Suppose the window leads to an inhabited room?" observed Girdel.

"Then we can explain our perilous position. We will not be likely to tumble into a policeman's house."

"Let us hope for the best," replied Girdel.

At the same moment a terrific crash was heard and Fanfaro saw his foster-father sink away. Girdel had unconsciously trodden on a window-pane and fallen through!

"That is a new way of paying visits," cried a voice which Fanfaro thought he recognized, and while Girdel made desperate attempts to swing himself again on the roof, a hand armed with a tallow candle appeared in the opening.

"I will light the gentlemen," continued the voice.

"Bobichel, is it you?" cried Fanfaro, joyously.

"Certainly, and I ought to know you," was the reply; "really, the master and Fanfaro."

"Bobichel," said Girdel, greatly astonished, "is it really you? We thought you were dead!"

"Bah! a clown can stand a scratch; but come quickly into my room, it is cold outside."

Girdel and Fanfaro entered the small attic and Bobichel received his old comrades cordially.

"The ball did not hit you, then?" asked Girdel: "we thought you were gone."

"Almost," replied the clown; "I dragged myself a few steps further, with the bullet in my side, and then sank down unconscious. When I awoke I found myself in the hospital at Remiremont, where I remained until a week ago. Later on I will give you all the details. For to-day I will only say that I arrived in Paris yesterday and rented this room here. I expected to find you here, and I intended to look about to-morrow morning. What happy accident brought you here?"

"In the first place, the police," replied Fanfaro; "they hunted us like a pack of dogs a wild animal, and if we had not escaped over the roofs we would now be behind lock and key."

"But why are you pursued?" asked Bobichel, anxiously. "Do you belong to the conspiracy of which there is so much talk?"

"Probably," replied Girdel.

"Is there a place for me in the conspiracy?" asked

the clown, vivaciously, "I am without employment just now, and if you wish to take me in tow, I—"

"We shall attend to it," said Fanfaro, cordially.

"How is little Caillette getting on?" asked Bobichel, after a pause.

"Very well, thank you. We shall let her know to-morrow morning that we are safe."

"Then she is in Paris, too?"

"Certainly. We lived up till now in the Golden Calf. However, we must look for other rooms now. We can speak about that to-morrow. Let us go to sleep now, it must be very late," said Girdel; and looking at his watch, he added: "Really it is two o'clock."

"Bobichel's eyes knew that long ago," laughed Fanfaro. "Go to bed, old friend, you are tired."

"Oh, I am not tired," said the clown, yawning in spite of himself. "I will not go to bed after I have found you again."

"You must do so, Bobichel," said Fanfaro, earnestly. "You are still weak and must husband your strength. Go calmly to bed. Girdel and I have still a great deal to consider, and we are both glad that we need not camp in the street."

Bobichel hesitated no longer; he threw himself on his hard couch and in less than five minutes he was fast asleep.

As soon as Girdel found himself alone with Fanfaro, he said, in an anxious voice:

"Fanfaro, tell me what ails you. I know you too well not to be aware that something extraordinary has happened. Place confidence in me; perhaps I can help you."

"If you only could," sighed Fanfaro; "but you are

right, I will tell you all. First, Papa Girdel, I must ask you a few questions about my past—"

"Speak; what do you wish to know?"

"What did you find out about my mother?"

"That she was the victim of a conflagration. She was in a farmhouse which had been set fire to by Cossacks."

"And my father?"

"He died the death of a hero, fighting for his country."

"As far as my memory goes," said Fanfaro, pensively, "I was in a large, dark room. It must have been a subterranean chamber. My parents had intrusted my little sister to my care. I held her by the hand, but suddenly I lost her and could never find her again."

"I know, I know," said Girdel, sorrowfully.

"Since this evening," continued the young man, "I have been thinking of my poor little Louison. I have not been able to tell you yet that a respectable young girl, who earns her living by singing, was forcibly abducted from the Golden Calf this evening."

"Impossible! Monsieur Aube is a brave man," exclaimed Girdel, impatiently.

"Ah! Aube knows nothing of the matter. He is innocent. The villain who did it is a bad man, who has already crossed our path."

"And his name?"

"Vicomte de Talizac."

"Talizac? Has this family got a thousand devils in its service? It was the vicomte's father, the Marquis of Fougereuse, who wished to kill us at Sainte-Ame; his steward ran to Remiremont to get the police."

"Like father like son. The proverb says that the

apple doesn't fall far from the tree. The young girl whom Talızac abducted is named Louison, and I—"

"My poor boy, you do not really think—"

"That this Louison is my poor lost sister? Yes, I fear so, Papa Girdel. When I heard the name, I trembled in every limb, and since then the thought haunts me. If I knew that Louison were dead I would thank God on my knees, but it is terrible to think that she is in the power of that scoundrel. The fact that Robeckal has a hand in the affair stamps it at once as a piece of villany."

"Robeckal is the vicomte's accomplice?" cried Girdel, springing up. "Oh, Fanfaro, why did you not say so at once? We must not lose a minute! Ah, now I understand all! Robeckal abducted the poor child and brought it to Rolla. I know they are both in Paris, and I will move heaven and earth to find them!"

"May God reward you, Papa Girdel," said Fanfaro, with deep emotion. "I will in the meantime try to find the invalid with whom the street-singer lives, and—"

"Is there nothing for Bobichel to do?" asked the clown, sitting up in his bed.

"Oh, Bobichel!" exclaimed Fanfaro, gratefully, "if you want to help us?"

"Of course I do. I will accompany master to Robeckal, for I also have a bone to pick with the scoundrel.'

CHAPTER XIV

LOUISE

LOUISON'S crazy mother had passed a miserable night. Accustomed to see Louison before going to sleep and hear her gentle voice, and not having her cries answered on this particular evening, the poor woman, who had not been able to move a step for years, dragged herself on her hands and feet into the next room and shoved the white curtains aside.

The painful cry of the invalid as she saw the bed empty, drowned a loud knock at the door, and only when the knocking was repeated and a voice imploringly cried: "Open, for God's sake, open quick!" did the burned woman listen. Where had she heard the voice?

"Quick, open—it is on account of Louison," came again from the outside. It was Fanfaro who demanded entrance.

A cry which was no longer human came from the breast of the burned woman, and, collecting all her strength, she crawled to the door and tore so long at the curtains which covered the pane of glass that they came down and Fanfaro could see into the room. As soon as he saw the position of the poor woman, he understood at once that she could not open the door, and making up his mind quickly, he pressed in the window, and the next minute he was in the room.

"Where is Louison, madame?" he exclaimed.

The woman did not answer; she looked steadily at him and plunged her fingers in her gray hair.

"Madame, listen to me. Louison has been abducted. Don't you know anything?"

The poor thing still remained silent, even though her lips trembled convulsively, and the deep-set eyes gazed steadily at the young man.

"Madame," began Fanfaro, desperately, "listen to my words. Can you not remember where Louison told you she was going? You know who Louison is; she nurses and cares for you. Can you not tell me anything?"

At length a word came from the burned woman's breast.

"Jacques, Jacques!" she stammered, clutching the young man's knees and looking at him.

Fanfaro trembled. Who was this horrible woman who called him by the name of his childhood?

"Louison! Jacques!" uttered the toothless lips, and hot, scalding tears rolled over the scarred cheeks.

A flood of never-before-felt emotions rushed over Fanfaro; he tenderly bent over the poor woman, and gently said:

"You called me Jacques. I was called that once. What do you know of me?"

The burned woman looked hopelessly at him; she tried hard to understand him, but her clouded mind could not at first grasp what he meant.

"I will tell you what I know of the past," continued Fanfaro, slowly. "I formerly lived at Leigoutte in the Vosges. My father's name was Jules, my mother's Louise, and my little sister Louison — where is Louison?"

At last a ray of reason broke from the disfigured eyes, and she whispered:

"Jacques, my dear Jacques! I am Louise, your mother, and the wife of Jules Fougeres!"

"My mother!" stammered Fanfaro with emotion, and taking the broken woman in his arms, he fervently kissed her disfigured face. The poor woman clung to him. The veil of madness was torn aside and stroking the handsome face of the young man with her broken fingers, she softly murmured:

"I have you again. God be thanked!"

"But where is Louison?" broke in Fanfaro, anxiously.

Still the brain of the sick woman could not grasp all the new impressions she had received, and although she looked again and again at Fanfaro, she left the question unanswered.

At any other time Fanfaro would have left the sick woman alone, but his anxiety about Louison gave him no peace. He did not doubt a minute but that his mother had recognized Louison long ago as her daughter, and so he asked more urgently:

"Mother, where is Louison? Your little Louison, my sister?"

"Louison?" repeated the sick woman, with flaming eyes. "Oh, she is good; she brings me fruit and flowers."

"But where is she now?"

"Gone." moaned the invalid.

"Gone? Where to?"

"I do not know. Her bed is empty."

"Then I was not deceived. She has been abducted by that scoundrel, Talizac!"

"Talizac?" repeated the maniac, with a foolish laugh. "Oh, I know him, do not let him in; he brings unhappiness—unhappiness!"

"Then he has been here?" cried Fanfaro, terror-stricken.

"No, not here—in—Sachemont—I—oh! my poor head."

With a heart-rending cry the poor woman sank to the ground unconscious. The excitement of the last hour had been too much for her. Fanfaro looked at the fainting woman, not knowing what to do. He took her in his arms and was about to place her on the bed when the door was softly opened and three forms glided in.

"Girdel, thank Heaven!" cried Fanfaro, recognizing the athlete, "have you found Robeckal?"

"No, the wretches moved out of their former residence in the Rue Vinaigrier, yesterday, and no one could tell us where they went."

"I thought so," groaned Fanfaro, and then he hastily added: "Girdel, the unhappy woman I hold in my arms is my mother. No, do not think I am crazy, it is the truth; and the girl who was abducted is my sister Louison."

"Impossible!" stammered Girdel.

"His mother!" came a whisper behind Fanfaro, and turning hastily round he saw Caillette—who stood at the door with tears in her eyes—with Bobichel, who said:

"Caillette will take care of the invalid until we have found Louison; I say that we move heaven and earth so that we find her."

"You are right, Bobichel," said Fanfaro, and, pressing a kiss upon his mother's forehead, he ran off with Girdel and the clown.

CHAPTER XV

SWINDLED

WHILE Montferrand and Talizac were struggling, Robeckal slipped up to the door and winked to Louison. She hurried out and implored Robeckal to bring her out of this miserable house. This was just what the wretch had been waiting for, and hardly five minutes later he was in a small street with the betrayed girl. In this street a carriage stood. Robeckal seized the unsuspecting girl by the waist, lifted her into the carriage, and sprang in himself. The driver whipped up the horses and away they went at a rapid gait.

"Where are you bringing me to?"' cried Louison in terror, as she saw the carriage take a wrong direction.

"Keep still, my little pigeon," laughed Robeckal, "I am bringing you to a place where it will please you."

Louison for a moment was speechless; she soon recovered herself, however, comprehended her position at a glance, hastily pulled down the carriage window, and cried aloud for help.

"Silence, minx!" exclaimed Robeckal roughly, and pulling a cloth out of his pocket he held it in front of Louison's face.

"Ah, now you are getting tame," he mockingly

laughed, as the young girl, moaning softly, fell back in the cushions. The carriage hurried along and finally stopped in an obscure street of the Belleville Quarter.

Robeckal sprang out, and taking the unconscious Louison in his arms, he carried her up the stairs of a small house, and pulled the bell, while the carriage rolled on.

"Ah, here you are; let me see the chicken!"

With these words Rolla received her comrade.

She put the lamp close to Louison's face, and then said:

"Your Talizac hasn't got bad taste; the little one is handsome."

"Is everything in order?" asked Robeckal, going up the stairs after the "Cannon Queen."

"Certainly, look for yourself."

Robeckal entered an elegantly furnished room, and, placing Louison on a sofa, he said in a commendatory tone:

"It's pretty fair."

"Don't you think so? Leave the rest to me; I have a grand idea."

"An idea?" repeated Robeckal, doubtingly.

"Yes, an idea that will bring us in a nice sum of money."

"Then I am satisfied. If the little one only does not cause us any embarrassment."

"No fear of that. In the first place she should sleep."

The virago poured a few drops of a watery liquid in a spoon and approached Louison. The latter had her lips parted, but her teeth were tightly drawn together. Robeckal carefully put the blade of his knife between

them, and Rolla poured the liquid down Louison's
throat.

"Now come downstairs with me," she said, turning
to Robeckal, "and if your vicomte comes you will praise
me."

The worthy pair now left Louison, who was sleeping; and after Rolla had tightly locked the door and
put the key in her pocket, they both strode to the basement. Here they entered a small, dirty room, and Rolla
had just filled two glasses with rum when a carriage
stopped in front of the door.

"Here they are," said Robeckal, hastily emptying his
glass and going to the street door, from whence came the
sound of loud knocks.

Shortly afterward he returned in company with Talizac
and Velletri. The vicomte's face was flushed with the
wine he had been drinking; spots of blood were on his
clothes, and his walk was uneven and unsteady. Velletri,
on the other hand, showed not a trace of excitement, and
his dress was neat and select.

"A glass of water!" commanded the vicomte, in a
rough voice, turning to Rolla.

The fat woman looked angrily at him, and while she
brought the water she muttered to herself:

"Wait now. You shall pay dearly for your coarse-
ness."

Talizac drank, and then said:

"Is the little one here?"

"Yes."

"You haven't done anything to her, have you?"

"What do you take me for?" growled Rolla.

"Bring me some wash water," said the vicomte, without noticing Rolla's sensitiveness, and turning to Velletri, he added: "Montferrand handled me roughly; I look as if I had been torn from the gallows."

"As if you won't get there one of these days," growled Rolla; and, lighting a candle, she said aloud, "If the gentlemen wish I will conduct them to the 'Marquise.'"

"Go on; where is she?"

"In the upper story—she is sleeping."

"So much the better. I will lavish my affection on her, and see if she is still as prudish."

Rolla preceded the vicomte up the stairs. As she went past she exchanged a quick glance with Robeckal, and the latter growled to himself:

"There is something up with her; I will watch and help her should it be necessary."

Rolla and Talizac were now in front of the door which led to Louison's room. The vicomte looked inquiringly at his companion and said:

"Open it."

"One moment, we are not as far as that yet. Just look at the little one first."

With these words Rolla opened a sliding window in the door and stepped back, while the vicomte bent down and looked into the partly lighted room.

Louison lay fast asleep on the sofa. The pretty head rested on the left arm, while the right hung carelessly down, and the long eyelashes lay tightly on the slightly flushed cheeks. The small, delicate mouth was slightly compressed, and the mass of silky hair fell in natural curls about the white forehead.

"Isn't she charming?" giggled Rolla.

Talizac was a libertine, a dissipated man, and yet when he saw the sleeping girl, a feeling he could not account for overcame him. He forgot where he was, that the miserable woman at his side had helped to carry out his dastardly plans, and all his longing now was to throw himself at Louison's feet, and say to her:

"I love you dearly!"

"Open," he hastily ordered.

Rolla let the window fall again and looked impertinently at him.

"My lord," she said, with a courtesy, "before I open this door you will pay me twenty thousand francs."

"Woman, are you mad?"

"Bah! you would shout so! I said twenty thousand francs, and I mean it. Here is my hand. Count in the money and I will get the key."

"Enough of this foolish talk," cried the vicomte, in a rage. "I paid your comrade the sum he demanded, and that settles it."

"You are more stupid than I thought," laughed Rolla. "If you do not pay, nothing will come of the affair."

"But this is a swindle," said the vicomte.

"Do not shout such language through the whole house," growled Rolla. "Do you think it is a pleasure to abduct girls? Robeckal had enough trouble with the little one and—"

What Rolla said further was drowned by the noise Talizac made as he threw himself against the door. It did not move an inch though; and before the vicomte could try again, Robeckal hurried up with a long knife in his hand.

"What is the matter?" he angrily cried.

"Your friend the vicomte forgot his purse and thinks he can get the girl on credit," mockingly replied Rolla.

The noise brought Velletri up too; but as soon as he saw Robeckal's long knife, he turned about again. The vicomte too became pacified.

"I will give you all the money I have with me," he said, as he turned the contents of his purse into Rolla's big hand. "Count and see how much it is."

"Ten, twenty, eight hundred francs," counted the Cannon Queen; "we shall keep the money on account, and when you bring the rest, you can get the key."

"This is miserable," hissed Talizac, as he turned to go; "who will vouch to me that you won't ask me again for the money?"

"Our honor, vicomte," replied Rolla, grinning. "We think as much of our reputation as high-toned people."

"Scoundrels," muttered Talizac, as he went away with Velletri. "If we could only do without them!"

CHAPTER XVI

MACHIAVELLI AND COMPANY

THE Marquis of Fougereuse was sitting in his study, and Simon stood beside him.

"So he has escaped from us again?" remarked the marquis frowning.

"God knows how it happened, my lord; my plans were all so well laid that I cannot understand how the affair fell through?"

"Postponed is not given up," observed the nobleman; "and as Fanfaro does not yet suspect who he really is, he can go on compromising himself. Have you any further details with regard to the conspiracy?"

"Yes, my lord, we have trustworthy witnesses, who can swear, in case of need, that Fanfaro planned an attempt upon the sacred person of the king."

"Very good; but still the attempt must be really made, so that Fanfaro could be convicted."

"I have attended to that. One of our agents will set the harmless attempt in motion, and the individual selected—who, by the way, has escaped the gallows more than once—will swear in court that Fanfaro is the intellectual head of the assassination and chief conspirator."

Before the marquis could express his satisfaction, the Marquis of Montferrand was announced.

"A visit at this hour!" cried Fougereuse, in amazement; "it is hardly seven o'clock."

"The gentleman comes on important business, as he informed me," said the servant.

"Bring the marquis in," ordered the nobleman; and as the servant went away he hastily said to Simon: "Hide behind the curtain, and remain there until the interview is over; perhaps you might hear something that will further our plans." Simon nodded and disappeared, while the marquis was led in.

Arthur's father was a man of imposing presence. He looked down upon the beggar nobility which fawned about the court, to receive money or favors.

The old man looked pale. He hastily approached the marquis and said:

"Marquis, you imagine you are a faithful adherent of the monarchy, but scandals such as take place to-day are not calculated to raise the Fougereuse and Talizacs in the estimation of the court."

"You are speaking in riddles, marquis!" exclaimed Fougereuse, in amazement.

"So much the worse for you, if your son's conduct must be told you by another party," said the old man, sternly.

"What is the matter with my son?"

"The Vicomte de Talizac has dishonored himself and the cause you serve."

"My son is young and wild. Has he again committed one of his stupid follies?" asked the marquis, uneasily.

"If it only were a stupid folly! The vicomte had a quarrel last night with my son, because my son wished to hinder him from committing a dastardly act. My son boxed the vicomte's ears, upon which the latter tried to stab him with a knife."

"Impossible!" cried Fougereuse, in a rage.

"I am speaking the truth," declared the old gentleman, calmly.

"What was the nature of this dastardly act?"

"The vicomte was drunk and employed people to abduct a respectable young girl, a street-singer. My son was in the society of yours, in a restaurant of a low order. When he heard what the affair was, he energetically protested and tried to hinder the vicomte and his friend Velletri from carrying out their plot. They quarrelled, the vicomte was boxed on the ears and my son was stabbed. They both received what they deserved. What brought me here is another matter. You are aware that I consented to speak to my cousin the Comtesse of Salves in relation to the marriage of her daughter with your son. From what happened last night, I should regard it as a misfortune for Irene if she becomes the vicomte's wife. I came here to tell you this."

Fougereuse became pale and clutched the back of a chair to keep from falling. At this moment the rustle of a silk dress was heard, and Madeleine, the marquis's wife, entered the room.

The marquis excitedly approached her.

"The vicomte is a scoundrel!" he cried, in a rage; "he has dragged the old noble name in the mud, thanks to his mother's bringing up. You have never refused him a wish."

Madeleine's blue eyes shot gleams of fire; she looked above her husband as if he had been empty air, and turned to the Marquis of Montferrand.

"Monsieur le Marquis," she politely said, "my son desired me to offer you his apologies."

"Apology?" repeated Montferrand, coldly, "for the box on the ear he got?"

"No, my lord, but because he was so intoxicated as to raise the ire of your son. He would not have gone so far if he had been sober. As to the affair with the street-singer, it is not so serious as you imagine. My son regrets very much that such a trivial affair has been the means of causing a rupture between him and your son. He has already taken steps to indemnify the girl for the wrong he did her, and I am positive the little one will have her liberty restored to her before many hours have passed. Is the word of the Marquise de Fougereuse sufficient for you, my lord?"

"Perfectly sufficient," said Montferrand, gallantly kissing the marquise's hand.

"Then we can count on seeing you to-night at our house?" asked Madeleine. "I have a surprise in store for my friends."

"Can one find out in advance the nature of it?" asked Montferrand, while Fougereuse looked anxiously at Madeleine.

"Oh, yes; his majesty has condescended to appoint the vicomte a captain in the Life Guards with the decoration of St. Louis," said the marquise proudly.

"Oh, I call that a surprise," cried Fougereuse, more freely, and Montferrand hastened to extend his congratulations.

"The Countess of Salves and her daughter have signified their intention of being present," continued Madeleine, "and as soon as my son receives his commission, the engagement of the young couple will be announced."

"It is only what one might expect from the Marquise of Fougereuse," said Montferrand politely, as he rose. "Good-by then, until this evening."

The marquis accompanied the old man to the door, then returned to his wife and excitedly asked:

"Madeleine, is all this true?"

Instead of answering, the marquise contemptuously shrugged her shoulders and left the room to hunt up her son.

"It is all settled," she said; "here are the twenty thousand francs you need to silence the girl; and now try to bring honor to your new position."

Madeleine placed a pocket-book on the table and went away. Talizac laughed in his sleeve. He did not think he could obtain the money so easily.

CHAPTER XVII

LOUISON

TOWARD noon Louison awoke from the lethargic sleep in which Rolla's liquid had thrown her, and her first look fell upon the virago, who was sitting in a half-drunken condition near the window. The young girl unconsciously uttered a cry when she saw the repulsive woman, and this cry aroused Rolla from out of her dreams about well-filled brandy bottles into reality.

"Well, my pigeon, how goes it?" she asked, grinning.

"My head hurts," replied Louison faintly, and throwing an anxious look about the strange apartment, she timidly added: "Where am I?"

"Where are you? Among good people certainly, who have become interested in you and will do what's right."

Louison was silent and tried to collect her thoughts. But it was no use, she had to close her eyes again from exhaustion.

"Ah, you are sensible I see; that pleases me," said Rolla, giggling. "Robeckal thought you would stamp and cry, but I said right away: 'The little one is smart, she will not throw her fortune away.' What is the use of virtue, anyway? It hardly brings one dry bread, so the sooner you throw it overboard the better it is. Oh, you will make your way, never fear. Your face is handsome, and who knows but that you will have your own elegant house and carriage one of these days? The little vicomte is certainly no Adonis, with his high shoulder, but one cannot have everything and—"

Louison had listened to Rolla's words with increasing loathing, and when she heard the name of the vicomte pronounced, her memory returned to her. Hastily springing up, she uttered a loud cry, and clutching Rolla tightly about the shoulder she exclaimed:

"Let me go or you shall be sorry for it!"

Rolla looked at the street-singer with a foolish laugh, and, shaking her thick head, she laconically said:

"Stay here."

"But I will not stay here," declared Louison firmly. "I will go away! Either you let me go or I shall cry for help. I am a respectable girl, and you ought to be ashamed to treat me in this way."

"So you—are a respectable girl," said the woman, in a maudlin voice. "What conceit—you have! You might have been so yesterday, but to-day—try it—tell the people that you spent a few hours in the Cannon Queen's house in Belleville and are still a respectable girl. Ha! ha! They will laugh at you, or spit in your face. No, no, my pretty dear, no one will believe that fairy story, and if an angel from heaven came down and took rooms in my house, it would be ruined. Give in, my chicken, and don't show the white feather! No one will believe that you are respectable and virtuous, and I think you ought to save yourself the trouble. It is too late now."

"You lie!" cried Louison, in desperation.

"So—I lie—it is about time that I shut your bold mouth," growled the virago, and raising her voice, she cried: "Robeckal, bring me the bottle."

The next minute hurried steps were heard coming up the stairs, and Rolla hastened to open the locked door. It was Robeckal, who entered with a small bottle in his hand. When Louison saw him she turned deathly pale, and running to the window she burst the panes with her clinched fist and called loudly for help.

"Minx!" hissed Robeckal, forcibly holding her back and throwing her to the ground.

With Rolla's assistance he now poured the contents of the bottle down her throat. When he tried to open the tightly compressed lips, Louison bit him in the finger. He uttered an oath, put a piece of wood between her teeth, and triumphantly exclaimed:

"For the next few hours you are done for, you little hussy."

"If it were only not too much," said Rolla, as Louison, groaning loudly, sank backward and closed her eyes.

"Have no fear; I know my methods," laughed Robeckal. "I am not so foolish as to kill the little one before we have the vicomte's money in our hands. She will sleep a few hours, and wake up tamed. Come, let us put her on the sofa and leave her alone."

The worthy pair laid the unconscious girl on the sofa and went away. Rolla, on closing the door, put the key in her pocket. They began to play cards in the basement, a pursuit which agreed with them, and at the same time swallowed deep draughts of brandy.

Toward six o'clock the vicomte entered. He threw

a well-filled pocket-book on the table, and in a tone of command said: "The key!"

"First we will count," growled Rolla; and opening the pocket-book with her fat hands she passed the contents in review.

"It is correct," she finally said; and taking the key out of her pocket she handed it to the vicomte.

As soon as the latter had left the room, Rolla shoved the pocket-book in her dirty dress, and hastily said:

"Come, Robeckal, the little one might make a noise. Let him see how he will get through with her."

Robeckal acquiesced, and they both quickly left the house, leaving all the doors open behind them.

They had hardly been gone, when a cry of rage rang through the house, and immediately afterward the vicomte burst into the room.

"You have deceived me," he cried, in a rage; "the window is open and the girl is gone!"

CHAPTER XVIII

THE CANAL

BY WHAT miracle had Louison escaped? In his anxiety to make the young girl harmless, Robeckal had given her such a strong dose that the narcotic had just the opposite effect, and before an hour had passed, a hammering and beating of her temples awakened her again. The excited state in which she was made her unable to grasp a clear thought; but one thing stood plainly before her—she must leave this horrible house at any price.

Slowly rising, she felt for the door; it was locked. She then walked softly to the window and looked at the street. It was deserted and empty of pedestrians, a fog hung over it, and if Louison could only reach the street she would be safe.

Through the broken pane the fresh air entered, and she tried then to collect her thoughts. The horrible woman had spoken about Belleville; if she were only in the street she would soon reach the Boulevard du Temple, and then—further than this she did not get with her plans. Away, only away, the rest would take care of itself.

What had the virago said? "Too late, too late, too

late!'' The horrible words rang in her ears like a death-knell; every pulse-beat repeated, ''Too late!''

Pressing her hand to her temples, Louison began to sob. Just then the coarse laughter of her torturers sounded from the basement and her tears immediately dried.

Softly, very softly, she opened the window, stood on the sill and swung herself to the outer sill. A pole which served to support a grapevine gave her a hold. She carefully climbed down its side, reached the street and ran as if pursued by the Furies.

The fog grew denser, and more than once Louison knocked against a wall or ran against passers-by, but these obstacles did not hinder her from running on.

How long she had been going in this way she did not know, but suddenly a blast of cold air grazed her burning face, and looking up she perceived that she had reached the Canal St. Martin. She had only to cross the bridge to reach those quarters of the great city which were known to her, but still she did not do it. A short while she stood there not knowing what to do. Then she strode on, timidly looking around her and walked down the damp stone steps leading to the water.

For a long time she stood on the last step. All around everything was still, and only the monotonous ripple of the waves reached the deserted girl's ears. With her arms folded across her bosom, she gazed at the black waters; the murmuring waves played about her feet and then she paused so long—long—

Robeckal and Rolla hurried through the streets with feverish haste. The ground burned under their feet, and they did not dare to breathe before they had turned their back upon the capital. They were just turning into the Rue St. Denis, when an iron fist was laid upon Robeckal's shoulder, and forced the frightened man to stand still.

"What does this mean?" he angrily cried, as he turned around, "a—"

He paused, for he had recognized Fanfaro. Bobichel had clutched Rolla at the same time, and shaking her roughly, he cried:

"Monster, where is the street-singer?"

"What do I know of a street-singer?" cried Rolla, boldly. "Let me go or I shall cry out."

"Cry away," replied Bobichel. "You must know best yourself whether you desire the interference of the police or not."

Rolla thought of the well-filled pocket-book and kept silent. Robeckal, in the meantime, had almost died of strangulation, for Fanfaro's fingers pressed his throat together; and when he was asked if he intended to answer, he could only nod with his head.

"Where is Louison?" asked Fanfaro, in a voice of thunder.

"No. 16 Rue de Belleville."

"Alone?"

"I do not know."

"Scoundrels, God help you, if all is not right," hissed Fanfaro, "bring us quickly to the house named."

"Oh, it is very easy to find," began Rolla, but Bobichel threatened her with his fist and cried:

"So much the better for you, forward march!"

Robeckal and the Cannon Queen, held in the grips of Fanfaro and the clown, proceeded on the way to Belleville. They stopped in front of No. 16, and it required the application of force to get them to enter.

Rolla, in advance of the others, went to the top story. The door was wide open and the room empty.

"Really, he has taken her along?" she exclaimed in amazement.

"Of whom are you speaking?" asked Fanfaro, trembling with fear.

"Of whom else but the little vicomte."

"His name?"

"Talizac."

"The villain!" muttered Fanfaro to himself.

Bobichel was still holding Rolla by the arm. His gaze, roving about the room, had espied a note on the table. Rolla saw it, too, but before she could take it the clown had called Fanfaro's attention to it.

"You have swindled me," the young man read; "you have helped her to escape, confound you!"

"Thank God all is not lost yet," whispered Fanfaro, handing Bobichel the paper.

"One moment," said the clown; "I have an idea which I would like to carry out."

With a quick movement Bobichel threw Robeckal to the ground, bound him with a thick rope and threw him into a closet. He locked it and putting the key in his pocket, he turned to Rolla.

"March, away with you," he said, roughly, "and do not attempt to free him; he can ponder over his sins."

Rolla hurried to leave the house. If Robeckal died she would be the sole possessor of the twenty thousand francs. Bobichel and Fanfaro left the house likewise, and Robeckal remained crying behind.

CHAPTER XIX

SPLENDOR

THE Fougereuse mansion was resplendent with light. Madeleine intended to celebrate the vicomte's appointment to a captaincy in a fitting way, and hundreds of invitations had been issued and accepted.

One fine carriage after another rolled up; the marquise, dressed in princely style, received her guests in the fairy-like parlors, and soon a brilliant assembly crowded the rooms.

The marquis and his wife looked proudly at the vicomte, who, however, could hardly restrain his disappointment. He did not know what hurt him most, the loss of Louison or the twenty thousand francs, and he railed against himself for being so foolish as to imagine that Robeckal and Rolla would keep their word.

"Do not frown so," whispered Madeleine to her son, "here comes Irene."

The vicomte bit his lips until they bled, and then approached Irene de Salves, who had just entered, accompanied by her mother and the Marquis de Montferrand.

Irene was dazzlingly beautiful, and her rich dress enhanced her charming appearance. There was, however, a melancholy look in her dark eyes, but her voice sounded clear and strong as she replied to the vicomte's greeting.

Brought up in the traditions of the nobility, Irene did not think of resisting her mother when the latter told her that her engagement with the Vicomte de Talizac would be announced that evening. Irene loved Fanfaro with all the fervor of her soul, but she would never have dared to tell her mother of her attachment for the acrobat.

When the vicomte pressed her hand upon his arm, she trembled violently, and a gleam of rage shot out of the dark eyes, while Talizac thought to himself that the young girl had every reason to be proud of him. Captain in the Life Guards and Knight of St. Louis. The more he considered it the more he came to the conclusion that he could demand more, and only the circumstance that the young countess possessed several millions caused him to submit to the match.

The first notes of a polonaise were heard now, and the guests, grouping themselves in pairs, strode through the wide halls. A quadrille followed the polonaise, and it was a charming sight to see all these graceful women and young girls dance. Irene kept up a cross-fire of words with the vicomte and Velletri. Talizac had just whispered some gallant sentence to her, when a high officer of the Royal Life Guards appeared and handed the vicomte his commission.

Great enthusiasm arose. The vicomte and his parents were congratulated from all sides, and the young girls envied Irene, for it was an open secret that she would be the future Vicomtesse de Talizac.

Arthur de Montferrand was the only one who could not force himself to congratulate the vicomte. It was only on his father's account that he came at all, and while Talizac was being surrounded on all sides, Arthur's thoughts went back to the scene of the previous evening. He saw Louison's pleading looks, he heard her contemptuous words, and could never forgive himself for having given her good reason to believe that he was one of Talizac's accomplices.

The vicomte's voice aroused him from his dreams.

"Well, Arthur," said Talizac laughing, "have you no congratulation for me?"

Arthur looked penetratingly at the vicomte, and in a low voice replied:

"Vicomte, if I cannot discover any traces of the punishment you received yesterday on your cheeks, I hope to be able to pay up for what I have lost. For to-day you must excuse me."

Deathly pale, Talizac looked at Montferrand, but before he had a chance to reply, a commotion was heard in the corridor, followed by a war of words.

The marquis looked uneasily at the door, and was about to give an order to a servant to inquire after the cause of the disturbance, when the folding doors were thrown open and a man who carried the lifeless, dripping form of a young girl in his arms rushed into the ballroom.

"Fanfaro!" cried Montferrand in amazement.

Fanfaro, for it was really he, laid the young girl's body tenderly upon the ground, and, turning to the assembled guests, cried with threatening voice:

"Ladies and gentlemen, here is the corpse of a young girl whom the Vicomte de Talizac murdered."

The women uttered cries of terror and the men looked threateningly at Talizac, who was trembling and trying hard to appear indifferent.

The Marquis of Fougereuse was as white as a spectre. Was this Fanfaro going to pursue him forever?

"Who is the bold fellow?" he audaciously said. "Throw him out."

"Don't be so quick, marquis," said Fanfaro earnestly; "it is a question of a terrible crime, and your son the Vicomte de Talizac is the criminal! Oh, the shame of it! Does he think that because he is a nobleman he can do what he pleases? This young girl lived modestly and plainly; she was pure and innocent. The Vicomte de Talizac regarded her as his prey. He bribed a couple of scoundrels and had the poor child abducted.

"Half crazed with horror and despairing of humanity, the victim sought peace and forgetfulness in suicide. Marquis, do you know of any infamy equal to this?"

Proud, with head erect like an avenger of innocence, Fanfaro stood in the centre of the room and his eyes shot forth rays of contempt.

Montferrand hurried toward him and cordially shook him by the hand.

"Is she dead—is she really dead?" he asked.

"I fear so," replied the young man, slowly, "yet I do not like to give up all hope. Is there no lady here who will take care of the poor child and try to soften the vicomte's crime?" continued Fanfaro, raising his voice. "Does not a heart beat under these silks and satins?"

From the group of timid ladies came a tall figure clad in a white silk dress, and kneeling next to Louison she softly said:

"Here I am."

"The farce is becoming uproarious," cried the Marquis of Fougereuse, nervously laughing.

"Do not call it a farce; it is a drama, a terrible drama, my lord," replied Fanfaro, earnestly. "Ask your son, who is leaning pale and trembling against the wall, whether I am telling you the truth or not?"

"Yes, it is a lie!" exclaimed Talizac, hoarsely.

"It is no lie," declared Arthur de Montferrand, stepping in front of Talizac. "Vicomte, you have a bad memory, and if my hand had not fortunately stamped your face you might have even denied it to my face. Look at the vicomte, gentlemen; the traces which burn on his pale cheeks he owes to me, for I was present when he made the first attempt to scandalize this poor girl. I chastised him, and he stabbed me."

"He lies! He is crazy!" cried the vicomte, in despair.

But none of those who had a quarter of an hour before overwhelmed him with congratulations condescended to look at the wretch, and with a moan Talizac sank back in a chair.

In the meantime Irene had busied herself with Louison, and now triumphantly exclaimed:

"She lives, she breathes, she can still be saved! Mamma," she said, turning quickly to her mother, "we will take the poor child home with us and nurse her."

The countess assented with tears in her eyes; she was proud of her daughter.

"The poor thing is my sister," said Fanfaro in a low voice to Irene.

Irene bent over Louison and kissed her pale forehead. This was her answer to Fanfaro's information.

Talizac had now recovered his senses. He tore open the door and angrily cried:

"Is there no one here who will show this impudent fellow out? Come in, lackeys and servants; lay hands on him!"

"I would advise no one to touch me," said Fanfaro, coldly.

At this moment a hand was laid on Fanfaro's shoulder, and a deep voice said:

"In the name of the king, you are my prisoner!"

As if struck by lightning, the young man gazed upon an old man who wore a dark uniform with a white and gold scarf. All the entrances to the ballroom were occupied by soldiers, and Fanfaro saw at once that he was lost.

"My lord marquis," said the officer, turning to the master of the house, "I regret very much to disturb you, but I must obey my order. Less than an hour ago a man with a knife in his hand entered the apartments of his majesty and said that he intended to kill the king."

A cry of horror followed these words, and, pale and trembling, the guests crowded about the officer, who continued after a short pause:

"Asked about his accomplice, the would-be murderer declared that he was an agent for a secret society whose chief the prisoner Fanfaro is."

"Oh, what a monstrous lie!" exclaimed Fanfaro, beside himself with rage, while Irene de Salves rose upright and with flaming eyes said:

"He a murderer? Impossible!"

"Prudence," whispered Arthur to the young woman, "what I can do for him I will."

"Save my sister, Irene," said Fanfaro softly, and sorrowfully turning to the official, he declared with a loud voice: "Sir, I must deny the accusation that I am a murderer. I have openly fought against the present government, but have never employed any assassin! Do your duty, I will follow you without resistance and calmly await the judge's sentence."

With head erect Fanfaro strode toward the door and disappeared in company with the soldiers. Montferrand approached Talizac and hissed in his ear:

"It might be doing you an honor, but if there is no other remedy I will fight a duel with you to rid the world of a scoundrel—I await your seconds."

"You shall pay for this," said the vicomte, "I will kill you."

Half an hour later the splendid halls of the Fougereuse mansion were deserted; the guests hurried to leave a house where such things had occurred.

CHAPTER XX

IN LEIGOUTTE

LIKE so many other places, Leigoutte had risen from the ashes after the war was over. A great sensation was caused one day by the appearance in the village of an old gray-headed man. He said he intended to erect a new building on the spot where the school and tavern house formerly stood. The old man paid without any haggling the price asked for the ground, and shortly afterward workmen were seen busily carting the ruins away and digging a foundation.

The villagers thought a new and elegant house would replace the old one now, but they deceived themselves. Strange to say, the new building resembled the old one even to the smallest details. In the basement was the kitchen from which a door led to the low narrow tavern-room, and in the upper story were two bedrooms and the large schoolroom.

When the house was finished, a sign half destroyed by fire was fastened to one end, and the peasants swore it was the sign of the former innkeeper, Jules Fougeres. In the right corner the words "To the welfare of France" could be clearly seen.

The new owner did not live in the house himself. He

gave it free of charge to the poorest family in the village, with the condition that he be allowed to live there a few weeks each year. A schoolmaster was soon found in the person of a former sergeant, and as Pierre Labarre—such was the name of the new owner—undertook to look out for the teacher's salary, the inhabitants of Leigoutte had every reason to be thankful to him. When Pierre came to the village, which was generally in spring, the big and little ones surrounded him, and the old man would smile at the children, play with them, and assemble the parents at evening in the large tavern-room, and relate stories of the Revolution.

He had come this spring to Leigoutte and the children gleefully greeted him. On the evening of a March day he was sitting pensively at the window of the tavern, when he suddenly saw two curious figures coming up the road. One of the figures, apparently a young, strong girl, had her arm about a bent old woman, who could hardly walk along, and had to be supported by her companion.

Pierre felt his heart painfully moved when he saw the two women, and following an indefinable impulse he left the room and seated himself on a bench in front of the house.

The wanderers did not notice him. When they were opposite the house the old woman raised her head, and Pierre now saw a fearfully disfigured face. The woman whispered a few words to her companion; the young girl nodded and began to walk in the direction of the school-house. The paralyzed woman climbed the few steps which led into the house, and walking along the corridor she entered the parlor.

Pierre could not sit still any more. He noiselessly arose

and entered the corridor. The parlor door was wide open, and he saw the gray-haired woman sitting at a table and looking all around her. Her small, fleshless lips parted, and half aloud she muttered:

"Where can Jules be? The dinner has been ready a long time, the children are getting impatient, and still he does not come! Come here, Jacques; father will be here soon. Louison, do not cry or I shall scold! Ah, little fool, I did not mean it: be quiet, he will soon be here!"

Pierre Labarre felt his heart stand still. The crippled, disfigured woman who sat there could be none other than Louise, Jules's wife! But who could her companion be?

No longer able to control himself, he softly entered the room. The young girl immediately perceived him, and folding her hands, she said, in a pleading tone:

"Do not get angry, sir! We shall not trouble you long."

"Make yourselves at home," replied Pierre, cordially; "but tell me," he continued, "who is this woman?"

Caillette, for she was the young woman, put her finger to her forehead, and looked significantly at the old woman.

"She is crazy," she whispered.

Pierre Labarre laid his hand over his eyes to hide his tears, but he could not prevent a nervous sob from shaking his broad frame.

"Tell me," he repeated softly, "who is the woman?"

"Ah! the poor woman has gone through a great deal of trouble," replied Caillette, sorrowfully. "She has lost her husband and her children, and was badly injured at a fire. Only a few weeks ago she could hardly move a limb, but since a short time her condition has wonderfully improved, and she can now walk, though not without assistance."

"But her name—what is she called?"

"Ah, my dear sir, I do not know her real name; the people who live in her neighborhood in Paris call her the 'Burned Woman,' and Louison calls her mamma or mother."

"Louison? Who is that?"

"A young girl who has taken care of her. She earns her living through singing, and is a charming girl. Her brother is named Fanfaro. Ah! it is a curious story, full of misfortune and crime."

Pierre was silent for a moment, and then asked:

"Who is this Fanfaro whom you just spoke about?"

Caillette did not answer immediately. Fanfaro was to her the incarnation of all that was good and noble in the world, but of course she could not tell the old man this.

"Fanfaro is a foundling," she finally said; "of course he is a man now, and just as energetic and brave as any one."

"Fanfaro, Fanfaro," repeated the old man, pensively; "where have I heard the name before?"

The maniac now raised her eyes, and, seeing Pierre, she politely said:

"Excuse the plain service, sir; it is very little, but comes from our hearts."

Pierre Labarre uttered a cry of astonishment.

"Louise—Louise Fougeres!" he cried, beside himself.

The invalid looked sharply at Pierre, and tremblingly said:

"Who called me? Who pronounced my name just now?"

"I, Louise," replied Pierre. "Louise Fougeres, do you

not recollect your husband, Jules, and your children, Jacques and Louison?"

"Of course I remember them. Ah, how glad I would be if I could see them again! Where can Jules be? and Jacques—Jacques—"

The maniac was silent, and ran her crippled fingers through her gray hair, as if she were trying to recollect something.

"Yes, I know," she murmured pensively, "Louison is here, she sleeps in a neat white bed, but she is away now —and—and—"

Expectantly Pierre gazed at the poor woman, who was palpably confounding imagination with reality, and after a pause she continued:

"Oh, the door opens now, and Jacques enters! Welcome, my dear child. How handsome you have become. Thank God, I have you again!"

"Has she really found Jacques again?" asked Labarre, tremblingly, and turning to Caillette. "Is he living?"

"Yes, he is the same person as Fanfaro."

"God be praised. And Louison?"

"Louison has been abducted and—"

"Abducted? By whom?"

"By the Vicomte of Talizac."

"By Talizac? O my God!" stammered Labarre, in horror.

Louise, too, had heard the name, and raising herself with difficulty, she whispered:

"Talizac? He must know it! Jacques—the box, O God! where is the box?"

. . . .

How did these two women get to Leigoutte?

When Fanfaro went to search for Louison, his mother

had remained behind under the protection of Caillette. The day passed, night came, but neither Fanfaro, Girdel nor Bobichel returned. The maniac screamed and cried. She wanted to see Jacques, and Caillette could hardly calm her. Finally long past midnight she fell into a slumber, and Caillette, too, exhausted by the excitement of the last few hours, closed her eyes.

When she awoke it was daylight. She glanced at the maniac's bed. Merciful Heaven, it was empty!

Trembling with fear, Caillette hurried downstairs and asked the janitress whether she had seen anything of the "Burned Woman." The janitress looked at her in amazement and said she had thought at once when she saw the old crippled woman creeping down the stairs two hours before that all was not right in her head.

"But she cannot walk at all, how could she get out?" groaned Caillette. "Suppose Fanfaro came now and found that his mother was gone?"

"A milk-wagon stopped in front of the door," said the janitress, "and the driver let the old woman get in. I thought it had been arranged beforehand and was all right."

Caillette wrung her hands and then hurried to the station house and announced the disappearance of the "Burned Woman."

If her father and Bobichel, even Fanfaro, had come, she would have felt at ease. But no one showed himself, and Caillette, who knew that Girdel and Fanfaro were wanted, did not dare to make any inquiries.

She ran about in desperation. The only clew was the milkman, but where could she find him? Caillette passed hours of dreadful anxiety, and when a ragpicker told her that he saw a woman who answered her description pass the Barrière d'Italie on a milk-wagon, she thought him a messenger of God.

As quick as she could go, she ran to the place designated; a hundred times on the way, she said to herself that the wagon must have gone on; and yet it struck like a clap of thunder when she found it was really so. What now? Caillette asked from house to house; every one had seen the woman, but she had gone in a different direction; and so the poor child wandered onward, right and left, forward and backward, always hoping to discover them. Finally, after she had been thirty-six hours on the way, she found the maniac in a little tavern by the roadside. She was crouching near the threshold, and smiled when she saw Caillette.

"God be praised! I have found you," cried the young girl, sobbing; and when the hostess, who had been standing in the background, heard these words, she joyfully said:

"I am glad I did not leave the poor woman go; she spoke so funny, I thought at once that she had run away from her family."

"What did she say?" asked Caillette, while the "Burned Woman" clung to her.

"Oh, she asked for bread, and then inquired the way to the Vosges."

"Yes, to the Vosges," said the maniac, hastily.

"But, mother, what should we do in the Vosges?" asked Caillette, in surprise.

"To Leigoutte—Leigoutte," repeated the maniac, urgently.

"Leigoutte—that is Fanfaro's home!" exclaimed the young girl, hastily.

"Not Fanfaro—Jacques," corrected the old woman.

"But what should we do in Leigoutte, mother?"

"The box—Jacques—Talizac—the papers," the woman replied.

And so we find Caillette and her patient, after weary wanderings, in Leigoutte. The young girl had sold, on the way, a gold cross, the only jewel she possessed, to pay the expenses of the journey. Charitable peasants had given the women short rides at times; kind-hearted farmers' wives had offered them food and drink, or else a night's lodging. Yet Caillette thanked God when she arrived at Leigoutte. What would happen now, she did not know. Nothing could induce the maniac to return, and the young girl thought it best not to oppose her wish. Little by little, she began to suspect herself that the journey might be important for Fanfaro; who could tell what thoughts were agitating the mad woman's brain; and, perhaps, the unexpected recovery of her son might have awakened recollections of the past.

"I must speak to old Laison," said the "Burned Woman," suddenly; "he must help me."

She arose, shoved Caillette and Pierre aside, and hobbled toward the back door. Opening it, she reached the open field, and without looking around, she walked on and on. Pierre and Caillette followed her unnoticed. She had now reached the spot on which the old farm-house of Laison stood, and, looking timidly around her, she turned to the right.

Suddenly she uttered a loud scream, and when Caillette and Pierre hurried in affright to her, they found the maniac deathly pale, leaning against a hollow tree, while her crippled fingers held a box, which she had apparently dug out of the earth; for close to the hollow tree was a deep hole, and the box was covered with dirt and earth.

"There it is!" she cried to Pierre, and from the eyes in which madness had shone before, reason now sparkled. "Jacques is not my son, but Vicomte de Talizac, and Louison is the Marquise of Fougereuse—here are the proofs."

She clutched a number of papers from the box and held them triumphantly uplifted; but then nature demanded her right, and, exhausted by the great excitement. she sank senseless into Caillette's arms.

CHAPTER XXI

EXCITED

THE street-singer was resting in the beautiful boudoir of the young countess, Irene de Salves. The poor child lay under lace covers, and Irene's tenderness and attachment had banished her melancholy.

After the terrible scene in the Fougereuse mansion, the young countess, with the help of Arthur, brought Louison to a carriage, and, to Madame Ursula's horror, she gave the young girl her own room and bed. For Fanfaro's sister nothing could be good enough, and the young countess made Louison as comfortable as possible.

After the young girl had rested a few hours, she felt much stronger, but with this feeling the recollection of what she had gone through returned, and in a trembling voice she asked Irene:

"Who saved me?"

"Don't you know?" asked the countess, blushing. "It was Fanfaro."

"Fanfaro? Who is that?"

Irene looked at her in astonishment. Was it possible that Louison did not know her own brother, or had the excitement of the last days crazed her mind?

"Won't you tell me who Fanfaro is?" asked Louison, urgently.

"Don't you really know your own brother?" asked Irene in surprise.

"My brother?"

Louison laid her hand on her head and became thoughtful.

"I had a brother once," she said, pensively; "he was a few years older than I, and did everything to please me, but it is long ago since I saw Jacques—many, many years."

"Jacques and Fanfaro are identical," replied Irene, softly.

She had been told this by her cousin Arthur, who took a great interest in the brother and sister.

"Fanfaro," repeated Louison, pensively. "Ah! now I know who this man is. He belongs to a company of acrobats who give performances in the Place du Chateau d'Eau. They have all such peculiar names. One of them is named Firejaws—"

"Perfectly right; he is Fanfaro's foster-father, and Fanfaro is your brother."

"Who told you so?"

"He, himself; he begged me to care for his sister."

"But why does he not come? I long to see him."

Irene, too, longed to see Fanfaro.

"Let me speak a little about him," said Louison, vivaciously; "perhaps Fanfaro is identical with Jacques; he must be twenty years of age."

"That may be so."

"And then he must be very handsome. Jacques was a very pretty boy."

"That is correct, too," replied Irene, blushing.

"Has he black eyes and dark, curly hair?"

"I think so," stammered Irene, who knew all these details, yet did not wish to confess it.

"You think so," repeated Louison; "you haven't looked carefully at him?"

"I—I—" stammered the countess, in confusion; "what do you look at me for?"

A smile flitted across Louison's lips, but she kept silent, and Irene thanked God, as Madame Ursula now came in and softly said:

"Irene, a word."

"What is the matter?" asked the countess, hastily.

"There is a man outside who would like to speak to you."

"His name?"

"Bobichel—"

"Bobichel? Ah! bring him in the next room directly!"

Madame Ursula nodded and disappeared, while Irene turned to Louison and said in explanation:

"Excuse me a moment; I will not leave you long alone."

She went to the next room, where Bobichel was already awaiting her. He did not look as jolly as usual, and, twirling his cap between his fingers in an embarrassed way, he began:

"Mademoiselle, excuse me for disturbing you, but—"

"You come from him—from Fanfaro?" said Irene, blushing.

"Unfortunately no," replied Bobichel, sorrowfully; "I was not allowed to see him."

"Who sent you here?"

"His foster-father—Girdel."

"Why does he not come personally?"

"I do not know. I have something to give you."

"What is it?"

"Here it is," said Bobichel, pulling a small package out of his pocket and handing it to Irene.

The young countess hastily unfolded the package. It contained two letters, one of which was addressed to "Mademoiselle Irene," while the other bore, in clear, firm letters, her full name, "Countess Irene de Salves."

Without accounting for her feelings, Irene feverishly broke the last letter. Did she suspect from whom it came?

"Countess, you are brave and noble!" wrote Fanfaro, "and therefore I dare to ask you to take care of my sister, whom I barely rescued from death. The hour is near at hand in which my sentence will be pronounced. You have never doubted me, and I thank you from the bottom of my heart! I have fought for the rights of humanity, and I hope at some future time to be enrolled among those to whom right is preferable to material things. One thing, however, I know now: a powerful enemy pursues me with his hatred, and if the sentence should turn out differently from what this enemy expects, he will find the means to make me harmless. I therefore say farewell to you—if forever, who can say? Irene, do not despair, eternal heavenly justice stands above human passions. But if I should succumb, I will die peacefully, knowing that my mother and my sister will not be deserted."

The letter bore no signature. Irene read again and again the words of her beloved, and hot tears fell on the paper.

Bobichel, deeply affected, observed the young girl, and to console her he said:

"Who knows, he might not be found guilty anyhow?"

"Whom are you talking of? Who will be found guilty?" came from a frightened voice behind Irene, and as the latter hastily turned round, she saw Louison, who, enveloped in a soft shawl and pale as a spectre, stood in the doorway.

"Louison, how did you get here?" cried Irene, beside herself. "O God! I am neglecting you. Quick, go to your room again, you shall know all to-morrow."

"Sister," whispered Louison, softly, "why do you wish to conceal something from me which I already know? Tell me what has happened to Fanfaro? I know danger threatens him, and two can bear the heaviest burden easier than one."

"Yes, you are right," replied Irene, embracing Louison, and, gently leading her to her room, she sat down beside her and hastily told her what she knew about the conspiracy and the part Fanfaro took in it. Bobichel put in a word here and there, and when Irene had finished he said with a smile:

"Mademoiselle, in your eagerness to read one of the letters you forgot to open the other."

"That's so!" exclaimed Irene blushing, and unfolding Girdel's letter she read the following words, written in an original orthographical style:

"We must reskue Fanfaro and this is only posibel in one way. You have great inflooence; try to make the thing which Popichel will give you all right, but not

until after the trial, which will take place in two days.
I trust in you.   GIRDEL."

"What answer shall I bring master!" asked the clown
after Irene had read the letter.

"That I will do as he says," replied Irene. "Where
is the thing Girdel intrusted to you?"

"Here," said Bobichel, handing the young lady a pin
with a pretty large head; and as Irene, amazed, looked
inquiringly at him, he quickly tore off the head and
showed her a small hollow in which a note lay.

"You see, mademoiselle," he laughingly said, "presti-
digitation is sometimes of use. And now good-by. I will
tell master that he struck the right person."

He disappeared, and the two young girls looked after
him filled with new hope.

From the time that the old Countess of Salves had
informed the Marquise of Fougereuse that under existing
circumstances a marriage between her daughter and the
Vicomte de Talizac was out of the question, violent scenes
had taken place in the Fougereuse mansion.

Financial ruin could now hardly be averted, and, far
from accusing her son of being the cause of this ship-
wreck of her plans, Madeleine placed the blame entirely
on her husband. It was already whispered in court cir-
cles that the newly appointed captain in the Life Guards
and Knight of St. Louis would lose his position, and
though the other young noblemen were no better than
the vicomte, they had the advantage that this was not
universally known.

The marquis and Madeleine had just been having a
quarrel, and the marquis, pale and exhausted, lay back

in his chair, when Count Fernando de Velletri was announced. The marquis bathed his face and forehead in cold water, and ordered the Italian to be sent up. He attached great importance to this visit, for Simon had told him that Velletri was a member of the Society of Jesus, and a man of great influence.

Velletri entered and his appearance was so different from what it ordinarily was that the marquis looked at him in amazement. He wore a long black coat, a black cravat, and a round hat of the same color. These things marked Velletri at once as a member of an ecclesiastical society. The dark cropped hair lay thick at the temples, and his eyes were cast down. The Italian was inch by inch a typical Jesuit, and his sharp look made the marquis tremble. He knew Loyola's pupils and their "energy."

Velletri bowed slightly to the marquis, and then said in a cold voice:

"Marquis, I begged for an interview with you which I desire principally for your own good. Are we undisturbed here?"

"Entirely so," replied the marquis, coldly.

The Italian sat down in a chair which the marquis had shoved toward him, and began in a business tone:

"Marquis, it is probably not unknown to you that the conduct of your son, the Vicomte de Talizac, compromises his own position and that of his family. I—"

"But, count," interrupted the marquis vivaciously, "you were the chum of my son, and you even encouraged his dissipations."

Velletri laughed maliciously.

"The Vicomte of Talizac," he said, weighing each

word, "is no child any more, and not influenced either in a bad or good way by any of his companions. If I have apparently taken part in his dissipations, it was in the first place to prevent something worse and to shield the honor of the Fougereuse, which was often at stake."

"You, count—but I really do not understand," stammered the marquis.

"It seems to me," interrupted the Italian, sharply, "that we are swerving from the real object of our interview. Let me speak, marquis. A powerful society, with which I have the honor of being associated, has had its eye on you for a long time. Your influence, your opinions and your family connections are such that the society hopes to have in you a useful auxiliary, and I, have therefore received the order to make arrangements with you. The society—"

"You are no doubt speaking of the Society of Jesus?" interrupted the marquis.

Velletri bowed and continued:

"Thanks to the assistance of the pious fathers, his majesty has foregone his original intention of stripping the Vicomte de Talizac of all his honors—"

The marquis made a gesture of astonishment, and Velletri went on:

"The society is even ready to give you the means to put your shattered fortune on a firm basis again."

"And the conditions?" stammered Fougereuse hoarsely.

"I will tell them to you directly; they are not very difficult to fulfil."

"And should I refuse them?"

"Do you really intend to refuse them?" asked the Jesuit, softly.

Fougereuse bit his lips; he had already said too much. The Jesuit was a worthy pupil of his master, and the marquis felt that should he oppose him he would be the loser.

"What does the society ask of me?" he said, after a pause.

"Two things—an important service and a guarantee."

"And what does it offer?"

"The position of his majesty the king's prime minister."

The marquis sprang up as if electrified.

"I have misunderstood you," he said.

"Not at all; it is a question of the premiership."

Cold drops of perspiration stood on the marquis's forehead; he knew the society had the power to keep its promises. Prime minister! Never in his dreams had he even thought so high. The position guaranteed to him riches, influence and power.

"You spoke of an important service and a guarantee," he said, breathing heavily; "please explain yourself more clearly."

"I will first speak of the service," replied Velletri, calmly; "it is of such a nature that the one intrusted with it can be thankful, for he will be able to do a great deal of good to His Holiness the Pope and the Catholic world."

Fougereuse closed his eyes—this outlook was dazzling.

Fernando de Velletri continued with:

"Marquis, you are no doubt aware that the Jesuits have been expelled from France under the law of 1764. About two years ago, in January, 1822, his majesty the king allowed them to stay temporarily in his kingdom.

The good prince did not dare at that time to do more for us. The time has now come to put an end to the oppression under which the Jesuits have so long suffered. What we desire is the solemn restoration of all their rights to the fathers. They should hold up their heads under their true names and enjoy anew all their former privileges. To secure this end we must have a law—not a royal edict, a sound constitutional law—which must be passed by the Chamber of Peers. It is a bold undertaking, and we do not deceive ourselves with regard to the difficulties to be encountered, and the man who does it must be quick and energetic, but the reward is a magnificent one. The man we shall elevate to the prime ministership will be in possession of great power. Marquis, do you think you have the necessary strength to be this man?"

Fougereuse had arisen. Excited, flushed with enthusiasm, he looked at Velletri.

"Yes, I am the man!" he firmly exclaimed, "I will easily overcome every obstacle, conquer every opposition—"

"With our assistance," added the Jesuit. "We are already in possession of a respectable minority, and it will be easy for you, with the aid of promises and shrewd insinuations, to win over those who are on the fence. Marquis, the work intrusted to you is a sublime one—"

"I am yours body and soul," interrupted the marquis impatiently. "And to-day—"

"One moment," said the Jesuit, placing his hand lightly on the marquis's shoulder; "I also spoke about a guarantee."

"Really," cried Fougereuse sincerely, "I forgot all about that, but I should think my word of honor would be sufficient."

Velletri did not reply to his last observation, but coolly said:

"The man in whom the society places such entire confidence as to give him the weapons which must lead to victory must be bound to us by ties which cannot be torn asunder."

The marquis's face expressed naïve astonishment.

"The strongest chains," continued the Jesuit, "are, as is well known, the golden ones, and the guarantee we desire is based on this fact. Marquis, I am the secretary of the general of the order, and it is my mission to ask you whether you are ready to assist the society financially by founding new colonies such as the Montrouge and Saint-Acheul houses in Parma and Tuscany?"

"Certainly," stammered Fougereuse, "I am ready to help the Society of Jesus to the extent of my means, and should like to know beforehand how high the sum is that is required. My finances are at present exhausted and—"

"Have no fear," interrupted Velletri dryly; "the sum in question is not so immense that you need be frightened about it."

Fougereuse breathed more freely.

"To found the houses named only a very modest sum is necessary, not more than a million!"

"A million!" stammered the marquis, "a million!"

"The sum is very small in comparison to the office you buy with it, and only the particular friendship our order had for you caused it to give you the preference, to the exclusion of numerous applicants."

"But a million!" groaned Fougereuse, "the sum is impossible to secure! If I were to sell or pawn everything, I would not succeed in raising a quarter of this sum."

"Then you refuse?" asked Velletri.

"God forbid, only I do not know how I shall satisfy the demand of the society. A million is, under the circumstances, a terrible sum!"

"Marquis, the house of Fougereuse possesses a fortune which is fabulous in comparison to the demands of the society."

"If it were only so," groaned Fougereuse, "but unfortunately you are mistaken; I am ruined, totally ruined!"

"Impossible! The fortune your father left behind him was too immense to have been spent in a few years! No matter what your embarrassments previously were, the fortune must have been sufficient to cover them and enrich you enormously besides!" replied Velletri.

"Count, I was robbed of my legacy—dastardly robbed," whined Fougereuse.

The Italian rose up angrily.

"Marquis," said he, "I am not used to bargaining and haggling. I ask you for the last time, what is your decision? I offer you peace or war. Peace means for you power and influence, while war—"

"War?" repeated Fougereuse, confused. "I—do not understand you!"

"Then I will express myself more clearly. When the society reposes its confidence in a man like you and discloses its most secret plans, it always has a weapon in the background, to be used in case of necessity. A comrade sometimes becomes an opponent—"

"I—should I ever become an enemy of the fathers? Oh, you do not believe that yourself!"

"Our measures are such that it cannot be done very easily, anyhow," replied Velletri, with faint malice; "this is our ultimatum: Either you accept my proposition and hand over the sum named within five days, or one of our emissaries will place certain papers in the hands of the district-attorney!"

Fougereuse trembled with fear and his teeth chattered as he stammeringly said:

"I—do not—understand—you."

"Then listen. The papers are drafts whose signatures have been forged by the Vicomte de Talizac, and which are in our hands."

"Drafts? Forged drafts? Impossible—my son is not a criminal!" cried the marquis, desperately.

"Ask the vicomte," replied Velletri, coldly, and rising, he added: "Marquis, I give you time to consider. As soon as you have made up your mind, please be so kind as to let me know."

"One moment, count. Are your conditions unchangeable?"

"Perfectly so. Inside of the next five days the preliminary steps must be taken in the Chamber of Peers—"

"I will do them to-morrow," cried the marquis, hastily.

"But only in case you are able to give the necessary guarantee. Marquis, adieu!"

The Italian went away, and Fougereuse, entirely broken down, remained behind.

He was still sitting thinking deeply, when Simon, who had remained behind the curtain and overheard the interview, softly stepped forth, and said:

"Courage, marquis; there is no reason for despair. Write to the pious fathers that you will satisfy their demands within the required five days."

"But I do not understand—"

"And yet it is very clear. Fanfaro is in prison—"

"Even so—he will not be condemned to death."

"If the judges do not kill him, there are other means."

"Other means?"

"Yes, my lord; the legacy of the Fougereuse will fall into your hands, and then the cabinet position is sure."

"Simon, are you mad?"

"No, my lord. I will kill Fanfaro!"

CHAPTER XXII

THE TRIAL

POLITICAL trials are in all ages similar; and then, as now, the verdict is decided upon long before the proceedings have begun.

It was only after Fanfaro had been brought to the court-room that he caught a glimpse of the man who had allowed himself to be used as a tool to set the assassination of the king in motion. A contemptuous smile played about the young man's lips when he saw it was Robeckal. The wretch looked like the personification of fear; his knees quaked together, his face was covered with cold perspiration, and his teeth chattered audibly.

Robeckal had been still half intoxicated when he under-took to carry out Simon's proposition to play the regicide. Not until now, when he found himself in the presence of his judges, had he comprehended that it might cost him his head, and his bold assurance gave way to cowardly despair.

Fanfaro answered the questions put to him briefly and clearly. He described Robeckal's actions during the time he had been a member of Girdel's troupe. He declared that the wretch had cut the chain in Sainte-Ame for the purpose of killing the athlete, and said everything in such a passionless way that the judges became convinced that he was speaking the truth. As soon as the indictment had been read, the proceedings began. Robeckal whiningly declared that he bitterly regretted what he had done. He had been seduced by Fanfaro, and would give his right hand if he could blot out the recollection of the attempted assassination.

"Thanks be to God that Providence protected our king!" he concluded, bursting into tears, the presence of which were a surprise even to himself, while a murmur of sympathy ran through the courtroom. He certainly deserved a light punishment, poor fellow, and—

Now came Fanfaro's turn.

"You are a member of a secret society which bears the proud title of 'Heroes of Justice'?" asked the presiding judge.

"I am a Frenchman," replied Fanfaro, "and as such I joined with the men who desire to free their country."

"And to do this you attempted assassination?" asked the judge, sharply.

"I am not an assassin," replied the young man, coldly; "these men who negotiated with foreign powers to cut France in pieces for the sake of conquering a crown sunk in mud have more right to the title."

"Bravo!" came from the rear of the hall, and then a terrible tumult arose. With the help of the policemen, several dozen men were hustled out of the room, while the man who had uttered the cry was let alone. It was Girdel, who wore the dress of a lackey and consequently aroused no suspicion.

Irene de Salves was also one of the spectators. Her sparkling eyes were directed at Fanfaro, and whenever he spoke, a look of pride shone in them.

When quiet had been restored, the judge turned once more to Fanfaro. He asked him to tell everything he knew about the attempt, and shook his head when the young man declared on his honor that he was the victim of a conspiracy.

"My father," Fanfaro concluded, "fell in defence of his country, and it would be a bad way of honoring his memory were I to stain his name with the shame of regicide."

Fanfaro's defender was a very able lawyer, but he was stopped in the middle of his speech, and when he protested he was forced to leave the courtroom.

Fifteen minutes later the verdict was given. Robeckal was condemned to death by strangulation, and Fanfaro to the galleys for life.

But at the moment the sentence was pronounced a terrible thing occurred.

Fanfaro arose, opened his mouth as if he wished to speak, stretched out his arms, turned around in a circle, and then fell heavily to the floor!

Loud cries broke forth.

"He has committed suicide," some cried.

"He has been poisoned," came from others, and all rushed toward the unconscious man.

Irene de Salves had hurried toward Girdel, she wished to ask him a question; but when she finally reached the place where she had seen the athlete he had disappeared. All attempts at recovery remained fruitless, and Fanfaro was carried off. Robeckal, too, was almost dead from fright. The sentence came upon him like a stroke of lightning.

CHAPTER XXIII

THE CRISIS

"A T LAST," cried the Marquis of Fougereuse, when he heard of Fanfaro's sudden death, and in great good humor he went in search of his wife.

"Madeleine!" he exclaimed, "all our troubles are at an end now; he who stood between us and fortune is dead."

"Of whom are you speaking?"

"Of whom else but that common regicide."

"What, of that Fanfaro who lately had the audacity to come into our parlor and create that terrible scene?"

"Of him—he is dead."

"Heaven be praised. We shall now receive the legacy."

"Without a doubt. All that is now necessary is to get Girdel to speak, and that can be easily arranged. He has only to repeat before witnesses what he has told me already."

"I had hardly dared to hope any more that this dream would be realized," said Madeleine. "The cabinet position is now sure, and our son has a brilliant future before him. Where is Frederic staying? He has been gone already several hours."

The marquis paid no attention to Madeleine's last words.

He was thinking about Simon and the great service the latter had done for him.

"Where can Simon be?" he uneasily remarked, "I have not seen him in two days."

"Bah! he will turn up, let us rather speak about our son. I—"

A knock was heard at the door.

"Come in," said the marquis expectantly; but instead of Simon, as he thought, a servant entered.

"My lord," he stammered, "the vicomte—"

"Ah, he is outside!" cried the marquise eagerly; "tell the vicomte we are awaiting him."

Saying which she advanced toward the door. The servant, however, prevented her from opening it, and placing his hand on the knob, he hesitatingly said:

"Madame—I—"

"What do you mean?" cried the marquise, angrily. "You announce the vicomte and lock the door instead of opening it?"

"My lord," said the servant, turning to the marquis.

The expression of the man's face was such that the nobleman felt his heart stand still with terror, and in a faint voice he stammered:

"Madeleine, let Baptiste speak."

"The—vicomte—is dead," stammered Baptiste.

A cry of despair came from the marquise's lips, while the unfortunate father looked at the messenger in a daze. He did not seem to know what was the matter.

But soon the terrible significance of the words was made clear to him. Heavy steps were heard in the corridor. They ceased at the door, and now—now four men entered the parlor and laid gently on the floor the burden they had been carrying. The burden was a bier, covered with a cloth, under which could be seen the outlines of a human form.

Neither the marquis nor Madeleine had the courage to raise the cover. In a daze they both stared at the bier and the pallbearers, and only when Gaston de Ferrette, Talizac's friend, stepped on the threshold of the door did life return to the unhappy parents.

"Gaston, what has happened?" cried the marquis in despair, as he imploringly held his hand toward the young man.

"He is dead," replied Gaston, in a hollow voice.

"Who is dead? For Heaven's sake speak!" moaned Madeleine.

"Your son, the Vicomte de Talizac, fell in a duel," said Gaston, earnestly.

Madeleine uttered a loud cry and sank unconscious to the floor. While Baptiste and the marquise's maid hurried to her assistance, Fougereuse gazed vacantly before him, and then raising his head, he passionately exclaimed:

"You lie—my son had no duel!"

"Would to God you were right, marquis," replied Gaston, sorrowfully; "unfortunately it is the truth. The vicomte and Arthur de Montferrand fought a duel, and the sword of the latter ran through Talizac's heart!"

The marquis still remained unconvinced, and carefully gliding toward the bier, he shoved the cloth aside with a trembling hand.

Yes, it was his son who lay on the bier. The pale face was stiff and cold. The eyes were glassy and on the breast was a deep red wound.

The marquis uttered a hoarse cry and his hand nervously grasped the cloth. His eyes shone feverishly and he stammered forth disconnected sentences.

Gaston de Ferrette consoled the unhappy father, but his words made no impression, and as Madeleine had in the meantime been brought back to consciousness by her maid, Gaston thought it best to go away for the present.

He softly strode to the door, but had hardly reached it when the marquis sprang up, and, laying his hand heavily on the young man's shoulder, said:

"Do not leave this room. I must know how he died."

A wink from Gaston sent the servants away, and as soon as he was alone with the parents he began his story.

"The vicomte sent his seconds to Arthur de Montferrand," he said; "the motive for the duel was to be kept secret by both combatants, and I of course had nothing to say to this. The meeting was agreed upon for this morning and took place in the Bois de Boulogne. When the vicomte arrived on the spot, he was so terribly excited that the seconds thought it their duty to ask for a post-ponement of the affair. This proposition was agreed to by Monsieur de Montferrand, but the vicomte firmly opposed it. We tried in vain to change his determination. He became angry, accused his seconds of cowardice, and threatened to horsewhip them. Under such circumstances nothing could be done. The distance was measured off and the duel began. The vicomte was already lost after the first tourney. In his passion he ran upon his opponent's sword, the blade of which penetrated his heart, and death immediately followed."

Pale, with eyes wide open, the marquis and Madeleine listened to Gaston's story. The marquise clinched her fist and angrily exclaimed:

"My son has been murdered, and I will avenge him!"

The marquis remained silent, but his silence made a deeper impression on the young man than Madeleine's anger.

"Did my son leave any letter?" asked the marquise, suddenly.

"Yes, my lady. Before we rode to the Bois de Boulogne the vicomte gave me a sealed letter, which I was to give to his parents in case of his death."

The young man thereupon handed the marquise the letter. Madeleine tore the envelope with a trembling hand. There were only a few lines:

"You have brought me up badly. You are the cause of my death. I hate you!"

A terrible laugh, the laugh of madness, came from the marquise's breast, and, rushing upon her husband, she held the paper before his eyes.

"Read," she cried, "read these words, which our only child sends us from his grave. He hates us—ha, ha, ha! —hates—hates!"

The cup of sorrow caused the marquise to become unconscious again, and this time Gaston ordered the servants to take her away. Madeleine was carried to her bedroom, and Gaston, who saw the marquis kneeling at his son's bier, noiselessly went away.

Hardly had he left the room, when the door was slowly opened and a gray-haired man entered. He saw the grief-stricken father beside his son's corpse, and an expression of deep sympathy crossed his stony face. Softly walking behind the marquis, he laid his hand upon his shoulder. Fougereuse looked up and an expression of dumb terror appeared on his features, while he tremblingly murmured: "Pierre Labarre!"

Yes, it was really Pierre Labarre who had accompanied Caillette and Louise to Paris, and had heard there that Fanfaro's trial had begun. As soon as he could he hurried to the court house and heard there what had happened. Several physicians stood about the so suddenly deceased young man, and they declared that death was brought about by the bursting of a vein.

Crushed and annihilated, Pierre Labarre hurried to the Fougereuse mansion, and the marquis trembled at sight of him, as if he were a spectre.

"Pierre Labarre," he cried in a hollow voice, "you come to gloat over my grief. Ah, you can triumph now. I know you are glad at my misfortune. Get out!" he suddenly exclaimed in angry tones, "get out, I have nothing to do with you!"

"But I have with you, marquis," replied Pierre calmly. "I have something to tell you, and you will listen to me!"

"Aha! have you finally become reasonable?" mockingly laughed the marquis. "Now you will no longer dare to prevent me from claiming my rights or dispute my legal title."

"No," replied Pierre, sorrowfully; "the real Vicomte de Talizac is dead, and from to-day on you are for me the Marquis of Fougereuse."

"I do not understand you," said the marquis, confused. "What has the death of my son got to do with my title?"

"I do not speak of the son who lies here a corpse, but of the other—"

"Which other?" asked the nobleman, more and more surprised.

"You will soon understand me—it is about Fanfaro—"

"Ah, I could have thought so; to his death I owe the fact that Pierre Labarre calls me the Marquis of Fougereuse, and that now that no one is living to whom he can give the hidden millions he must necessarily deliver them up to me!"

With a mixture of surprise and horror Pierre looked at the man, who could still think of money and money matters in the presence of his dead son.

"Why do you not speak?" continued the marquis, mockingly. "You are, no doubt, sorrowful at the death of Fanfaro, whom you imagine to be the legitimate heir of the Fougereuse? Yes, I cannot help you; gone is gone; and if it interests you, you can learn how Fanfaro came to his death. I killed him!"

"Impossible—do not say that!" cried Pierre Labarre in terror. "Say that it was a joke, my lord, or a misunderstanding. You did not kill him!"

"And why not?" asked the nobleman. "Yes, I got rid of him; I hired the murderer, who freed me of him! Ha! ha! ha! I knew who Fanfaro was—I recognized him immediately on account of his resemblance to my father and my brother, and as he stood in my way I got rid of him by means of poison! What are you staring at? I really believe you are getting childish in your old age!"

Pale as a ghost, Pierre leaned against the wall, and his hand was clasped over his eyes, as if he wished to shut the marquis out of his sight.

"Unhappy father," he murmured, in a broken voice;

"would to God somebody took the duty off my hands of telling you what you have done."

"Spare your pity," said Fougereuse, proudly; "if anything can console me for the death of my son, it is the knowledge that my brother Jules's son, who was always a thorn in my side, is at last out of the way."

"For Heaven's sake be silent: this Fanfaro was not your brother's son!"

"So much the worse!"

"My lord, in the presence of this corpse which lies before us, I beseech you do not blaspheme, and listen to what I have to say. Do you recollect the village of Sachemont?"

"Sachemont?" repeated Fougereuse, pensively.

"Yes—Sachemont. On the 16th of May, 1804, you and another officer took lodgings in the cottage of a peasant in Sachemont. You were running away from France. You had taken part in Cadoudal's conspiracy, and barely escaped from the hands of the officers of the law. The peasant received you hospitably, and, in return, the wretches insulted their host's daughters. One of the officers, a German, was repulsed by the young girl he had impudently approached, but the other one, a Frenchman, took advantage of the other sister, and after committing the dastardly outrage, he ran away with his companion. Marquis, shall I name you the man who acted so meanly? It was the then Vicomte de Talizac!"

Fougereuse looked at the old servant in amazement. Where had Pierre Labarre found all this out?

"The nobleman left the cottage like a thief in the night, and left behind him despair and shame," continued Pierre; "and this despair increased when the unhappy victim of the Vicomte de Talizac gave birth to a son, about the commencement of the year 1805—''

''Go on! What else?'' asked Fougereuse, mockingly, as Pierre paused.

''The unhappy girl died, and the child, which had neither father nor mother, stood alone in the world,'' said the old man softly; ''it would have died wretchedly if a brave and noble man had not made good the misfortune another caused. Jules de Fougereuse, the brother of the Vicomte de Talizac, married, under the name of Jules Fougeres, the sister of the dead woman, and both of them took care of the child. They brought the boy up as if he had been their own, and in the village of Leigoutte no one suspected that little Jacques was only an adopted child. In the year 1814 you induced the Cossacks to destroy Leigoutte. Jules Fougeres, your only brother, died the death of a hero, and if the wife and children of the victim did not get burned to death, as was intended, it was not the fault of the instigator of the bloody drama.''

This time the nobleman did not reply mockingly; pale and trembling he gazed at Pierre Labarre, and cold drops of perspiration stood on his forehead.

''My information is at an end,'' said the old man now, as he advanced a step nearer to the nobleman. ''Fanfaro and Jacques Fougeres are identical with the Vicomte de Talizac's son.''

''It is a lie,'' hissed Fougereuse, ''this Fanfaro was my brother's son; tell your fables to others.''

Instead of answering, Pierre Labarre searched in his breast-pocket and handed the marquis a package of papers. With trembling hands Fougereuse opened the ones on top and tried to read, but a veil was before his eyes and he tremblingly said:

"Read them, Pierre, I cannot see anything."

Pierre read the following aloud:

"I, Jules de Fougereuse, elder son of the marquis of the same name, swear that the child, Jacques Fougeres, which is supposed to be my own and bears the name of Fougeres, which I at present answer to, is not my son, but the son of my sister-in-law Therese Lemaire, and my brother, the Vicomte de Talizac.

"JULES FOUGERES."

"Those words have been written by some unmitigated liar!" cried the marquis. "Pierre Labarre, say that it is not true, or else—I must have poisoned my own son!"

"Would to God I could say no," replied Pierre, shuddering, "but I cannot! Fanfaro was your son—his blood lies on your head!"

"No! no!" cried the marquis, pale as death; "his blood will not fall upon me, but upon the devil who led me to do the dastardly deed."

"His name?" asked Pierre.

"Is Simon—my steward! He advised me to poison Fanfaro, so that I could force you to give up the legacy. I acceded to his proposition, and he committed the deed."

Pierre looked contemptuously at the coward who did not hesitate to throw the responsibility of the terrible deed on his servant.

"I am going now," he said, coldly; "I have nothing more to do here."

"No, remain. Do not leave me alone with the dead—I am frightened!" whined the marquis.

"I must go. I want to look after your other dead son," replied Pierre.

"Ah, take me along! Let me see him, let me beg forgiveness of the corpse against which I have sinned so," implored the broken-down man.

Pierre thought for a while, and then said earnestly:

"Come then—you are right."

"Thanks, a thousand thanks! But tell me, Pierre, what will become of the fortune you have in safe keeping. It exists yet, I hope?"

Labarre trembled with contemptuous rage; the man before him was more mercenary and wicked than he thought could be possible. He buried both his sons almost at the same hour, but he still found time and opportunity to inquire about the legacy for which he had made so many sacrifices.

"Well," exclaimed Fougereuse impatiently, "tell me, where are the millions of my father?"

"In a safe place," replied Pierre dryly.

"God be praised! I could draw a million then this evening?"

"My God, marquis! do you need a million to confess your sins?"

"Later! Later! Now answer me, when can I get the million?"

"To-morrow; the documents and bonds are deposited with a lawyer here."

"So much the better."

The marquis hurried to his writing-table, wrote a few lines and rang.

"Here, this note must be brought at once to Count Fernando de Velletri," he said to Baptiste. "Wait for an answer and bring it at once to me; you will find me in the court-house."

While the servant was hurrying away, the marquis hastily put on a cloak, and left the house with Labarre.

CHAPTER XXIV

THE AUTOPSY

IN A HOUSE opposite the court-house, which stood at the corner of a street which has long since disappeared, were two men who were earnestly conversing.

"Doctor," said one of them, "you guarantee a success?"

"Have no fear; I have often made such experiments, and always with success. I haven't grown gray in the service of science for nothing. I know what I am speaking about."

"But the long time," said the other anxiously. "You know we can operate only at night, and forty hours are sometimes an eternity."

"Before I entered upon the plan I weighed everything carefully," said the physician earnestly, "otherwise I should not have taken the responsibility. Have confidence in me; what my knowledge and care can do will be done to bring everything to a good end."

The other man shook the physician's hand heartily.

"Thank you, faithful friend," he cordially said. "I wish I could stop the uneasy beating of my heart, but I suppose it is only natural that I am anxious."

"That's it exactly," replied the doctor; "and to quiet you I will stay here from now on until the decisive hour. Good-by, I must go. You know where I am to be found."

The doctor went, while the other man struck his face with his hands and softly murmured:

"God grant that he be right. I would rather die a thousand deaths than lose the dear boy in this way."

Hot tears ran over the man's brown cheeks, and his broad breast rose and fell, torn by convulsive sobs.

"Shame yourself, Firejaws!" he murmured, "if any one saw you now! Let us hope everything will be all right, and then—"

A loud knock at the door interrupted Girdel's self-conversation, and upon a hasty "Come in," Bobichel entered the room.

"Well, Bobi, how goes it?" asked the athlete.

"She is downstairs," said the clown, with a significant gesture.

Without asking another question, Girdel hurried out, while Bobichel looked observantly around the room, and soon found a well-filled bottle of wine and a glass; he filled the glass and emptied it with one swallow.

In the meantime Girdel had met Irene de Salves in the corridor of the house.

The young lady wore a black dress, and when she saw the athlete she ran to meet him and sobbingly cried:

"He's not dead, is he?"

"No, he is not dead," confirmed Girdel; and seeing Irene's pale face, he said, more to himself: "I knew how the news would work, and yet it could not be helped —as God pleases, it will all be right again."

"But where is he?" asked Irene anxiously.

"Countess," began the athlete, somewhat embarrassed, "at present he is a corpse on a bier and whoever sees him thinks he is dead; but to-morrow at this time he will be well and at liberty."

"Ah, if I could only believe it—"

"You can do so," cried Girdel, hastily; "if I had not thought you were more courageous than women in general, I would have kept silent; but I thought to myself you were in despair, and I therefore concluded to speak."

"A thousand thanks for your confidence, but tell me everything that has happened—I can hardly understand the whole thing."

"I believe you. If you were to accompany me to the cellar now you would see one of the chief actors in the drama. Downstairs in a cage lies a wild beast which we have captured. I just want to call Bobichel and give him a message, then I will accompany you downstairs."

A low whistle from the athlete brought the clown directly to him, and Girdel ordered him to slip into the court-house and watch what occurred there. He then accompanied Irene into the damp cellar. Lighting a pocket lantern and holding it aloft, he said:

"Follow me, countess; we will soon be there."

The countess followed her guide without hesitation; she had perfect confidence in Girdel, and after a short journey they both stood in front of a heavy iron door.

"Here we are," said the athlete, triumphantly; and taking an iron bar which stood in a corner in his hand, he cried in stentorian tones:

"Get up, scoundrel, let us look at you!"

Low moans answered the gruff command, and Irene uttered a cry of terror, for in the cell a human form moved.

"Step nearer, mademoiselle," said Girdel, putting on the manners of a circus proprietor; "the wild beast is pretty tame now—we have taken out its teeth and chained it."

"But I do not understand—" stammered Irene.

"Who this beast is? You shall know it at once; the magnificent personage is Simon, the factotum of the Marquis Fougereuse. In his leisure hours the miserable wretch occupies himself with poisoning experiments, and it would not be a loss to humanity if he should never see daylight again. Come, boy, play your tricks; the performance begins."

"Mercy," whispered Simon, for he was really the prisoner, "let me free."

"Really? Perhaps later on, but now you must obey. Quick, tell us what brought you here."

"I am hungry," growled Simon.

"Really? Well, if you answer my questions probably you shall have food and drink. Why did you want to poison Fanfaro?"

"I do not know," stammered the steward.

"How bad your memory is. What interest did your master, the Marquis of Fougereuse, have in Fanfaro's death?"

Simon was silent. Girdel nudged him gently in the ribs with the iron bar, and turning to Irene, said:

"Would you believe, mademoiselle, that this fellow was very talkative a few days ago when he tried to bribe Fanfaro's jailer. Growl away, it is true, anyway!

You promised fabulous sums to the jailer if he would mix a small white powder in Fanfaro's food. Fortunately I have eyes and ears everywhere, so I immediately took my measures. With Bobichel's assistance I captured this monster here, and then I went to the bribed jailer and gave him, in the name of his employer, the white powder. He took it without any objection. That I had changed the powder in the meantime for another he was unaware of. If I only knew," he concluded with a frown, "what object this marquis has to injure Fanfaro. This beast won't talk, and—"

"Let me speak to him," said the countess, softly. And turning to the grating, she urged Simon to confess his master's motives and thereby free himself. At first Simon looked uneasily at the young girl; he made an attempt to speak, but reconsidered it and closed his lips.

"Let us leave him alone, mademoiselle," said Girdel; "solitude will do him good."

When Simon saw that Girdel and Irene were about to depart, he groaned loudly, but the athlete ordered him to keep still if he did not wish to be gagged, and this warning had the desired effect.

When Girdel and Irene reached the room, the latter sank, sobbing, upon a chair, and "the brave athlete" tried his best to console her.

"It will be all right," he assured her; "Fanfaro has swallowed a strong narcotic which makes him appear as if dead. To-morrow he will be buried; we shall dig him up again, and then bring him away as soon as possible."

At this moment Bobichel breathlessly rushed into the

room, and Irene uttered a cry of terror when she saw his pale face.

"What has happened?" she cried, filled with gloomy forebodings.

"O God—he is lost!" stammered the clown.

"Who is lost?"

"Fanfaro."

"Speak clearly," cried Girdel, beside himself.

"They have brought—Fanfaro—to the—Hotel Dieu," said Bobichel, sobbing.

"Well, that isn't such a misfortune," said the athlete, breathing more freely. "You need not have frightened us."

"But the worst is to come—they want to hold an autopsy over him to find out the cause of death."

"Merciful God! that must not be," cried Irene, wringing her hands. "We must run to the hospital and tell all."

"Who is the physician that is going to undertake the autopsy?" asked Girdel.

"Doctor Albaret, as I was informed."

"Then rely on me, countess," cried the athlete, rushing away; "either I rescue Fanfaro or else I die with him."

CHAPTER XXV

FROM SCYLLA TO CHARYBDIS

BOBICHEL unfortunately had not said too much. The fact that Fanfaro had dropped dead so suddenly had caused great excitement in the scientific world, and Dr. Albaret, the king's private physician, was the first to propose the autopsy. His colleagues immediately consented, and Fanfaro was at once brought to the Hotel Dieu and placed upon the marble table in the anatomy room. The attendants busily rushed here and there, and while they brought in the necessary instruments—lances, needles, knives, saws and bandages, —numerous disciples of Esculapius stood about the dead man and admired his beautiful proportions and strong muscles.

"He could have lived to a hundred years," said the physician, as he beat Fanfaro's breast, and his colleagues agreed with him. Fanfaro lay like a marble statue upon the table; the dark locks covered the pale forehead, and a painful expression lay over the firmly closed lips. Did the poor fellow suspect that he would become a victim of science and be delivered over to the knife?

In the meantime the hall had become crowded, and

when Dr. Albaret appeared a murmur of expectation ran through the ranks of the students and physicians.

Dr. Albaret, a sturdy old man, bowed to all sides, and hastily taking off his coat he took the dissecting knife in his hand and began to speak: "Gentlemen! a death so sudden as this in a person apparently in the best of health demands the attention of all physicians, and I hope that we will be able to discover the cause of this surprising phenomenon. There are different ways of beginning an autopsy such as this. The German professors, for instance, make a cut from the chin to the pit of the stomach, the Italians from the underlip to the breast-bone, while the French—"

"Dr. Albaret," cried a stentorian voice at this moment—"where is Dr. Albaret?"

The physician frowned, he did not like such interruptions, but when he saw that the man who was hurriedly pressing through the rows of listeners wore the livery of a royal lackey, his face became clear again.

"A message from his majesty the king," said the man breathlessly.

"A message from his majesty?" repeated the physician eagerly, as he grasped the note the messenger gave him.

Hurriedly running over the few lines, Albaret nodded, and quickly putting his coat on again, he said, in a tone of importance:

"Gentlemen, much to my regret I must leave you; an urgent matter requires my immediate attendance at the Tuileries, and I shall go there directly."

"But the autopsy?" remarked an elderly colleague.

"It isn't worth the trouble to postpone it," replied

Albaret, indifferently; "let the poor fellow, who is stone-dead, be buried. Death undoubtedly was produced by the bursting of a blood vessel in the brain, and the excitement under which the deceased was laboring proves this very clearly. Adieu, gentlemen, next time we shall make up for what we have lost now."

He hurried out. In the corridor he was stopped by the superintendent of the hospital, who asked him to put his signature under the burial certificate. Albaret signed it standing, got into the carriage which was waiting at the door, and rode rapidly away, while the royal servant, who was no other than Girdel, ran in an opposite direction, and took off his livery in a little house where Bobichel was awaiting him.

"Bobi, just in time," he breathlessly cried, "five minutes more and Fanfaro would have been done for."

Girdel's further arrangements were made with the utmost prudence. Irene de Salves had given him unlimited credit, and the well-known proverb that a golden key opens all doors was conclusively proved in this particular case. The man whose duty it was to bury those who died in the Hotel Dieu had, for a good round sum, consented to allow Girdel to do his work, and so the athlete had nothing else to do than to clothe himself appropriately and hurry back to the hospital.

The superintendent had just ordered the hearse to be put in readiness, when the Marquis of Fougereuse was announced. On the upper corner of the visiting card was a peculiar mark, and hardly had he seen it than he hurried to meet the marquis.

The nobleman leaned on Pierre Labarre's arm, and returning the superintendent's greeting, he tried to speak, but his voice was broken by sobs, and so he handed the official a folded paper and looked inquiringly at him.

Hardly had the official read the paper, than he respectfully observed that the marquis's wish should be complied with, and that he would give the necessary orders at once.

The note contained an order from the Minister of Justice to hand over to the Marquis of Fougereuse the body of Fanfaro; thus it will be seen that the marquis's present of a million to the Society of Jesus had already borne fruit, and Pierre Labarre felt his anger diminish when he saw for what purpose the marquis had demanded the money. He no longer thought of the cabinet position, he had bought the right with his million to have the son who had never stood near to him in life buried in the Fougereuse family vault.

"I should like—to see—the deceased," stammered the broken-down father.

The official bowed, and accompanied his guide up to the operating room where Fanfaro's body still lay.

The marquis sank on his knees beside the dead man, and murmured a silent prayer; how different was the son who had fallen in a duel to the brother whom the father had sacrificed for him.

"Marquis, shall I call the carriers?" asked Pierre, gently.

The nobleman nodded, and soon Fanfaro's body was laid upon a bier, which was carried to the Fougereuse mansion by four men. The marquis and Pierre followed the procession with uncovered heads. When they arrived at the Fougereuse mansion, Fanfaro was laid beside his brother, and the marquis then said:

"There is only one thing left for me—I must bury my sons and then die myself."

"But Madame la Marquise," said Pierre, anxiously.

"The marquise will have the same wish as I have to suffer for our sins," said the marquis, frowning; "and—"

At this moment Baptiste rushed into the room, and with a frightened look exclaimed:

"Madame la Marquise is nowhere to be seen, and her maid fears she has done herself an injury—she was talking so strangely."

Pierre and the marquis exchanged a silent look, and then the nobleman gently said:

"She did right. Of what further use was she in the world? Oh, I envy her!"

.   .   .   .

Girdel and Bobichel waited almost a full hour at the rear entrance of the Hotel Dieu. The athlete finally became impatient. He went inside of the house and asked if the body wasn't going to be put in the hearse.

"I really forgot all about it," cried the superintendent to whom Girdel had gone for information. "The body has been taken away long ago."

"Taken away?" repeated the athlete, astonished.

"Yes; the Marquis of Fougereuse claimed him and took him along. I believe he intends to bury him in his family vault."

"Almighty God! Is that true?" asked Girdel, horror-stricken.

"Yes, certainly; he brought carriers along, and that settled the matter."

"Where is the family vault of the Fougereuse?" asked Girdel.

"Oh, far from Paris; somewhere in Alsace, if I remember aright."

"God have mercy on me!" muttered Girdel to himself.

The official looked at him with amazement. What was the matter with the man?

CHAPTER XXVI

MISTAKEN

BEFORE Robeckal had consented to play the part of a regicide, he had made his conditions, and not before they were accepted had he undertaken the job. He had been told that he would be condemned to death *pro forma*, and set free at the right moment. He would then be given an amount necessary for him to go to England or America and live there.

Notwithstanding these promises, Robeckal felt a cold shudder run down his back when he heard the death sentence, and when he was taken back to jail again he impatiently awaited further developments. He thought it very strange that he should be left to his fate, and when hour after hour had passed and neither Simon nor any one else came to his cell, he began to feel seriously uneasy.

Suppose they no longer remembered the compact?

Cold drops of perspiration stood on the wretch's forehead, and his hands clinched nervously as these thoughts ran through his mind, and he tried to banish them. No, that must not be done to him. The rescue must come—he had not committed the fatal act for nothing. At last, the heavy iron door swung open, and Vidocq, the great detective, entered his cell. Robeckal knew him, and breathed more freely. Vidocq, no doubt, came to release him.

"Thank God you have come, Monsieur Vidocq," cried Robeckal to the official; "the time was becoming rather long for me."

"I am sorry that I have kept you waiting," replied Vidocq, quietly; "but there were certain formalities to be settled, and I—"

"Ah! no doubt in regard to the money?" said Robeckal, laughing. "Have you brought the yellow birds along?"

"Slowly, slowly—first let me inform you that the death sentence has been torn up."

"Really? I did not expect anything else."

"You do not say so," observed the official, ironically. "Then you already know your fate?"

"Yes, I am going to England and from there to America."

"I don't know anything about that; my information is that you will not leave France."

Robeckal's face became a shade paler, still he did not lose courage.

"Where am I to be sent?" he hastily asked.

"For the present to the south of France."

"To—the—south—of—France," repeated Robeckal.

"To Toulon."

"To Toulon?" cried the wretch, in terror. "That is impossible!"

"And why should it be impossible?" asked Vidocq, smiling maliciously.

"Because—because," stammered Robeckal, faintly, "the sentence—"

"Was death by strangulation. Thanks to the efforts of your friends, it has been commuted to the galleys for life, and I think you ought to be satisfied with the change."

"But—the—promise?" whined the criminal. "But, come, now, you are only joking?"

"I never joke," said the detective, earnestly; "besides, you must have been very innocent to imagine any one would make a compact with a scoundrel like you. It would be a crime against society to allow you to continue your bad course. No, thank God, the judges in France know their duty."

With these words, Vidocq beckoned to four muscular men to enter the cell. They seized Robeckal and put handcuffs and chains on him, in spite of his cries and entreaties. As the wretch continued to shout louder, a gag was put in his mouth, and in less than a quarter of an hour he was on the way to Toulon, which place he never left alive.

CHAPTER XXVII

FREEDOM

IN A POOR fisherman's cottage in Havre a young man was walking up and down in feverish uneasiness.

From time to time he looked through the window which opened on to the sea. The waves ran high, the wind whistled, while dark clouds rolled over the starless sky.

A slight knock was now heard at the door of the cottage.

"Who is there?" asked the young man, anxiously.

"We are looking for Fanfaro," came from the outside; and, when the man hastily shoved back the bolt, two slim female forms, enveloped in dark cloaks, crossed the threshold.

Before the young man had time to greet the strangers, another knock was heard, and upon the question, "Who is there?" the answer came this time, in a soft, trembling voice:

"We have been sent here to find Fanfaro."

"Come in," cried the young man, eagerly; and two more female forms entered the cottage. One of them was young and strong; the other, old, grayhaired and broken-down, clung to her companion, who almost carried her.

They all looked silently at each other; finally, one of those who had first entered let her cloak, the hood of which she wore over her head, sink down, and, turning to the young man, she vivaciously said:

"Arthur, have you sent me this invitation?"

With these words, she handed Arthur de Montferrand, for he was the young man, the following note:

"Whoever wants to see Fanfaro once more should come to the fisherman's cottage of Antoine Michel, in Havre, on the 18th day of March."

"I received a similar invitation," said Arthur. "I was told, at the same time, to come in the afternoon; to answer any inquiries that might be made; and to see that no stranger be admitted. Who invited us here, I do not know; but I think we shall not be kept waiting long for an explanation."

"As God pleases, this hope may be confirmed," replied Irene de Salves, and turning to her companion, who was softly sobbing, she whispered consolingly to her: "Courage, Louison, you will soon embrace your brother."

The two other women were Caillette and Louise; the latter looked vacantly before her, and all of Louison's caresses were of no avail to cheer her.

"Jacques—where is Jacques?" she incessantly repeated, and the fact that Louison was really her daughter seemed to have entirely escaped her.

Arthur de Montferrand never turned his eyes from the girl for whose honor he had fought so bravely, and every time Louison looked up she met the eyes of the young nobleman.

A skyrocket now shot up in the dark sky; it exploded

aloft with a loud noise, and a golden rain lighted up the horizon for a while.

"That was undoubtedly a good sign," thought Arthur, hastily opening the cottage door.

Loud oar-sounds were now heard, and a light boat struck for the shore with the rapidity of an arrow.

The keel now struck the sand and a slim form sprang quickly out of the bark and hurried toward the cottage.

"Fanfaro!" joyously exclaimed the inmates of the cottage, and the young man who had been rescued from the grave was soon surrounded on all sides. He, however, had eyes alone for the broken-down old woman who clung to Caillette in great excitement and gently implored:

"Jacques—where is Jacques? I do not see him!"

"Here I am, my poor dear mother," sobbed Fanfaro, sinking on his knees in front of the old lady.

With trembling hands she caressed his hair, pressed her lips upon her son's forehead, and then sank, with a smile, to the floor. Death had released her from her sufferings after she had been permitted to enjoy the last, and, to her, highest earthly joy.

. . . .

Here Fanfaro's story ended. Girdel knew something to add to it after Fanfaro had closed. He and Bobichel had succeeded in overtaking the funeral cortege which the marquis and Pierre Labarre conducted to the family vault. In a few words Pierre was informed of the condition of things, and as the marquis had become thoroughly exhausted, the faithful old servant had undertaken to bring Fanfaro's body to a place of safety. Girdel had been prudent enough to take along the physician who had given him the narcotic, and soon Fanfaro opened his eyes.

As soon as he had sufficiently recovered, Pierre told him, in short outlines, who he was. The young man listened with deep emotion to the story, and then he swore a sacred oath that he would never call another man father than the one who had taken pity on him, the helpless child; the Marquis of Fougereuse had no right to him, and he would rather have died than touch a penny of his money. No power on earth could induce him to have anything to do with the marquis. He would leave France, and try to forget, in a foreign country, what he had suffered.

That very night Fanfaro travelled, in company with his sister, Girdel, Bobichel, and Caillette, to Algiers. Before the ship lifted anchor, Fanfaro had received from Irene's lips the promise that she would become his wife. Her mother's life hung on a thread, and as long as she remained on earth the daughter could not think of leaving her.

The old countess died about six months afterward, and as soon as Irene had arranged her affairs, she prepared herself for the journey to Africa.

She was not surprised when Arthur offered to accompany her. She was aware that a powerful magnet in the person of Louison attracted him across the ocean, and when the young nobleman landed in France again, after the lapse of a few months, he was accompanied by a handsome young wife, whom the old Marquis of Montferrand warmly welcomed to the home of his fathers—for was she not a scion of the house of Fougereuse, and the sole heiress of all the property of that family? Louison's uncle, the Marquis Jean de Fougereuse, had ended his dreary life shortly after the Vicomte de Talizac's death, and it was not difficult for Arthur, with Pierre Labarre's assistance, to maintain Louison's claims as the daughter of Jules de Fougereuse and sole heiress of the legacy. Of course, the Society of Jesus was much put out by the sudden apparition of an heiress, for it had hoped to come into possession of the millions some day.

Bobichel had become Caillette's husband; and though the handsome wife did not conceal the fact from him that not he, but Fanfaro, had been her first love, the supremely happy clown was satisfied. He knew Caillette was good to him and that he had no ground any more to be jealous of Irene's husband.

The life which the colonists led in Africa was full of dangers, but had also its pleasures and joys, and through Louison and her husband they remained in connection with their fatherland, whose children they remained in spite of everything.

. . . .

At the end of a week Spero had entirely recovered, and the count prepared to depart for France. Before he parted from his kind host, he turned to Fanfaro and begged him in a solemn tone to stand by his son with his assistance and advice, should he ever need them, and Fanfaro cheerfully complied with his request.

"Rely on my word," he said, as the little caravan was about to start. "The son of the Count of Monte-Cristo is under the protection of all of us, and if he should ever call us to his assistance, whether by day or night, we shall obey the call!"

CHAPTER XXVII

BENEDETTO'S REVENGE

A Letter of the Count of Monte-Cristo to his son, Vicomte Spero

"MY DEARLY BELOVED SON—To-day is the anniversary of your rescue from the hands of that terrible Maldar, and although twelve years have passed since then, I still feel the effects of the fright I sustained. Thanks to faithful friends, you were saved to us; God bless them for it, and give you and me an opportunity to repay them for what they have done for us.

"In regard to myself this opportunity must come soon, for I have passed my sixtieth year, and my strength is failing.

"Yes, my dear Spero, your father, who was to you the incarnation of energy, is now only a broken-down man; since my poor wife died, all is over with the Count of Monte-Cristo. Five years, five long years, have passed since your dear mother breathed her last in my arms, and I, who never wept before, have cried like a child. How insignificant, how feeble I thought myself when I saw the cheeks of my dear wife become paler day by day and her beautiful eyes lose their sparkle. What good was all the art and science I had learned from the Abbé Faria to me if I could not rescue her? Like avenging spirits, the shades of all those upon whom I had taken revenge rose up before me: Villefort, Danglars, Morcerf, Benedetto, Maldar, had all been overcome by me, but death was stronger than I am—it took her from me!

"My blood, my life, I would have given for that of your mother, but it was all of no use, death would not give up its prey. At that time, my dear son, you were sixteen years old. Your tears mingled with mine and you cried out in deep grief: 'Ah, mother, if I could only die for you!'

"Spero, do you know what it is to feel that a person has deceived himself? I spent my life to carry out what I thought to be right, the punishment of wrong-doers and the rewarding of those who do good. I was all-powerful as long as it was a question of punishing the guilty, but as weak and feeble as a child when I attempted to make good the wrong I did in an excess of zeal, and all my tears and entreaties were of no avail.

"What good did it do that I rescued Albert, the son of the Countess Mercedes, from the murderous flames of Uargla? Two years later he was shot in the *coup d'état* of December, and his mother died of a broken heart.

"Maximilian Morrel and Valentine de Villefort met an early and a fearful death—they fell victims to the insurrection of the Sepoys in India, in the year 1859.

"You inherited from your mother everything that is good, noble, and sublime; from me a thirst for knowledge, energy, and activity. Would to God I could say that you did not also inherit my arrogance, my venomous arrogance. Spero, by the time you receive this letter, I shall be far away; yes, I am going away, and voluntarily place upon myself the heaviest burden, but it must be.

"Will you be able to understand me and my motives?

Ah, Spero, I cannot help domineering over those about me, and that is why I am going.

"So long as you are at my side, you are not yourself. You look at life with my eyes, you judge according to my ideas, and my opinion is decisive for you in everything you do and think.

"You do not regard me as a man, but as a supernatural being. Far from me you will learn the meaning of responsibility for one's acts, and if not now, later on, you will be grateful to me for this temporary separation.

"Spero, I have furnished you with the best weapons for the struggle of life, and it is about time that you take up your arms and begin your first battle with life.

"You are now twenty-one years of age. You are brave and courageous, and will not shrink from any obstacle. You are rich, you have knowledge—now it must be seen whether you possess the will which guarantees success.

"Your path is smooth—no enemy threatens you, and a crowd of friends stand at your side. I have never had a real friend. Those who acted as such were either servants or poor people, and only those who are situated similarly and think alike can understand the blessings of friendship.

"My son! give generously, believe in humanity, and do not distrust any one; real experience is gained only by mistakes.

"Murder is the worst crime, for it can never be made good again. Of the old servants, I shall leave only Coucou with you. He is devoted to you and loves you enthusiastically. The brave Zouave will yearn for me, but console him by telling him I have gone for your good and tell yourself the same thing, should you feel likewise. With best love,   YOUR FATHER."

CHAPTER XXVIII

SPERO

THE Vicomte of Monte-Cristo was a wonderfully handsome man. The grace of his mother and the stalwart build of his father were united in him. His dark hair fell in wavy locks over his high white forehead, and the long eyelashes lay like veils upon his cheeks.

The young man's surroundings were in every particular arranged with consummate taste. The vicomte had inherited from his parents a taste for Oriental things, and his study looked like a costly tent, while his bedroom was furnished with the simplicity of a convent cell. The Count of Monte-Cristo had taught his son to be strict to himself and not become effeminate in any way. Nice pictures and statues were in the parlors, the bookcase was filled with selected volumes and he spent many hours each day in serious studies. Spero was a master in all physical accomplishments. His father's iron muscles were his legacy, and the count often proudly thought that his son, in case of need, would also have found the means and the way to escape from the Chateau d'If.

The vicomte sat at his writing-desk and was reading

his father's letter when Coucou entered. The Zouave had changed somewhat. He no longer wore a uniform or the little cap of a Jackal, but had changed them for a dark brown overcoat. His eyes, however, still sparkled as merrily as ever, and Coucou could laugh as heartily as ever.

"When did the count leave the house?" asked Spero, whose voice reminded one of his father's.

"This evening, vicomte," replied Coucou, with military briefness.

"Why was I not called?"

"The count forbade it. He ordered me to place the letter which you found on the writing-table and—"

"Did the count go alone?"

"No, Ali accompanied him."

"In what direction did he go?"

"I do not know. I was called to the count at two o'clock this morning, and after I had received the letter, I went away."

"Without asking any questions?"

"Oh, vicomte, no one asks the Count of Monte-Cristo for a reason," cried Coucou, vivaciously. "I am not a coward, but—"

"I know you possess courage," replied the young man.

"*Sapristi*—there, now, I have allowed myself to go again. I know that my way of speaking displeases you, vicomte, and I will try next time to do better."

"What makes you think that your language displeases me?" asked Spero, laughing.

"Because—excuse me, vicomte, but sometimes you look so stern—"

"Nonsense," interrupted Spero; "I may sometimes look troubled, but certainly not stern, and I beg you not to speak differently from what you were taught—speak to me as you do to my father."

"Ah, it is easy to speak to the count," said Coucou, unthinkingly; "he has such a cheering smile—"

A frown passed over Spero's face, and he gently said:

"My father is good—he is much better than I am—I knew it long ago."

"Vicomte, I did not say that," cried the Zouave, embarrassed.

"No, but you thought so, and were perfectly right, my dear Auguste; if you wish to have me for a friend, always tell the truth."

"Yes, sir," replied Coucou, "and now I have a special favor to ask you, vicomte."

"Speak, it is already granted."

"Vicomte, the count never calls me Auguste, which is my baptismal name, but Coucou. If you would call me Coucou, I—"

"With pleasure. Well, then, Coucou, you know nothing further?"

"Nothing."

"It is good. You can go."

The Zouave turned toward the door. When he had nearly reached it, Spero cried:

"Coucou, stay a moment."

"Just as you say, vicomte."

"I only wished to beg you again," said Spero, in a low, trembling voice, "not to think me stern or ungrateful. I shall never forget that it was you who accompanied my father and me to Africa, and that you placed your own life in danger to rescue mine."

"Ah, vicomte," stammered the Zouave, deeply moved, "that was only my duty."

"That a good many would have shirked this duty, and that you did not, is why I thank you still to-day. Give me your hand in token of our friendship. Now we are good friends again, are we not?"

With tears in his laughing eyes, Coucou laid his big brown hand in the delicate hand of the vicomte. The latter cordially shook it, and was almost frightened, when the Zouave uttered a faint cry and hastily withdrew his fingers.

"What is the matter with you?" asked Spero, in amazement.

"Oh, nothing, but—"

"Well, but—"

"You see, vicomte, my hand is almost crushed, and because I was not prepared for it, I gave a slight cry. Who would have thought that such a fine, white, delicate hand could give you a squeeze like a piston-rod?"

Spero looked wonderingly at his hands, and then dreamily said:

"I am stronger than I thought."

"I think so, too," said Coucou. "Only the count understands how to squeeze one's hand in that way. I almost forgot to ask you, vicomte, where you intend to take breakfast?"

"Downstairs in the dining-room."

"Are you going to breakfast alone?"

"That depends. Perhaps one of my friends may drop in, though I haven't invited any one."

"Please ring the bell in case you want to be served," said Coucou, as he left the room.

Spero stood at the writing-desk for a time, and his dark eyes were humid. He shoved a brown velvet curtain aside and entered a small, dark room which opened from his study. A pressure of the finger upon the blinds caused them to spring open, and the broad daylight streamed through the high windows. The walls, which were hung with brown velvet, formed an octagon, and opposite the broad windows were two pictures in gold frames. The vicomte's look rested on these pictures. They were the features of his parents which had been placed upon the canvas by the hand of an artist. In all her goodness, Haydee, Ali Tebelen's daughter, looked down upon her son, and the bold, proud face of Edmond Dantes greeted his heir with a speaking look.

"Ah, my mother," whispered Spero, softly, "if you were only with me now that father has left me. How shall I get along in life without him? The future looks blank and dark to me, the present sad, and only the past is worth having lived for! What a present the proud name is that was laid in my cradle. Others see bright light where the shadow threatens to suffocate me, and my heart trembles when I think that I am standing in the labyrinth of life without a guide!"

From this it can be seen that the count had not exaggerated in his letter to his son. He domineered, consciously or unconsciously, over his surroundings, and so it happened that Spero hardly dared to express a thought of his own.

Spero was never heard to praise or admire this or that, before he had first inquired whether such an opin-

ion would be proper to express. The father recognized
too late that his son lacked independence of thought.
He had, as he thought, schooled his son for the battle
of life. He had taught him how to carry the weapons,
but in his anxiety about exterior and trivial things he
had forgotten to make allowance for the inward yearning.
The form was more to him than the contents, and this
was revenging itself now in a telling way. The demands
of ordinary life were unknown to Spero. He had put
his arm in the burning flame with the courage of a
Mucius Scævola, and quailed before the prick of
a needle.

Suddenly the door-bell rang, and breathing more freely
the vicomte left the little room. When he returned to his
study he found Coucou awaiting him. The Zouave presented a visiting card to the vicomte on a silver salver,
and hardly had Spero thrown a look at it, when he joyfully cried:

"Bring the gentleman to the dining-room, Coucou,
and put two covers on; we shall dine together."

CHAPTER XXIX

FORWARD, MARCH

WHEN Spero entered the dining-room, a handsome young man about twenty-five years of age hurried toward him with outstretched arms.

"How are you, my dear Spero?" he vivaciously cried.

"Oh, thank you, very well. Do you know, Gontram, that you couldn't have come at a more appropriate hour?"

"Really? That pleases me," said the new-comer, a painter who in spite of his youth enjoyed a great reputation. Laying his hand on Spero's shoulder, he looked steadily at him and earnestly asked: "Has anything disagreeable happened to you?"

"No; what makes you think so?" replied Spero, confused.

"Your appearance is different from usual. Your eyes sparkle, and you are feverishly excited. Perhaps you have some secret to intrust to me?"

In the meantime the young men had seated themselves at table, and while they were eating they indulged in general conversation.

"Do you know that my father has left Paris suddenly?" asked Spero in the course of the conversation.

"No. Where has the count gone to?"

"I do not know," said the vicomte.

Gontram Sabran had been acquainted with Spero for two years.

He had attracted the vicomte's attention through a picture he had exhibited, and as Spero admired painting, he paid a visit to the creator of the wonderfully natural painting.

The picture represented a young gypsy who was playing the violin. The vicomte sent his father's steward to the artist with an order to buy the canvas at any price. Gontram Sabran had refused to sell the painting, and the vicomte went personally to the painter.

"Sir," said Gontram, politely, "you offered me twenty thousand francs for a picture which is worth far less; that I have nevertheless refused to sell the picture needs an explanation, and if you are willing, I shall be happy to give it to you."

Spero had become curious, and upon his acquiescence Gontram told him the following.

"I had a girl once who suffered from an incurable disease. We were very happy together, enjoyed the present, and thought very little of the future. One day, as was customary with us, we undertook a little promenade. It led us however further than we intended to go, and before we knew it we were in the woods of Meudon. Curious and wonderful sounds awoke us from our reveries, and going to an opening, we saw a young gypsy who was playing the violin and moving her body to and fro to the time of the instrument. Aimee listened attentively to the heavenly playing of the almost childish girl, but suddenly I felt her head lean heavily on my shoulder

—she had fainted, and I brought a very sick girl back to Paris.

"One week later death knocked at her door. Aimee knew she was going to die, and with tears in her eyes she begged me to hunt up the gypsy girl and have her play a song to her before she died.

"What was I to do? I could not find the gypsy, and was almost in despair. On the morning of the fourth day, the invalid suddenly rose in her bed and cried aloud:

"'There she is, I hear the gypsy's violin—oh, now I can die peacefully! Open the window, Gontram, so that I can hear the music better.'

"I did as she said, and now the tones of the violin reached my ears. The dying girl listened breathlessly to the sweet sounds. When the song was over, Aimee took my hand and whispered:

"'Bring her up and beg her to play at my bedside.'

"I hurried into the street and asked the gypsy to fulfil the wish of the dying girl. She did so at once, and sitting beside Aimee she played upon her instrument. How long she played I do not know, but I was thrilled by the sudden cessation of the music, and when I looked in terror at Aimee, I saw she had drawn her last breath—she had gone to her eternal slumber to the music of the violin.

"The gypsy disappeared, and I have never seen her since. But I have put her features on canvas as they are engraved in my memory, and you can understand now why I do not wish to sell the picture."

"Monsieur Sabran," said Spero when the painter had

finished, "your little romance is interesting, and I am now ready to pay fifty thousand francs for the picture."

Gontram looked pityingly at the vicomte and dryly replied:

"I stick to my refusal."

Spero went away disappointed. Two days later he hurried to the painter's studio and hesitatingly said:

"Monsieur Sabran, I treated you the other day in a mean way. Please excuse me."

Gontram was surprised. Taking the vicomte's hand, he cordially said:

"I am glad I was mistaken in you; if features such as yours are deceitful, then it is bad for humanity."

From that day on they became firm friends. When the painter saw Spero's disturbed features on this particular day, and heard that the count had departed, he had an idea that it would do him good.

"Where did your father go to?" he asked.

"I do not know," replied Spero, uneasily.

"What? Your father did not inform you?" asked Gontram.

"No," replied Spero; "he departed this evening and left a letter for me behind him."

"Ah, really, every one does as he pleases," said Gontram. "Do you know I came here to-day to ask a favor of you?"

"You couldn't do me a greater pleasure," replied Spero, cheerfully; "everything I possess is at your disposal."

"I thought so; the next time you will offer me your millions," cried Gontram, laughing.

"I hope you will ask me for something besides

wretched money," said Spero, warmly. "I could gladly fight for you, or do some other important service for you."

"And suppose I was to keep you at your word?" asked Gontram, seriously; "suppose I came here only to demand a sacrifice of you?"

"Oh, speak!" cried the vicomte, eagerly.

"H'm, would you for my sake get on top of a stage?" asked Gontram, earnestly. "No, do not look so curiously at me. I know you never did such a thing before, and knew what I was talking about when I said I would ask a sacrifice of you."

"I—would—do it—to please you," replied Spero, hesitatingly.

"I thought so," cried the painter, laughing; "yet I made you the proposition, because I thought you were boring yourself to death here."

"But—"

"No, do not protest. You are not happy because you are the slave of propriety, and if you were to get in a stage with me it would be a heroic act on your part. If you want to go out, a carriage is at the door, the horses already harnessed. You have your own box at the theatre, and so on. Nowhere do you come in contact with the great world; your life is no life."

Spero gazed at the painter in astonishment.

"Why have you not told me all that long ago?" he slowly asked.

"Because a great deal depends on time and opportunity. If I had told you this at the commencement of our friendship you would have thought me impertinent, and I did not come here to-day either to give you a lecture.

The words came unconsciously to my lips. Your life is that of a drop of oil which when put in a bottle of water feels itself in a strange element and decidedly uncomfortable.''

Spero bit his lip.

"Am I ever going to hear what service I can do for you?" he asked with a calmness which reflected honor on his powers of self-control.

"Bravo, you have already learned something. First fill your wine-glass, otherwise I shall drink all your fine sherry alone.''

The habit of drinking moderately Spero had also learned from his father.

Upon the remark of the painter, he filled his, glass and impatiently said:

"Well?"

"I would like to make a loan. Don't laugh, but hear what I have to say. I intend to give a little party in my studio—''

"In your studio?" said Spero in surprise.

"Yes, it is certainly not as large as the Place Vendome, but that doesn't matter. Diogenes lived in a hogshead, and a dozen good friends will find plenty of room in my house. Let me tell you what gave me the idea. While I was studying in Rome, an aristocratic Italian, Count Vellini, took an interest in me. He was my friend, my Macænas, and I owe a great deal to him. The day before yesterday he arrived in Paris, and I should like to revenge myself for his kindness. As he is a millionnaire —not a millionnaire like you, for he has, at the utmost, five or six millions—I must offer him certain pleasures which cannot be obtained with money. I am going to turn my studio into a picture gallery and exhibit the best works of my numerous friends and my own. He shall see that I have become something in the meantime, and from what I know of him he will be delighted with my idea. I want to furnish my house properly, and for this I need some costly tapestries. You have real treasures of this description. Would you loan me a few pieces?"

"Is that all?" said Spero, cordially. "You give me joy, and I hope you will allow me to attend to it."

"That depends. What do you intend to do?"

"I would like to ask you to let my decorator take charge of the furnishing of your studio. To-morrow morning he can select from my storehouse whatever he thinks best—"

"And spoil my fun?" interrupted Gontram, frowning. "No, no, I cannot consent to that. Your decorator may be a very able man, but that isn't the question. I know of no greater pleasure than to do everything according to my own taste. But I had almost forgotten the principal thing; I count on your appearance."

"I generally work at night," replied Spero, hesitating.

"No rule without an exception," declared the painter; "I have invited ladies too, and I hope you will enjoy yourself."

CHAPTER XXX

JANE ZILD

ON THE night of the party, Gontram's room looked lovely, and when the guests arrived they could not refrain from expressing their admiration. The Oriental hangings gave the whole a piquant appearance, and Gontram knew where to stop, an art which few understand. The society which assembled in the painter's studio was a very exceptional one. Many a rich banker would have given a great deal if he could have won some of the artists who assembled here for his private *soirées*, for the first stars of the opera, the drama and literature had accepted the invitation. Rachel had offered to do the honors; Emma Bouges, a sculptress, assisted her, and Gontram was satisfied.

The painter had told the vicomte that he desired to revenge himself upon Count Vellini. The other reason he had for giving this party he said nothing of, and yet it was the one which did honor to his heart. Under the pretence of surprising the count, he had asked his numerous friends to loan him their pictures, and had hung them in splendid style. Of his own works he only exhibited the gypsy, and when the guests strode up and down the studio to the music of a small orchestra, it was natural that they criticised or admired this and that painting.

Count Vellini, a splendid old gentleman, was enthusiastic over the cause of the party. He gave the secretary who accompanied him directions to buy several of the exhibited paintings, and the secretary carefully noted everything.

Signor Fagiano, the secretary, was not a very agreeable-looking gentleman. A blood-red scar ran clear across his face, his deep black eyes had a sharp, restless look, and one of the young partners jokingly said:

"If I did not know that Signor Fagiano had charge of the count's finances, I would suspect him of robbing his employer—he has a bad look."

While the young man uttered these joking remarks, new guests were announced, and their names, "Monsieur de Larsagny and Mademoiselle de Larsagny," created surprise among the guests. Monsieur de Larsagny was the manager of the new credit-bank, and every one was astonished at Gontram's acquaintance with him. However, as soon as Mademoiselle de Larsagny was seen to enter the room leaning on her father's arm, the riddle was solved. The classical head of the young girl graced the last *salon*, and as Gontram had painted the picture, no one wondered any longer at seeing the handsome Carmen and her father in the studio.

The young girl appeared to be somewhat eccentric, a thing which was not looked upon as strange in the daughter of a millionnaire. Nevertheless, the pranks of the young heiress never overstepped the bounds of propriety, and the numerous admirers of the beautiful Carmen thought her on this account all the more piquant. Her ash-blond hair fell in a thousand locks over a dazzling white forehead, and the small, finely formed mouth understood how to talk.

Hanging to Gontram's arm, Carmen walked up and down the studio. She sometimes directed her dark-blue eyes at the young painter, and who could scold Gontram if he loved to look in those magnificent stars?

"I am thankful to you, mademoiselle, for having come here," said Gontram, sparkling with joy, as he walked by the young girl's side.

"How could I have refused your cordial invitation?" replied Carmen, laughing; "even princesses have visited the studios of their court painters."

"The Duchess of Ferrara, for instance," said a young sculptor who had overheard the remark.

Gontram frowned, and whispered softly to the young artist:

"You ought to be ashamed of yourself, Raoul."

Carmen, however, laughed, and carelessly said:

"Let him alone; I knew the story long ago."

To make this little scene understood, we must observe that the young sculptor's words referred to that Duchess of Ferrara whom Titian painted in the primitive costume of Mother Eve, and it stung the young painter to the heart when he heard Carmen confess that she had heard the story before—who could have told it to the nineteen-year-old girl?

"What about the surprise you were going to give your guests?" asked Carmen, after an uncomfortable pause.

"I will keep my word," replied the painter, laughing. "Have you ever heard the name of Jane Zild, mademoiselle?"

"Jane Zild? That wonderful songstress who comes from the north, either Lapland or Finland? What is the matter with her?"

"Well, this songstress, who, by the way, comes from Russia, has promised to be here to-night," declared Gontram, triumphantly.

"Ah, really?" replied Carmen, breathing heavily, while her eyes shot forth threatening gleams.

"What ails you, mademoiselle?" asked Gontram uneasily, "have I hurt you in any way?"

"No; what makes you think so? But let us go to the parlor; my father is already looking for me, and you know he can't be long without me."

A curious laugh issued from the pale lips, and it seemed to Gontram as if she had accented the words "my father" in a peculiar way.

Just as Gontram and his companion re-entered the parlor, a short but unpleasant scene was being acted there. An accident had brought Signor Fagiano and Monsieur de Larsagny together. Hardly had the secretary caught a glimpse of the banker than he recoiled in affright and nearly fell to the ground. Larsagny sprang to his rescue, but Fagiano muttered an excuse and hastily left the parlor.

Carmen and her companion were witnesses of the meeting, and Gontram felt the young girl's arm tremble. Before he could ask for the cause of this, she laughed aloud and mockingly said:

"A good host has generally several surprises *in petto* for his guests; are you an exception to the general rule?"

Gontram was about to reply when the door was opened and the servant announced:

"Mademoiselle Jane Zild, the Vicomte of Monte-Cristo!"

"There you have my second surprise," said the painter, laughing; "are you satisfied now?"

Gontram did not find out whether this was the case, for the broker uttered a cry at the same moment and stretched his hands out as if to ward off a spectre.

"What has happened to you, Monsieur de Larsagny?" asked Gontram in amazement. "You are so pale and you tremble. Can I do anything for you?"

"No, thank you—it is the heat," stammered Larsagny. "Will you permit me to go on the terrace? I will recover in the fresh air."

Without deigning to notice Carmen, the banker turned toward the glass door which led to the terrace and disappeared. The young girl bit her lips, and the next minute she was the centre of a gay crowd of admirers.

Gontram in the meantime had gone to meet the young lady who had just entered. She was a wonderfully handsome girl, and taking the painter's arm she slowly walked through the decorated rooms.

Who Jane Zild was no one knew. Two months previously she had made her appearance in Paris society, and since then it was considered good form to patronize Jane Zild.

The members of the Opera and other theatres had arranged a performance for the relief of the inhabitants of a village which had been destroyed by fire, and the elegant world of the capital fairly grew wild with enthusiasm over the coming event.

The climax of the performance was to be a duet, to be sung by the great Roger and a diva who was past her youth. Half an hour before the number was to be sung a messenger arrived who announced the sickness of the diva. Roger immediately declared his willingness to sing alone, and loud applause ran through the crowded auditorium when he sang the charming song from the "White Lady," "Ah, what a joy it is to be a soldier!"

The success of the first part of the concert was assured. Before the second part began a strange young lady went to the celebrated singer and offered to take the part of Madame X——, and sing several songs.

"What is your name, mademoiselle?" asked Roger.

"My name will be unknown to you, as I have only been two days in Paris," replied the stranger, laughing. "I am Jane Zild. Perhaps you will allow me to sing something to you first. Will the beggar aria from the 'Prophet' be agreeable to you?"

Without waiting for answer Jane Zild went to the piano.

The accompanist struck the first notes of the well-known aria, and hardly had Roger heard the magnificent contralto of the stranger than he enthusiastically exclaimed:

"Thank God, Madame X—— is sick!"

"That is treason!" scolded the young lady; but the public seemed to be of the same opinion as Roger, and rewarded the young songstress, when she had finished, with round after round of applause. Encouraged by the applause, she sang the aria from "Orpheus"—"Ah, I have lost her, all my happiness is gone." This set the audience wild.

For two days nothing else was talked of in Paris but the young songstress. Jane Zild lived in a house in the

Champs-Elysées. She had arrived, as she said, but a few days before from Russia, in company with an elderly man, who was looked upon as her steward, and whom she called Melosan.

The reporters had seized upon these meagre details and magnified them. According to them, Jane Zild was the daughter of a rich Russian nobleman. An unconquerable yearning for the stage brought her in conflict with her father, and, burdened with his curse, she ran away from home. If in spite of this she did not go on the stage it was not the reporters' fault.

The young lady was very capricious, and had refused the most tempting offers from the management of the Opera. She also refused to sing for the Emperor at Compiegne, and it therefore caused a sensation among Gontram's guests when Jane Zild suddenly appeared.

"Gontram's luck is really extraordinary," said a colleague of the young painter laughingly, as he saw the majestic figure of the diva enter the room. What would he have said if he had heard in what way Gontram had secured Jane Zild as one of his guests?

While the young painter was breakfasting with Spero, a perfumed note was sent up to his residence in the Rue Montaigne, wherein Jane Zild declared her willingness to appear in the painter's parlors and sing a few songs.

Gontram did not say no, and immediately hurried to the diva's house to thank her.

Spero had entered just behind the songstress, and Gontram smiled when he saw the vicomte. Spero's carriage had driven up in front of the house almost simultaneously with that of the diva, and Spero assisted the young lady to alight.

When the vicomte entered the parlor, he felt humiliated when he saw all eyes turned in the direction of the diva. No one seemed to care to notice the heir of the Count of Monte-Cristo.

Jane Zild strode the rooms with the dignity of a queen.

"Heavenly! Admirable! Beautiful!" Such were the epithets which were murmured half aloud, and later when she sat down at the piano and sang a simple ballad, loud applause ran through the room. The ballad was followed by an aria; Jane then sang a Russian melody, and closed with a magnificent tarantella.

"Monsieur Sabran," said a low voice to Gontram, "I must confess that you are an obliging host! You are forgetting all your other guests on account of the beautiful songstress, and I will reflect upon a suitable punishment."

The one who spoke was Carmen de Larsagny. Gontram blushed and made excuses, but it took some time to appease the young lady's wrath.

"Well," she finally said, "I will forgive you, but only upon one condition. Have you a moment's time?"

"For you always," replied the painter, warmly.

"Good; then conduct me to the terrace."

"To the terrace?" repeated Gontram in surprise. "How do you know I have a terrace?"

"Oh, I heard my father mention it a little while ago."

"That's so," replied the painter. "Will you please accompany me?"

They both walked through the studio and turned into the gallery.

Suddenly Gontram paused, and uttered a low cry of astonishment.

Spero was leaning against a door sunk in thought.

"Can I introduce the young man to you?" asked Gontram softly of his companion.

"Who is he?" replied Carmen.

"The Vicomte of Monte-Cristo!"

"What? The son of the celebrated count?" asked the young lady, looking at Spero with increased interest.

"Yes. I have a high regard for the vicomte."

"I could have thought so," said Carmen, laughing.

"What do you mean by that, mademoiselle?" asked Gontram in surprise.

"Oh, you see you have the habit of caring very little for those whom you pretend to honor," replied the young girl, looking at the painter in such a way as made his heart beat fast.

"I hope to be able soon to prove my esteem for you," whispered the young man.

Carmen was for a moment silent, and then vivaciously said:

"Introduce me; I am curious to know your little vicomte."

Just then Spero raised his head, and, seeing Gontram, he cordially said:

"Gontram, am I not deserving of praise? You see I have accepted your invitation."

"I am very grateful to you," replied the painter warmly, and turning to Carmen he said:

"Mademoiselle de Larsagny, permit me to introduce the Vicomte of Monte-Cristo to you."

Spero bowed deeply. The young lady gazed steadily at the handsome cavalier, and admiration shone in her eyes.

"I really have not had the pleasure of seeing the vicomte. I should not have forgotten him."

"I believe you," said the painter; "the vicomte is, by the way, a man of serious ideas, an ascetic, who does not care for worldly pleasures."

Spero protested with a shake of the head, and muttered some disconnected words. Carmen, however, noticed that his thoughts were elsewhere.

"Mademoiselle de Larsagny," said Gontram, laughing now, "I hope that you and the other ladies here will succeed in converting the hermit."

Carmen was dissatisfied with the vicomte's indifference, and, bowing coldly, she went away, drawing the painter with her.

"Well, how does my eccentric please you?" asked Gontram.

"H'm, he is very handsome; whether he is intellectual, I cannot tell. Is the father of the little vicomte really the knight without fear and reproach, the hero of Dumas' novel?"

"The same."

"And has this man—Edmond Dantes was his right name—really had all the adventurous wanderings imputed to him?"

"I am sure of it."

"One more question. It might appear strange to you, but I must ask it nevertheless. Do you know whether Monsieur de Larsagny ever had any relations with the count?"

"I do not know, in fact I hardly think so. Your father has been living in Paris but a few years, and the count has not been in Paris for any great length of time during the past ten years. He is almost always travelling. I believe there is no country on earth which he has not visited, and he is again absent. However, if it interests you, I will make inquiries and—"

"Not for any price," interrupted Carmen, laughing; "let us drop the subject and hurry to the terrace before others get there ahead of us."

"We are there already," said Gontram, laughing, as he shoved a Japanese drapery aside and stepped upon a small balcony with his companion. A beautiful view of the Champs-Elysées was had from here.

At that time the many mansions which now fill the Champs-Elysées were not yet built, and the eye reached far down the beautiful lanes to the Place de la Concorde.

The two young persons stood upon the little terrace, and the spring wind played with Carmen's golden locks and fanned Gontram's cheeks.

The young girl now leaned over the railing, and, breathing the balsamic air, she sighed:

"Ah, how beautiful and peaceful it is here."

Gontram had his arm about the young girl's slim waist, and carried away by his feelings he pressed a kiss upon Carmen's coral-red lips. The young girl returned the kiss, and who knows but that they would have continued their osculatory exercise had not a voice close to the terrace said:

"Take care, Monsieur de Larsagny, that you do not try to find out my name. You will know it sooner than will be agreeable to you."

Carmen shuddered, and leaning far over, she tried to espy the speakers. However, she could not see any one, though some passionate words reached her from below; Gontram, on the other hand, felt like strangling the disturbers.

"Let us go back to the parlor," said the young girl, and it seemed to Gontram that her voice had changed in tone.

He silently opened the drapery and brought his companion back to the studio; when they entered it, the vicomte hurried to the painter, and said in a low tone:

"Gontram, have you a minute for me? I must speak to you."

CHAPTER XXXI

A THUNDERBOLT

THE vicomte's disturbed features and the tone of his voice caused Gontram to become anxious, and leading Carmen into the music-room, he stammered an excuse, and then returned to Spero.

"What has happened to you?" he asked, as he saw the young man was still excited. "I am afraid I am a very inattentive host."

"Oh, that is not it," said Spero, hesitating; "but—"

"Well, speak. You frighten me," said Gontram, uneasily.

"Gontram," began the vicomte, "you have confidence in me?"

"Certainly; but what have we to do with that now? You know that I esteem you—"

"And you do not think me capable of deceiving or lying to you?"

"Spero, I do not know you any more," cried Gontram, more and more confused.

"Have patience, you will soon learn to understand me," said the vicomte, smiling curiously; "let me now tell you what has happened to me."

Spero took a long breath, and then continued:

"About ten minutes ago I was standing here, listening

to the wonderful singing of that beautiful creature whom you call Jane Zild. The melody transported me to another world, and I saw and heard very little of what was going on about me. Suddenly I heard a slight noise behind the drapery, and these words reached my ears: 'Vicomte of Monte-Cristo, take care of yourself. A trap has been set for you, and woe to you if you are foolish enough not to notice it.'"

"A trap laid? What does that mean, and who was it that gave you this warning?" asked Gontram, in amazement.

"I do not know. Springing up I ran in the direction whence the words came. I shoved the drapery aside, but could see no one."

"No one?" repeated the painter, breathing more freely. "That looks like magic! Are you sure, Spero, that you didn't deceive yourself?"

"You do not believe me," said the vicomte, smiling sorrowfully.

"Spero, you misunderstand me. Let us proceed to work thoroughly, and, if possible, find out what has occurred. You yourself confessed that you were plunged in thought. In such half-dreamy conditions it often happens that we imagine we see things which have no foundation in fact. We believe we see persons, hear voices—"

"You speak of imagination," interrupted Spero, "while I told you of something that I actually have experienced. I heard the words clearly and legibly; the voice was strange to me, and yet there was something sincere in it which struck me."

"Curious! Perhaps some one has played a joke upon you."

"That would not be improbable, yet I do not believe it. The words were spoken seriously."

"But you are mad! A trap, if laid for you, could only be done by me. I must now ask you the same question you put to me: Have you confidence in me?"

"Perfect confidence," said the vicomte, warmly.

"God be praised! Now follow me to the parlor, and forget your black thoughts," and, shoving his arm under the vicomte's, he led him into the music-room.

"And where should the trap be?" asked Gontram, as they walked on; "not in Jane Zild's heavenly tones? Just look how the dark eyes are looking at you—really you are in luck."

Jane Zild had risen after the song was ended, and while the applause sounded about her, she looked steadily at the vicomte.

"Banish the black thoughts," whispered Gontram to the young man, "come and talk a little to the diva; she appears to expect it."

"Mademoiselle," he said, turning to Jane, "here is one of your most enthusiastic admirers, who would consider himself happy if you would make a tour of the gallery with him."

Gontram turned to other guests, and Spero timidly drew near to the young girl and offered her his arm. Jane hesitated for a moment to take it, and looked expectantly at the vicomte. She waited, no doubt, for a compliment or some word from him. As Spero remained silent, a satisfied smile crossed the classical features of the diva, and placing her hand on his arm she carelessly said: "Let us go."

Just then something unexpected happened. A burning candle fell down from the chandelier, and a flame licked the black lace dress of the diva and enveloped her.

A cry of horror came from the lips of the bystanders, and they all rushed away. Spero was the only one who showed self-possession. Quick as thought, he tore one of the draperies from the wall, and placing the thick cloth around the shoulders of the diva, he pressed her tightly to his bosom.

The next minute Jane stood with pale face, but otherwise uninjured, before her rescuer, and holding her little hand to him, she whispered cordially:

"Thanks, a thousand thanks!"

Spero took the long fingers and pressed his lips as respectfully upon them as if Jane Zild were a queen and he her subject. The diva, with the drapery still about her shoulders, looked really like a queen, and all eyes were turned admiringly toward her.

A man dressed in plain dark clothes hurried through the crowd, and looking anxiously at Jane he cried in a vibrating voice:

"Are you injured?"

The diva trembled when she heard the voice, and blushing deeply, she hastily replied:

"No, thank God, I am not hurt. The coolness of the Vicomte of Monte-Cristo prevented a misfortune."

The vicomte, too, trembled when he heard the unknown's words, for he felt certain that the voice was the same as that which had given him the mysterious warning.

The man bowed respectfully to the vicomte, and Jane, turning to Spero, said in cordial tones:

"Complete your good work, vicomte, and conduct me to my carriage."

Spero laid her little hand upon his arm and led her out. As Spero assisted her in the carriage she bowed again to him and whispered:

"I hope we shall see each other again."

Jane's companion looked at the vicomte in an embarrassed way; he evidently wished to say something to him, but had not the courage to do so. The next minute the horses started and the carriage rolled away.

Spero looked after the equipage as long as it could be seen and then called for his coachman, as he wished to go home too. Just as he was about to enter the carriage, the coachman, in surprise, exclaimed:

"You have forgotten your hat, vicomte. Jean, quick, go and get it."

Spero, in astonishment, felt his head; it was true, the coachman was right.

"Stay, Jean, I shall go myself," he briefly said, as he hurried back to the house.

Just as he reached the stairs, Monsieur de Larsagny and his daughter, whom Gontram escorted, and Count Vellini and his secretary came down.

"Vicomte," said Carmen, vivaciously, "you are a hero, and the rest of the gentlemen can take you for an example."

Monsieur de Larsagny coughed slightly, while Fagiano loudly cried:

"The vicomte is the worthy son of his father, the great count."

These words, although spoken in a respectful tone, displeased Spero, yet he kept silent and the guests departed.

"Stay a minute longer," begged Gontram, "I will take a walk with you, if it is agreeable; I am too much excited yet to go to bed."

"That is my position, too," replied the vicomte.

The servant brought them their hats and cloaks, and they both walked in the direction of the Champs-Elysées. Neither of them noticed a dark form which stood at a street corner and looked after them.

"Have a care," hissed Fagiano's voice, "you shall suffer for being his son."

CHAPTER XXXII

OLD ACQUAINTANCES

JANE ZILD lived in a modest room in a small house on the Champs-Elysées.

The interior was furnished in the ordinary style of a private house. In the basement was the reception-room, the sitting-room and dining-room. The owner of the house was Madame Vollard, the widow of an officer. One of her principles was, that it was better to have her rooms empty than to let them out to people whose reputation was not of the best.

She did not care much either for artists or actresses, but made some exceptions, and when Melosan, Jane Zild's secretary, offered her a considerable sum for a room on the first floor, she immediately accepted.

The bells of Notre-Dame struck one o'clock, when a carriage, which contained Jane and her companion, stopped in front of Madame Vollard's house.

In spite of the late hour, the landlady hurried to the street door to greet the young girl. When she saw the latter's disordered toilet, she uttered a cry of horror. Jane had thrown off the cloak, and the burned dress with the withered and crushed roses could be seen.

"What is the matter, my dear?" asked the worthy lady.

"Oh, nothing," replied Jane; "I am only tired."

"Then you tell me, at least, what has occurred," said Madame Vollard, turning to Melosan.

"Later on, later on. The young lady is excited and needs rest."

"Oh, I will give her some drops," said the good-hearted lady, "I—"

"Good-night, Madame Vollard," said the secretary, and taking a light from the lady's hands, he hurried up the stairs with Jane.

The young girl sank back in a chair exhausted. Melosan, a man about sixty years of age, with white hair and sunburned face, stood with folded hands before his mistress, and his dark eyes looked anxiously at Jane's pale face.

"You are suffering?" he said, after a pause.

Jane shuddered. "Ah, no," she said, "I am feeling perfectly well."

"But the fright?"

"Oh, that is nothing," replied Jane, sorrowfully; and, rising up wildly, she passionately added: "Why am I forced to enter a world which is not my own, and never can be! And it shall not be either," she sobbingly concluded, "never—never!"

Melosan held down his head.

"A queen would have been proud at the reception you had to-night."

"Why do you tell me this?" she exclaimed. "A queen? I? Oh, what bitter mockery!"

"But your eminent talent—your voice?"

"Would to God I had none! I—but go now, I want to be alone."

The man sorrowfully approached the door; on the threshold he paused and imploringly murmured:

"Pardon me, Jane, I did not wish to hurt you."

"I know it. I am sometimes hard and cruel, but my unhappy situation is the cause of it. Why did not the wretched fire consume me? Then all grief would have been at an end. O my God! my God!"

She sobbed as if her heart would break, and Melosan wrung his hands in despair.

"Jane, tell me what has happened," he said, in despair. "I have never seen you this way before. Has any one insulted you?"

"No one," said Jane, softly, "no one."

"Your fate is dreary and burdensome, but you are young and strong. You have life before you, and in time you'll forget the past and be happy."

Melosan's words caused the young girl to dry her tears.

"You are right," she said, half ashamed, "I was foolish and ungrateful. I will forget the past. Forgive me—grief overwhelmed me."

"You are an angel," cried Melosan, enthusiastically; "but now you must really go to bed. Good-night, Jane."

"Good-night," said the young girl, cordially, and then the door closed behind Melosan.

As the secretary was about to go to his room, Madame Vollard intercepted him on the stairs.

"Well, how goes it?" she asked; "has the poor child recovered?"

"Yes, thank you."

"What occurred?"

"She was almost burned to death; her dress had already caught fire."

"What a lucky accident—"

"Lucky accident?" repeated Melosan, not understanding.

"I do not mean the fire, but the fact that I just possess a walking suit, such as Mademoiselle Zild needs, and which I can let her have at a very moderate price. A silk dress with pomegranate leaves—"

"To-morrow, Madame Vollard, to-morrow," Melosan interrupted her. "I really feel fatigued, and should like to go to my room."

"You are right. I ought to have known it."

She disappeared, and Melosan walked up the stairs. On entering his room he locked the door, threw himself into a chair, and burying his face in his hands he sobbed bitterly.

"What is going to happen now," he muttered to himself; "my money is nearly all gone, and—"

Hastily springing up, he opened the bureau and took a torn portfolio out of it. Opening it, he sorrowfully counted its contents and shook his gray head.

"It is useless," he muttered in a hollow voice, "the day after to-morrow the rent is due, and what then remains to us is not worth speaking about. If I only could begin something, but everywhere my horrible past stares me in the face. I dare not go out in the broad daylight. I myself would be satisfied with dry bread, but Jane, the poor, poor thing! With her talent she could have had a brilliant life, and reign everywhere like a queen if it were not for the terrible past. Like a spectre, it stands in our path, and while she is innocent, the curse of being the cause of both our wretchedness strikes me. I—"

A slight noise caused Melosan to pause and listen. For a while all was silent, and then the noise recommenced.

He hurried to the door, but could not see any one, and returning to the room he shook his head and resumed his seat.

"I must have been deceived," he murmured uneasily, "and yet I thought—"

The knock was repeated, and this time so loudly that Melosan discovered from whence it came. Hastily going to the attic window he threw the curtain aside and peered out. A dark shadow moved here and there on the roof, and Melosan reached for his pistol.

"Who's there?" he cried.

"Some one who desires to speak to you," came back in firm tones.

"To me? At this hour?" asked the secretary in a daze.

"Yes, to you—open quickly or I shall burst in the window."

Melosan saw that it could not be a thief, and so he hesitatingly shoved back the bolt.

A powerful hand raised the window from the outside, and Melosan raised his weapon threateningly; but at this moment the light from the room fell full on the man's face, and the secretary let the pistol fall, and cried in a faint, trembling voice:

"You! You! O God! how did you get here?"

"Ha! ha! ha! Don't you see I came from the roof?" cried the man, mockingly.

"But you shall not come in," cried Melosan, angrily, as he cocked his pistol. "Get out of here, or I shall blow your brains out."

"You won't do any such thing," said the other, coolly. "Do you think because you are posing as an honest man that other people will imagine you are one? Ha! is the situation clear to you? A good memory is a good thing to have, and if one does not like to hear names it is better to acquiesce. Well, what do you say? Shall we talk over matters peacefully, or do you persist in firing off your pistol and attracting the attention of the police?"

A shudder ran through Melosan, and he looked at the floor in despair.

"Can I offer you a cigar?" continued the man. "No? Then permit me to light my own;" and turning himself in his chair, and reclining comfortably against the back of the fauteuil, the speaker lighted a cigar, and with the utmost calm of mind puffed blue clouds of smoke in the air.

Melosan was evidently struggling with himself. At last he had made up his mind, and, angrily approaching the other, said:

"Listen to me. The sooner we get rid of each other the better it will be for both of us. Why did you hunt me up? You ought to have known long ago that I did not wish to have anything to do with you. You go your way and I will go mine; let neither of us bother the other, and as I am called Melosan, I shall forget that you ever bore any other name than Fagiano."

"You have become proud!" exclaimed the man who called himself Fagiano, laughing mockingly; "upon my word, Anselmo, if I did not know that you were a former galley-slave, I would think you were a prince!"

"And I would hold you now and always for the incarnation of everything that is bad," replied Anselmo (for it was he). "You ought to be called Lucifer instead of Benedetto!"

CHAPTER XXXIII

THE CATASTROPHE

THE two men looked at each other with flaming eyes. In Toulon they were chained together, and now—

Anselmo had reversed the letters of his name and called himself Melosan. In Toulon they were both on the same moral plane, but since then their ways as well as their characters had changed. Benedetto sank lower and lower day by day, while Anselmo worked hard to obliterate the stigma of a galley-slave.

Benedetto, bold and impudent, looked at his former chain-companion, and a mocking smile played about his lips. Anselmo, however, lost little by little his assurance, and finally implored Benedetto to leave, saying:

"We two have nothing in common any more."

"That is a question. Sit down and listen to me."

"No, Benedetto, we are done with each other."

"Nonsense—you have become virtuous all of a sudden," mocked Count Vellini's secretary.

"Would to God it were so. When we were in Toulon an unfortunate accident brought us together; a far more unfortunate one separated us. Since then it has been my endeavor to have the sins which led me to the Bagnio atoned for by an honest life. I do not care to know what kind of a life you have led. All I ask is that in the future we meet as strangers, and I hope you will consent to my wish!"

"And if I do not do so?" asked Benedetto, laying his hand upon his former comrade's shoulder. "Suppose I will not forget you nor want to be forgotten by you?"

Anselmo moaned aloud.

"Moan away," continued Benedetto. "I know all the details of your past life, and if you have forgotten anything I am in a position to refresh your memory."

"I—do not—understand you," stammered Anselmo.

"Think of the past," replied Benedetto, frowning.

"Of the time when the smith fastened us to the same chain?"

"Oh, think again."

Anselmo trembled.

"Do you speak of the moment when we jumped into the sea and escaped from the galleys?" he softly asked.

"No; your memory seems to be weak."

"I do not know what you mean."

"Really? You seem to have drunk from the spring of Lethe," said Benedetto, contemptuously. "Anselmo, have you forgotten our meeting at Beaussuet?"

"Scoundrel! miserable wretch! Do you really dare to remind me of that?" cried Anselmo, beside himself.

"Why not?"

"If you can do so—no power on earth can induce me to say another word about that horrible affair," said Anselmo, shuddering.

"My nerves are better than yours," laughed Benedetto. "It was only to speak to you about that particular night that I braved the danger of hunting you up. I need you as a witness, and that is why you see me here.''

"As a witness?'' exclaimed Anselmo, in surprise. "Either you are crazy or else I shall become so. Benedetto, if I open my mouth the gallows will be your fate!''

"That is my business and need not worry you at all. Do you remember the night of the 24th of February, 1839? Yes or no?''

"Yes,'' groaned Anselmo.

"No jeremiads! Do you also remember the vicarage at Beaussuet?''

"Yes.''

"Well, a certain person came expressly from Toulon to see about a sum of money, a million—''

"I have not touched a penny of the money,'' interrupted Anselmo, shuddering.

"No, certainly not, you were always unselfish. Well, do not interrupt me. The person who came from Toulon (recte Benedetto) was just about to put the sum of money in his pocket, when the devil sent a stranger who—''

"Benedetto, if you are a human being and not a devil, keep silent,'' cried Anselmo, beside himself.

Benedetto shrugged his shoulders.

"You are a fool,'' he said, contemptuously. "I heard two persons on the stairs. I hid behind the door, with a knife in my right hand. The door opened. The shadow of a form appeared in the door, and I struck. I felt the knife sink deep into a human breast.''

"Wretch! It was the breast of your mother!'' stammered Anselmo.

"Ah, your memory is returning to you,'' mocked

Benedetto, with a cynical smile. "Yes, it was my mother. But how did you know it?"

"I met the unfortunate woman on the way in the gorges of Oliolles—"

"Ah! and there she told you the story of her life."

"She begged me to help her save her son, and I promised to do so; I knew that you were that wretched son."

"Did she tell you her name?" said Benedetto, uneasily.

"She hid nothing from me. I found out that the son she wished to save intended to murder her—"

"Facts," said Benedetto, roughly, "and less talk."

"And that this son was a child of sin."

"Ah, really; and her name?"

"She made me swear to keep it secret."

"So much the better! She really thought, then, that a galley-slave was a man of his word?"

"Galley-slave or not, I have kept silent, and will do so further."

"You are a hero! Nevertheless, you can tell me the name."

"No!"

"And if I demand it?"

"I won't tell you, either."

"Anselmo, have a care!" hissed Benedetto, angrily. "Tell me the name, or—"

"I am silent," declared Anselmo; "you do not know the name, and you will never learn it from me."

Benedetto broke into a coarse laugh.

"You are either very naive," he said, "or think I am. I only wished to see if you had not forgotten the name. The lady was Madame Danglars."

Anselmo uttered a cry of rage.

"Well, preacher of words, what do you say now?" asked Benedetto, politely.

"Since you know the name, we are done with each other," said Anselmo, "and I think you will now leave me in peace."

"You are wrong, my dear Anselmo; do you know that you are very disrespectful?"

Anselmo began to ponder whether it would not be better to appear more friendly to the hated comrade.

"Benedetto," he said, in a gentle voice, "why should we be enemies? I know you had reason to be angry a little while ago, but the recollection of that fearful night unmanned me, and I did not know what I was speaking about. At that time, too, I was terribly excited—"

"As I had reason to notice," interrupted Benedetto. "You were ready to kill me."

"Let us forget all that," said Anselmo, hastily. "You came here to ask a favor of me and I was a fool to refuse. We have both the same interests in keeping our past history from the world. Therefore speak. If what you desire is within the limits of reason, it shall be done."

"Bravo! you please me now, Anselmo," cried Benedetto, laughing. "At length you have become sensible. But tell me, is the little one handsome? For it is natural that your reform has been brought about by a woman; you always were an admirer and connoisseur of the fair sex."

Anselmo sprang upon Benedetto and, holding his clinched fist in his face, he said:

"Benedetto, if you care to live, don't say another word!"

"And why?" asked the wretch, with silent contempt.

"Because I shall not stand it," replied Anselmo, coldly. "You have me in your power, Benedetto. With an anonymous letter you could denounce me to-morrow as an escaped galley-slave and have me sent back to the galleys. I would not care a snap for that, but I most emphatically forbid you to throw a slur upon the reputation of the woman who lives with me under this roof."

"You forbid me? Come now, Anselmo, you speak in a peculiar tone," hissed Benedetto.

"I speak exactly in the tone the matter demands. You know my opinion; conduct yourself accordingly."

"And if I did not care to obey you?"

"Then I would denounce you, even though I put my own neck in danger."

"Ha! ha! I tell you you won't do anything of the kind."

"Listen," said Anselmo, "you do not know me. Yes, I was a wretch, a perjurer, worse than any highwayman. But I have suffered, suffered terribly for my sins, and since years it has been my only ambition to lead a blameless life as repentance for my crimes. I have taken care of a poor helpless being, and to defend her I will sacrifice my life. I bear everything to shield her from grief and misery; in fact, if it were necessary, I would accept her contempt, for if she ever found out who I am, she would despise me."

"Have you pen, ink and paper?" asked Benedetto, after Anselmo had concluded.

"Yes. What do you want to do with them?"

"You shall soon find out."

Anselmo silently pointed to a table upon which writing materials lay. Benedetto dipped the pen in the ink, and, grinning, said:

"My friend, have the kindness to take this pen and write what I dictate."

"I?"

"Yes, you. I only want you to write a few lines."

"What shall I write?"

"The truth."

"I do not understand you."

"It is very simple; you will write down what you have just said."

"Explain yourself more clearly."

"With pleasure; better still, write what I dictate."

Anselmo looked uneasily at the wretch; Benedetto quietly walked behind the ex-priest's chair, and began:

"On the 24th of February, 1839, Benedetto, an escaped convict from the galleys of Toulon, murdered Madame Danglars, his mother."

"That is horrible!" cried Anselmo, throwing the pen down; "I shall not write that."

"You will write; you know I can force you; therefore—"

Anselmo sighed, and took up the pen again.

"So, I am done now," he said, after a pause; "must it be signed, too?"

"Certainly; though the name has nothing to do with it. You can put any one you please under it."

It sounded very simple, and yet Anselmo hesitated.

"No," he firmly said, "I will not do it. I know you are up to some trick, and I do not intend to assist you."

Benedetto laughed in a peculiar way.

"I know you are not rich," said the pretended secretary, "and—"

Anselmo made a threatening gesture, but Benedetto continued:

"I was at this window for some time. Count Vellini's house is next door to this, and I had no difficulty in getting here. I saw you counting your secret treasure, and consequently—"

Unconsciously Anselmo glanced at the portfolio which lay on the table. Benedetto noticed it and laughed maliciously.

"Yes, there lies your fortune," he said contemptuously. "The lean bank-notes you counted a little while ago will not keep you long above board."

"But I have not asked for anything," murmured Anselmo.

"I offer you a price."

Benedetto drew an elegant portfolio from his pocket, and took ten thousand-franc notes out of it which he laid upon the table. "Finish and sign the paper I dictated," he coldly said, "and the money is yours."

Anselmo grew pale. Did Benedetto know of his troubles? Had he read his thoughts?

"I will not do it," he said, rising up. "Keep your money, Benedetto; it would bring me misfortune."

Benedetto uttered a cry of rage, and, grasping the pen, he seated himself at the table and wrote a few words.

"So," he said, with a satanic gleam in his eyes as he held the paper under Anselmo's nose, "either you do what I say or else these lines which I have just written will be sent to the papers to-morrow."

Anselmo read, and the blood rushed to his head. He

felt his brain whirl, and, beating his face with his hands, he groaned aloud. What had Benedetto written? Only a few words: "The lady who is known as Jane Zild is—"

"You will not send these lines off," cried Anselmo, springing up suddenly and clutching Benedetto by the throat. The latter, however, was too strong for him; in a minute he had thrown the ex-priest upon the bed.

"No nonsense," he sternly said, "either you write or I will send the notice to the papers to-morrow."

The ex-priest took the pen and with a trembling hand wrote what Benedetto had asked of him.

"Here," he said, in a choking voice, "swear to me —but no—you do not believe in anything—I—"

"My dear friend," interrupted Benedetto, "do not take the thing so seriously. I have no intention of disturbing your peace."

Anselmo sank upon a chair, and his eyes filled with hot tears.

Benedetto hastily ran over the paper and his lips curled contemptuously when he saw the signature.

"The fool wrote his own name," he murmured as he rubbed his hands, "may it do him good."

The next minute the secretary of Count Vellini disappeared, and Anselmo breathed more freely.

Suddenly an idea flew through his brain as his gaze fell upon the bank-notes.

"We will fly," he muttered to himself, "now, this very hour! This demon knows everything; we are not safe from him, and if an accident happens to Jane—"

In desperation he walked up and down the room and disconnected words came from his lips.

"Who will guarantee me that he will keep silent? Oh, he was always a wretch—to-morrow at four o'clock we can take the train—we will go to England and from there to America."

He paused, and, going to the window, listened. Everything was quiet and Anselmo noticed that a rain shed connected the count's house with that of Madame Vollard. Benedetto's visit was probably undiscovered, and a great deal depended on that.

"I will wake Jane," said Anselmo after a short pause, "I will tell her an excuse, and since she believes in me, she will be ready at once to follow me! I will tell her I am in danger and must leave France."

Anselmo carefully opened the door and listened. All was still in the house, and, going on tiptoe, he glided up to the next story and into Jane's room. Merciful God, it was empty!

Uttering a cry he rushed out of the room and down the stairs, and, a prey to despair, hurried out into the dark night.

CHAPTER XXXIV

A SHOT

IN DEEP silence Gontram and Spero walked along the Champs-Elysées, which at this time of the day was deserted. They were both indulging in day-dreams and permitted the magical spring air to affect them.

"Confound the slow pokes," cried the painter at length, after the two young men had been walking up and down for over an hour; "I will go directly to the point."

Spero looked up in amazement. Buried in thought, he believed his friend had spoken to him, and so he said confusedly:

"Excuse me, Gontram, I was thinking of something else and didn't catch your meaning."

"Oh, I was only thinking aloud," replied the painter, laughing, "but it is best if I talk the matter over with you. I will sooner reach a decision."

"I do not understand," stammered Spero.

"I believe you; but do you know that we are both in the same boat?"

"How so?"

"Oh, I do not wish to pry into your secrets, but hope that you will listen quietly to my confession and then give me your opinion."

"A confession? Have you any debts? You know very well—"

"That your purse is open to me I know, but I want to make a loan with your heart."

"Speak quickly; what is the matter?"

"It is about the solution of a problem which has already brought many a man to the brink of despair."

"Gontram!"

"Yes, look at me; it is unfortunately true. One of the most interesting chapters in Rabelais's 'Pantagruel' is devoted to the theme."

Spero was not in the humor for any literary discussion, and so he firmly said:

"If Rabelais handled this theme, he did it undoubtedly in a more worthy way than I could possibly have done."

"H'm, Rabelais merely gives the question, but does not answer it."

"You are speaking in riddles," said the vicomte, laughing, "and, as you know, I have very little acquaintance with practical life."

"But you know 'Pantagruel'?"

"Yes, but—"

"Panurge asks his master, 'Shall I marry or shall I not marry?' and Pantagruel replies, 'Marry or do not marry, just as you feel inclined.'"

"Ah, so that is the question you wish to place before me?" said Spero.

"Yes."

"But why do you come to me for my advice in such a delicate matter?"

"Because I have confidence in you," replied the painter, warmly.

"Thank you," said the vicomte, cordially; "in questions of ordinary life I know as little as a child. I think it is a misfortune to always live alone."

"Then you advise me to marry?"

"If the woman you have selected is worthy to be your wife."

For a time they were both silent, and then Spero continued:

"I think marriage must be based upon unlimited mutual esteem."

"You are right. You have, no doubt, observed that the young lady whom I conducted through the parlor this evening—"

Spero trembled and uttered a low cry. The painter looked suspiciously at him, but the vicomte laughingly said that he had knocked against a stone, and so the painter continued:

"The young lady has captivated me—"

"Of which lady are you speaking?" asked the vicomte, uneasily.

"Of the pretty blonde, Mademoiselle de Larsagny!"

"Ah! she is certainly very handsome," cried Spero, breathing more freely.

"Don't you think so?" exclaimed Gontram, enthusiastically. "That is the young lady I mean."

"In that case I can only congratulate you on the choice you have made."

"Thank you. Then you think Carmen de Larsagny charming?"

"Yes. From what I have seen of the young lady

she deserves the love of such a splendid fellow as you are."

"If I were to obey the voice of love," said Gontram, "I would go to her now and say: 'I love you—be mine!'"

"And why do you hesitate? You love her, do you not?"

"I suppose so; Carmen is charming. This evening I was at the point of proposing—"

"Well? and—"

"That is just the point. Spero, have you never had a feeling which caused you to leave undone something which your heart prompted you to do? Several times this evening a feeling of coming misfortune overcame me, so that I had great trouble to retain my cheerfulness."

"Such things are sometimes deceiving," said Spero.

"That may be, but every time I think of a marriage with Carmen a feeling of uneasiness overcomes me."

"That is merely nervous excitement."

"I am in love and—"

"Well, you hesitate?"

"I have not told you everything yet. I committed an indiscretion."

"Of what nature?"

"I embraced Mademoiselle de Larsagny and kissed her."

"Ah! and the young girl?"

"Did not repulse me. Now shall I marry or not?"

"What does your heart tell you?"

"My heart is like Pantagruel. It knows no decided answer."

"Good. If you follow my advice, marry the girl. A

kiss between two good young people is as binding as an engagement."

"You are right, a hundred times right, and yet the moment I pressed my lips to hers I felt a pain in my heart. If I only knew the cause of this fright which seizes me every time I think of Carmen."

"Perhaps it is her father, Monsieur de Larsagny, who does not inspire you with confidence?" said Spero after a pause.

In the meantime the two friends reached the Arc de Triomphe and walked up and down the woods.

"Perhaps you are right," said Gontram, answering the vicomte's last question. "I know very little of Monsieur de Larsagny, and yet I could swear that there are some dark spots in his past."

At this moment a shot sounded in the still night, and the friends stood still and looked at each other in surprise.

"What was that?" cried Spero.

"A shot, and, as I fear, a crime," said Gontram, softly.

The young men hurried in the direction from which the shot came, and were soon in a small pathway which was lighted up by the faint gleam of the moon. On the ground a motionless form lay. Spero bent over it, and, uttering a hollow cry, he took it in his arms and clasped the head with its long, black, streaming hair to his bosom. It was Jane Zild whom the vicomte held in his arms. Near her lay a revolver.

CHAPTER XXXV

WILL SHE LIVE?

SPERO hurried with his burden to the street, and Gontram could hardly keep up with him. Finally he overtook him, and, placing his hand on the vicomte's shoulder, he urgently cried:

"Spero, where are you going with this corpse?"

"She is not dead," replied the vicomte, tremblingly. "She lives; she must live—she dare not die!"

"And who is she?" asked Gontram, as he tried to get a glimpse of the face. Yes, he recognized her now as she lay in Spero's arms.

"Jane! Jane Zild?" stammered the painter, terror-stricken. "O my God!"

They had now reached the Place de l'Etoile, and Gontram looked around for a carriage.

"What shall we do?" he asked, turning in desperation to Spero. "Are you going to bring the poor thing to your house? I shall go and arouse the servants."

"Do so, Gontram, and hurry—every minute counts."

Soon the Monte-Cristo mansion was reached. Spero carried the unconscious girl up the stairs and gently laid her on the divan. He then got on his knees beside

Jane, and, hiding his face in his hands, he sobbed bitterly.

Gontram now approached his friend.

"Spero," he said, "calm yourself; we must rescue the poor child."

The vicomte sprang up.

"You are right, Gontram," he replied; "but if she is dead, I shall die, too, for I love her—I love her more than my life."

"She is no doubt wounded," said Gontram softly.

"Yes, just hold a light here," cried the vicomte. "I will examine her. I have not studied medicine for nothing."

The vicomte laid his ear to her bosom, and then said:

"She lives, but to tell whether there is any hope I must examine her more closely. Gontram, go to my study and bring me the cedar box which stands on my writing-desk."

Gontram left the room, and Spero was alone with the unconscious girl. Placing his hand upon her white forehead, he bent over the young girl and tenderly murmured:

"Poor dear child! Why did you wish to die? Oh, Jane, Jane! you must live—live for me, and no power on earth shall tear you from me!"

He pressed his lips upon her pale mouth, and with this kiss his soul was bound to that of the young girl.

Gontram now returned; Spero opened the box and took an instrument from it.

"Feel if my hand trembles," he said, turning to the

painter; "only if that is not the case can I dare to probe for the bullet."

Gontram took hold of the white hand. It did not tremble, and Spero began to probe for the bullet.

"The ball has not touched a vital part," whispered the vicomte at length; "it lies in the muscles. I touched it with the instrument."

"Do you think you can remove the bullet?" asked the painter.

"I hope so."

The vicomte motioned to Gontram to hand him the box again, and taking a bistoury and a pincette he bent over the unconscious girl again.

An anxious moment passed and then Spero triumphantly exclaimed;

"Saved!"

"Saved," repeated Gontram as he took the murderous lead from the vicomte's hand.

"Then we can call the housekeeper," said Spero, after he had poured a liquid down the young girl's throat.

He hurried out, and returned in less than five minutes with Madame Caraman.

The last time we saw the worthy governess she was in Africa, in company with Miss Clary. The latter fell in love with Captain Joliette and married him in spite of Lord Ellis's opposition. The young couple were very happy until the *coup d'etat* of the 2d of December, 1851, when Albert de Morcerf was killed by a murderous ball. Six months later Miss Clary died of grief. Four weeks after her death Madame Caraman became the housekeeper of the Monte-Cristo mansion. Thus it came about that Spero hurried to her for aid for the sick girl. She asked no questions, but, with the vicomte's assistance, placed a bandage upon the young girl's wound and wished to discreetly retire.

"Mamma Caraman," said Spero, imploringly, "stay here and watch over the young girl whom I place under your protection. Let no one know that she is in this house."

Spero thereupon withdrew, while Jane Zild remained under the care of the good-hearted woman.

CHAPTER XXXVI

MELOSAN'S SECRET

WE LEFT Melosan as he ran into the street in despair, hoping to find the missing girl. Had Jane run away? Had she been abducted?

Two policemen were patrolling the Champs-Elysées, and Anselmo went up to them and politely asked them whether they had not seen his mistress, a young lady?

The officials looked suspiciously at him, and remarked that the young lady would have something else to do than wander in the streets at this time of night. Anselmo sorrowfully bowed his head, and, after thanking them, continued on his way.

He had reached the polygon and listened attentively. He heard steps, but not the right ones. Suppose Jane had committed suicide?

She had been so painfully excited this evening, and Anselmo, who knew her past, shuddered when he thought that the Seine was not far away.

Without a pause he ran to the edge of the water; the dawning day was raw and chilly, and Anselmo shuddered as he looked in the dark waves. Were they taking his dearest treasure on earth along in their course?

What mysterious tie bound him to Jane Zild? the former galley-slave to the beautiful, talented creature?

.   .   .   .

Twenty-one years had passed since Anselmo had witnessed the killing of Madame Danglars by her son Benedetto and the latter's flight with the treasure. Anselmo was, of course, a scoundrel, too; but his whole being rose up in anger at such inhuman cruelty, and, grasping the knife, he had threatened to kill the parricide if he did not depart at once.

Benedetto was thrown into the sea, and was rescued upon the island of Monte-Cristo.

Anselmo had remained behind, half dazed, and only little by little did he recover his senses sufficiently to think over his own situation. It was a desperate one; yet he would not have exchanged with Benedetto for any price.

Suddenly, a faint glimmer of daylight shone through the open window, and Anselmo trembled when his gaze fell on the pale face of the murdered woman. Suppose she was not dead? Anselmo bent over her and listened; not the slightest sign of breathing was visible, and yet the convict thought he felt an almost imperceptible beating of the heart.

Should he call for help? That would be equivalent to delivering himself over to the hangman. If he hesitated, the woman would die, under all circumstances. Who would believe him, if he said that the woman's own son was the murderer? Appearances were against him, and, if the murdered woman really recovered consciousness again, and she should be asked who raised the knife against her, she would much sooner accuse him than the son whom she madly loved.

While Anselmo was still debating the question in his mind, he heard a noise in front of the house, and, hurrying to the window, he perceived the priest, who had just returned home from his journey. The convict uttered a cry of relief. He could now leave without having a murder upon his soul; for the clergyman would, no doubt, immediately discover what had happened, and take care of the victim. He waited until he had heard the priest's steps on the stairs, and then swung himself through the window on to the tree which had helped Benedetto to enter the room, and disappeared at the very moment that the horrified clergyman entered the room. Anselmo determined to leave France in an easterly direction. After great trials and difficulties he reached Switzerland, and from there he journeyed to Germany. Intelligent and active, he soon found a means of earning an honest living; he settled in Munich, and, under the name of Melosan, gave lessons in French.

Fifteen years passed in this way. Anselmo worked hard, and was satisfied with the reward of his activity. His scholars esteemed him. During this time an entire change had taken place in the former convict. But then a yearning to see France once more seized him, and he resolved to return to the fatherland.

He first went to Lyons, where he gave lessons in German and Italian. He lived in a modest apartment in the Faubourg St. Antoine. One evening Anselmo was walking along the quay when he heard quarrelling voices. A woman's voice cried aloud:

"Let me go! I want to go for my daughter. I have nothing to do with you. Help, help!"

Anselmo stood still. A woman was no doubt struggling with some men, and when her cries redoubled, he forgot his prudence and hurried toward the group.

As he suspected, he found three drunken workmen trying to force a sixteen-year-old girl from the grasp of an elderly woman.

The woman cried loudly for help and struck angrily around her. The young girl, however, silently defended herself.

"Don't be so prudish, Zilda," said one of the men. "You make as much noise as if we were going to hang the little one."

The speaker, as he said this, threw his arms around the slim waist of the young girl and tried to draw her to him. At this moment Anselmo appeared, and with a terrible blow he struck the fellow to the ground.

The young girl sobbed, and taking the hand of her rescuer she pressed a kiss upon it. Then turning to the old lady, who was leaning against the wall moaning, she cried, beside herself:

"Oh, mother, mother! What is the matter with you? My God, she is dying!"

This really seemed to be the case; the poor woman had become deathly pale, and sank to the ground.

"Let me help you," said Anselmo to the young girl. He bent down and took the unconscious woman in his arms. "Where do you live?"

As simple as the question was, the girl appeared to be embarrassed by it.

"Won't you tell me where you live?" said Anselmo, as the girl remained silent.

"We do not live far from here, in the Rue Franche-foin."

"I do not know that street."

"Ah, I believe you," stammered the poor child, shuddering; "I shall proceed in advance."

"Do so," said Anselmo.

The ex-priest followed her, bearing the unconscious woman in his muscular arms, and only gradually did he perceive that his companion was leading him into one of the most disreputable streets in the city.

The young girl stopped in front of a small house. A robust woman stood in the doorway, and when she saw the young girl she venomously said:

"Zilda has taken time. She stayed away a good two hours to get her daughter."

"My mother is dangerously ill, perhaps dying," said the young girl in a sharp voice.

"It won't be so serious," replied the woman, with a coarse laugh.

"Have you not heard that the woman is dangerously ill?" said the ex-priest.

"Is she sick?" asked the woman, coldly. "Well, if she dies, it won't be a great misfortune. I—"

"Madame, for God's sake!" implored the young girl.

"Show me to a room where I can lay the invalid down," said Anselmo roughly.

"Yes, yes, directly. Follow me if you are in such a hurry," growled the woman.

Just then two men who were intoxicated staggered into the hallway.

"Ah, there is Zilda," cried one of them; "quick, old woman; come in and sing us a song."

The woman opened a door and winked to the ex-priest to enter. The room was small and dirty. In the corner stood a slovenly bed upon which Anselmo deposited the invalid.

"Is there a physician in the neighborhood?" he asked.

"A physician? That is hardly worth the trouble," mocked the virago, "she is only drunk."

The ex-priest took a five-franc piece from his pocket and said:

"Get a physician, I insist upon it."

The next minute the virago was on the way.

Anselmo remained alone with the two women. The young girl sobbed silently, and the invalid remained motionless.

"Mademoiselle," he began, "I think you might loosen your mother's dress; the fainting fit lasts rather long."

The young girl looked at him, seeming not to understand.

"She is your mother, is she not?"

The young girl nodded, and, rising, pressed her lips upon the woman's forehead. Thereupon she loosened her mother's dress and held a glass of water to her lips. The invalid mechanically drank a few drops, but soon waved it back and whispered:

"No more, no water, leave me!"

"Mother," said the young girl, "mother, it is I; do you not know me?"

"No, I do not know who you are!" cried the invalid. "Away, I cannot sing to-day—my breast pains me. Oh—"

"Oh, mother," sobbed the poor child.

"Yes—I am cold—why do you put ice on my feet?" complained the invalid, and with a quick movement she raised herself up in bed.

Suddenly the delirious woman caught sight of Anselmo, and with a terrible cry she sprung at him with clinched fists.

"There you are, you wretch," she hissed; "where have you put your black coat?"

Just then the virago returned with the doctor.

The latter looked contemptuously at her, and in a gruff voice said:

"Lie down!"

He then beat her bosom, counted her pulse, and shook his head.

"Nothing can be done," he dryly declared; "her strength has been impaired by a fast and dissipated life, and—"

"But, doctor," interrupted Anselmo, "have some compunction for the poor woman. You see she is conscious and understands every word."

"Ah, you are probably a relative of hers, or has your warm interest in her some other ground?"

"Doctor, I only speak as a human being," replied Anselmo, sternly, "and if you do not do your duty as a physician I will notify the proper authorities."

This threat had the desired effect. The doctor drew his note-book from his pocket, rapidly wrote a prescription, and went away.

Anselmo took the prescription and hurried to the nearest drug-store. As he walked along the snow-covered streets, he muttered to himself:

"Merciful God, do not punish me so hard!"

When he returned he found the virago awaiting him at the door.

"Monsieur," she said, "it seems that Zilda interests you."

"Yes, like any other unhappy creature."

"Well, I have her papers. Her name is Zild—Jane Zild."

"Give them to me," said Anselmo, firmly; "I will take care of her."

"May God reward you; the sooner you get her out of my house the happier I shall be."

The woman hurried into the house, and Anselmo handed the invalid's daughter the medicine he had bought and waited for the return of the virago. In less than five minutes she returned and handed the ex-priest a package of papers.

"Where can I look through them?" he asked, uneasily.

"Oh, come into the kitchen."

Anselmo accepted her invitation, and by the flickering light of a tallow candle he unfolded the yellow and withered papers.

One of the papers contained a passport for the workman, Jean Zild, and his daughter Jane, made out by the commune of Sitzheim in Alsace. When Anselmo read this he grew pale and nearly fell to the floor in a faint.

"The reading seems to overtax your strength," said the woman giggling. "Zilda has travelled a great deal, and maybe you have met her before."

"I hardly think so," stammered Anselmo.

In company with the virago, Anselmo re-entered the sick-room, and, laying his hand on the young girl's shoulder, he said:

"My dear child, your mother is much better now, and if you follow my advice you will go to bed and take a rest. I shall stay with the invalid. The housekeeper here has kindly consented to give you a room."

"Not for any price," cried the little one in terror. "I cannot stay in this house overnight."

Little by little he managed to calm the poor child and make her understand his aim. She hesitatingly consented to stay overnight in the house, and the housekeeper conducted her to a little room. With inward terror the little one gazed at the unclean walls, and only her love for her mother induced her to stay and not return even now.

"Good-night, mother," she said, sobbing.

The woman looked vacantly at her and gave no sign of recognition of her daughter.

"Do not wake your mother up," said Anselmo, hastily. "Sleep is necessary to her and I will call you if she asks for you."

"Then you really intend to stay here?"

"Yes."

"Do you know us?"

"No," stammered Anselmo; "but go to bed now, it is late."

"You will surely call me?" asked the little one.

"Certainly; go now and rely on me."

She went, and Anselmo was alone with the invalid—the dying woman, as he shudderingly said to himself.

From time to time the sick woman would wake up in her sleep and utter a low moan.

Anselmo looked in terror at the face, which showed traces of former beauty. Whose fault was it that her life ended so early and so sadly?

Suddenly the invalid opened her big black eyes, and gazed at the ex-convict who was sitting by her bedside with folded hands.

"How did you get here?" she asked, timidly.

"You are sick, keep quiet; later on you shall learn everything," replied Anselmo.

"I am sick! Ha! ha! ha! I am cursed—cursed!" she cried.

"Keep still; go to sleep," begged Anselmo, frightened. "No one has cursed you."

"But he—my father—oh, I have brought shame and sorrow upon him; but it was not my fault—no, not my fault! Oh, I was so young and innocent. Father said, pray earnestly and often, and so I prayed. Oh, how nice it was in Sitzheim; the church lay upon a hill, hid in ivy, from which a view of the peaceful village could be had. A well was also in the village. Evenings we young girls used to go there to get water, and then—then he went past. How he frowned. He wore a black coat, and the bald spot on his shaved head shone like ivory. When he came near, we made the sign of the cross. We must honor the embassadors of God!"

The dying woman with trembling hands made the sign of the cross, and Anselmo groaned and moaned.

"I had not yet gone to confession," continued the delirious woman; "my father used to laugh at me and say: 'Stay at home, little Jane, you haven't any sins to confess yet.' I stayed. I was only sixteen. But one day as I was sitting in front of our door the man addressed me.

"'Why do you not come to confession?' he asked sternly.

"'Because my father said I was too young, and have no sins to confess.'

"'We are all sinners in God,' he earnestly replied. 'Do not forget that you will be eternally damned if you do not confess.'

"I got frightened; no, I did not wish to be damned, and so I went secretly to confession. He always gave me absolution and I was happy. He sometimes met me when I went walking, and was always very friendly to me."

Anselmo leaned his head against the hard bed-post and sobbed—they were the bitterest tears he had ever wept.

"He told me I was so pretty," continued the woman. "He promised me dresses, books and sweetmeats—my father must not know that I saw his reverence almost every day, and then—then he suddenly disappeared from the village—his superiors had transferred him, and I—I wept until my eyes were red. And then—then came, a terrible time. The girls at the well pointed their fingers in scorn at me—my father threw me out of the house! I ran as far as my feet would carry me—I suffered from hunger and thirst—I froze, for it was a bitter cold winter; and when I could no longer sustain my misery, I sprang into the water.

"I was rescued," she laughingly continued, "and then my child, my little Jane, was born, and to nurse her I had to keep on living. Yes, I lived, but how? The fault was not mine, but that of the hypocrite and scoundrel in clergyman's dress!"

"Mercy," implored Anselmo. "Mercy, Jane!"

"Ha! who—is it that—calls me?" stammered the dying woman, faintly. "I should know—that—voice!"

"Oh, Jane, it is I—the wretched priest!" whispered Anselmo; "forgive me for my crimes against you and tell me if that girl there is," he pointed to the other room— "my—our daughter?"

But the invalid could not speak any more; she only nodded, and then closed her eyes forever.

When day dawned a broken-down man rose from the bedside of the deceased. He had spent the night in torture, and now went to wake the daughter of the dead woman—wake his daughter! He must take care of her without letting her know that he was her father.

When he told the girl her mother was dead, she threw herself upon the corpse, covered the pale face with tears and kisses, and yet—curious phase of this girl's soul—when she thought she was not observed, she whispered faintly:

"God be thanked that your troubles are over, poor mother — now I can love you without blushing for you."

Anselmo ordered a respectable funeral, and when he returned from the cemetery with the young girl he said with deep emotion:

"Jane, I knew your mother—I promised her that I would look out for you. Will you stay with me?"

Jane Zild sorrowfully said "Yes." Anselmo left Lyons in company with the lonely child. He worked hard to place Jane above want, and tenderly loved her. Gradually he tried to win the young girl's confidence; he comprehended that Jane was on the brink of despair, and to distract her he began to educate her.

The result was well worth the work. Jane learned with the greatest facility, and took pleasure in study. Yet she remained pale and melancholy, and Anselmo knew what troubled her—the memory of the horrible past. It seemed as if she were branded—as if every one could read on her forehead whose daughter she was.

An accident revealed to Anselmo that Jane possessed eminent musical talents, and a magnificent contralto voice. He worked, saved and economized to be able to give Jane the best teachers. He removed with the young girl to a German city which possessed a celebrated conservatory; there Jane studied music and singing.

Three years father and daughter remained in Leipsic, and then Jane felt homesick—homesick for France. Anselmo selected Paris as their place of residence, and hoped that she would succeed in conquering a position at the Opera.

But Jane refused all offers from the managers, and when Anselmo reproached her she said, in bitter tones:

"If I were not my mother's daughter the matter would be different. Shame would kill me if some one were to discover in me the daughter of Jane Zild. No, I must remain in seclusion until God sees fit to end my miserable existence!"

It therefore surprised him when the young girl told him she thought of visiting the young painter's soiree and singing there. Was she in love with the painter, or did she expect to meet some one in his parlor?

Anselmo declared that he would not go to any party in Paris, and would only bring her to the Rue Montaigne and then call for her again. He was, however, not prepared for the surprise which awaited him in Gontram Sabran's parlor. He recognized in Count Vellini's secretary the demon Benedetto, and his heart ceased beating when he saw the wretch. He hoped Benedetto would not recognize him, but he was destined to be deceived, as we have seen.

When Anselmo heard the name of the Vicomte of

Monte-Cristo, he recollected the oath which the convict Benedetto had sworn against the Count of Monte-Cristo.

Hidden by the drapery, he had given Spero the mysterious warning. After the soiree was over he was sur prised at the excited condition of Jane. He attributed it to a recurrence of her thoughts to her horrible past.

And while he was promising to assist the former galley-slave in carrying out some deviltry to save himself from being unmasked, Jane disappeared. Anselmo regarded it as a new evidence of the wrath of God.

How long he lay crouched in a corner of the quay, buried in thought, he knew not; all he knew was that the sound of hurried footsteps, which were coming toward him, had aroused him.

Suppose it was Jane who wished to seek oblivion in the waters of the Seine? Anselmo listened. The footsteps drew near now—the spectral apparition of a woman went past him and swung itself on the bridge railing.

"Jane—my child!" cried the despairing father; but when he reached the spot where he had seen the apparition it was empty.

He bent over the railing. Something dark swam about. Anselmo thought he recognized Jane's black dress, and only filled with a desire to rescue his child, he plunged into the turbulent waters.

With a few powerful strokes he had reached the place where he had last seen the figure. Thank God! it was in front of him. He stretched out his arm clutched the hand of the drowning person, and tried to swim back to shore with his dear burden.

But the shore was still far away, the body lay heavy as lead on his left arm, and much as he tried to cleave the ice-cold water with his right he could not succeed in doing it. He felt his strength grow feeble—was he going to be overcome at the last moment?

"Help! help! we are sinking!" he cried aloud, and as he felt himself seized at that moment by a huge wave, whose power he could not resist—the water entered his mouth—he cried again:

"Help! help!"

"Patience! Keep up a moment longer! I am coming!" came back in a loud voice.

The water was parted with powerful strokes, four arms were stretched toward the drowning persons, and Anselmo and his burden were brought to the shore by two men.

"Confound the cold," said one of the men, shaking himself as if he were a poodle. "I should like to know what reason induced these two people to take a cold bath so early in the morning?"

"Bring them to my house, Bobichel," said the other, a strong, handsome man, "and everything will be explained there."

"Yes, if they are still alive," replied Bobichel. "I think, Fanfaro, that we came just at the right moment. What will Madame Irene say when we arrive home?"

"She will at once prepare for everything," said Fanfaro, laughing.

After they had both walked along with their burdens in their arms for about a quarter of an hour, they stopped in front of a small house which lay back of a pretty garden.

Five minutes later both the unfortunates lay in a comfortably warmed room, and Fanfaro, his wife, and Bobichel busily attended to them.

"Who can they be?" asked Irene, gently, of her husband.

"God knows," replied Fanfaro; "anyhow, I am glad that they both still live."

But the woman Anselmo had rescued at the risk of his life was not Jane, but a gray-haired old lady.

CHAPTER XXXVII

CARMEN

IN a magnificently furnished house in the Rue de Rivoli sat Carmen, the handsome daughter of the bank director Larsagny. She was pensively gazing at the carpet, and from time to time uttered a low sigh.

"Aha, bah!" she muttered; "he shall tell me all."

She rang a silver bell, and immediately after a maid appeared.

"Where is Monsieur de Larsagny?"

"In his office."

"Since when?"

"Since eight o'clock."

"And what time is it now?"

"Ten."

"Good. Tell Jean to serve breakfast here in my boudoir, and then go and tell Monsieur de Larsagny that I await him."

A quarter of an hour later the banker appeared in the boudoir.

He ate so greedily that Carmen impatiently exclaimed:

"Are you not yet satisfied?"

"Really, I have a good appetite this morning," nodded Larsagny.

"Do you know how your phenomenal appetite appears to me?" asked Carmen, laughing.

"No. What do you mean?"

"Well, I mean that you must have been starving at one time, and since then you always feel greedy."

Larsagny shuddered and his brow contracted.

"Do not speak of such things; I cannot bear it," he said, with a frown.

"Why not? Not every one comes to the world as a millionnaire. I, for instance, as a child, have suffered more than once from hunger, and—"

"Carmen, be silent," said the banker, sternly; "you'll spoil my appetite if you talk so."

"I should think your appetite would be stilled by this time. What you have already eaten would have fed an army."

Larsagny did not answer. He was busy eating an Edam cheese, and not until all the plates were empty did he lay his knife and fork on the table, and, breathing more freely, say:

"So, now I can stand it for a little while."

Carmen rang the bell. The table was cleared off, and as soon as the servant had brought the cigarettes and cigars, the girl motioned to him to leave.

Carmen lighted a cigarette, and, leaning back in her chair, said:

"I have something important to say to you."

"What is it?" asked Larsagny.

"Oh! different things," replied Carmen.

"About money? Do not be timid."

"It is not about money, but about an information."

"An information?" asked the banker.

"Yes."

"Really, Carmen, you are speaking in riddles to-day—"

"Which you will, I hope, solve for me," interrupted the young lady, dryly. "In the first place, what is the meaning of your gigantic appetite?"

"Ah! that's very simple; I am hungry."

"That isn't it. I have seen a great many hungry people. In fact, I have often suffered from hunger when mother had no money to buy bread."

"Carmen, how often have I told you that I do not like these reminiscences?"

"Why not? Take an example from me, and tell me a little of your past."

"Enough—enough!" cried Larsagny, growing pale.

"Answer my questions, and then you shall have quiet."

"Carmen, you are bothering yourself and me unnecessarily. I give you the assurance—"

"As if your assurances had the slightest value for me," interrupted Carmen.

Larsagny smiled in a sickly fashion.

"Carmen, you are childish," he said. "I should think you ought to have known enough of me by this time to—"

"To be able to hate you thoroughly. You have cheated me of my youth and innocence."

"Carmen, for God's sake, not so loud! Suppose some one heard you?" cried the banker, anxiously.

"What do I care? You are a baron, live in Florence, and have a good housekeeper, whose only joy is her eighteen-year-old daughter. One night the mother is away. The baron uses the opportunity to take advantage of the young girl. When the mother returns the next day and learns the truth, she becomes so frightened that she falls dead on the spot. The unhappy girl tries to throw herself into the river, but is prevented from doing so, and finally becomes the mistress of the villain."

"Carmen!"

"Yes, yes, I know I am no better than you. Monsieur de Larsagny, tell me why you do not make me your wife?"

"My God, because—"

"Well? Why do you pause? Do you know what I believe? You are a married man with a dreadful past!"

"Carmen, you are doing me an injury."

"Ha! ha! If I do you a wrong, I am at the most too easy with you."

"Carmen, what is the matter with you?" exclaimed Larsagny, in despair. "Only yesterday you were so affectionate, and now—"

"Bah! Yesterday is yesterday, and to-day is to-day. Either I find out from you who you really are, or—"

"Or?"

"Or I shall find out myself, and should I discover that you have committed some unpunished crime, I shall denounce you, even though you take revenge upon me for it."

Larsagny had sprung up, and looking at Carmen in amazement, he stammered:

"You—would—dare—to do—that?"

"Yes. And if you look at yourself in the glass, you will see that my wildest declarations are far behind the reality. Your answer shines in every color."

"Listen to me, Carmen," said the banker, in a tender voice. "It is time you dropped the subject. I am not an Adonis, and as you have rightly suspected, I have seen a great deal and gone through many troubles, but in spite of all that—"

"Well, in spite of all that?"

"I do not deserve your unjust accusations. Can you, for instance, reproach me for the hunger which bothers me continually?"

"No, only I should like to learn the cause."

"The cause?" repeated Larsagny.

"Yes."

"Then listen. I will tell you everything, even though you should laugh at me. Years ago I was travelling in Italy, and as I had a large sum of money in my pocket, I was attacked by robbers. The wretches locked me in a cell and let me starve. One day I asked for food, and to mock me they made the bandit who guarded me eat his meal in my presence.

" 'Can I get a meal here?' I asked of the bandit, who was swallowing some peas.

" 'Is your excellency hungry?' asked the fellow (his name was Peppino) in surprise.

"I was angry.

" 'What!' I exclaimed in a rage, 'since twenty-four hours I have not eaten a thing, and you ask me if I am hungry.'

" 'Then you wish to eat?'

" 'Yes, at once, if it is possible.'

" 'If you pay for it.'

" 'I will pay what you ask,' I cried.

" 'What do you wish?'

"'Anything, a chicken or a partridge.'

"'Good. Let us say a chicken.'

"'But have you a cook here?'

"'Certainly,' nodded the bandit, and, raising his voice, he cried: 'A chicken for the gentleman.'

"Ten minutes later a chicken was brought in by a waiter in a frock suit. For a moment I thought I was in the Café de Paris.

"I ate the chicken with my eyes, and asked for a knife and fork. Peppino gave them to me, but just as I was about to attack the chicken, he held my hand and said:

"'Pardon me, your excellency, but we get paid here before things are eaten.'

"I looked at him in astonishment.

"'What does the chicken cost?' I asked.

"'Five thousand louis d'ors, or one hundred thousand francs.'

"'Are you crazy? One hundred thousand francs for a chicken?'

"'Your excellency is not aware how hard it is to get chickens in this neighborhood.'"

"Well, and how did the matter end?" asked Carmen.

"I sent the chicken back, and asked for a piece of bread. It was brought to me by Battista, another bandit, on a silver salver.

"'How dear is the bread?' I asked, trembling.

"'One hundred thousand francs.'

"'What! A piece of bread one hundred thousand francs?' I cried in amazement.

"'One hundred thousand francs.'

"'But you asked no more for the chicken?'

" 'Prices here are fixed,' replied Peppino; 'pay and you can eat.'

" 'But with what should I pay ?' I cried in desperation; 'the money I have with me—'

" 'Is your whole fortune,' interrupted Peppino. 'You have five million and fifty thousand francs in your portfolio in drafts, and you can get fifty chickens and a half for it.

"I was astounded. The robbers knew exactly how much money I had, and I saw I had either to pay or to starve.

" 'Will I be able to eat in silence ?' I asked, 'if I pay ?'

" 'Certainly.'

" 'Good, then bring me some writing materials.'

"I wrote out a draft on Rome for one hundred thousand francs, and received the chicken."

"What was their motive ?" asked Carmen.

"Merely to plunder and blackmail me."

"Then they demanded more ?" asked Carmen.

"Oh, no. After I had eaten the chicken, I felt thirsty. I called Peppina and told him.

" 'You wish to drink something ?' he asked.

" 'Yes. I am dying with thirst.'

" 'I am very sorry to hear it. The wine this year is ry bad and very dear.'

" 'Then bring me water,' I cried.

" 'Oh, water is still dearer.'

" 'Then give me a glass of wine.'

" 'We only sell by the bottle.'

" 'Then bring me a bottle of Orreto.'

" 'Directly.'

" 'And the wine costs ?'

" 'Twenty-five thousand francs per bottle.'

" 'Swindler!   Robber!' I cried, beside myself.

" 'Do not talk so loud, master might hear you.'

" 'I don't care.   Who is your master?'

" 'Luigi Vampa.'

" 'Can I speak to him?'

" 'Yes.'

"Peppino went away, and two minutes later a slimly built, fine-looking man, with dark hair and eyes, stood before me!

" 'You want to speak to me?' he asked, politely.

" 'Are you the chief of the people who brought me here?' I said.

" 'Yes.'

" 'What ransom do you wish of me?'

" 'Only the five million francs you possess.'

" 'Take my life,' I cried, 'but leave me my money.'

" 'Your death wouldn't do us any good,' replied the bandit, 'but your money would.'

" 'Take a million then?'

" 'No.'

" 'Two?'

" 'No.'

" 'Three?'

" 'No.'

" 'Four?'

" 'We leave haggling to usurers.'

" 'Then take everything from me and kill me!' I cried in despair.

" 'We do not wish to do that.'

" 'And suppose I die of hunger?'

" 'Then we are not responsible for that.'

" 'Keep your wine and I will keep my money.

" 'Just as you please,' laughed Vampa, and went away.

"Two days later I asked for food. A fine dinner was served. I paid a million and stilled my hunger. This continued three days longer, and when I finally counted the contents of my portfolio, I found I had only fifty thousand francs left. I considered what I should do with this sum, and fell asleep over my plans. When I awoke, I was on the road to Rome. When I suddenly looked at myself in a mirror I found to my horror that my hair had turned gray. Since that time I have always feared that I would never have sufficient to eat; and now you know the cause of my ravenous appetite."

"Yet I cannot understand why they should have wanted to torture you so. It must have been an act of revenge," said Carmen.

"You are mistaken," replied Larsagny, "I fear no one and every one esteems me; I—"

"One moment," interrupted Carmen, as she looked fixedly at the banker. "Why did you get frightened at the *soiree* recently, when the servant announced the Vicomte of Monte Cristo? I thought you feared no one, baron?"

Larsagny stared at the young girl as if she had been a spectre. Carmen continued:

"I have not finished yet. In the evening I stood on the terrace and heard these words:

" 'Monsieur de Larsagny, take care you do not learn my name too soon.' "

"Ah, you are spying on me," cried Larsagny angrily; "have a care or—"

"I do not fear you,' said Carmen, calmly; "I will be

the first to urge your punishment, if some suspicious circumstance should arise and—"

"Be silent, wretched creature!" cried Larsagny angrily, "be silent, or—"

He grasped a knife and rushed upon Carmen. The latter stared at him in such a way that he dropped the weapon and stammered:

"Carmen, you will drive me crazy!"

At this moment the door opened, and the servant brought in a card which he handed to Larsagny.

"The gentleman is waiting in the parlor," he said; "will the baron receive him?"

Before Larsagny could throw a look at the card, Carmen had grasped it.

"Signor Fagiano," she read aloud, and as the banker with trembling voice said he would be down, she nodded to the servant to go away, and then mockingly said:

"Signor Fagiano has no doubt come to tell the baron his name. Good luck to him!"

CHAPTER XXXVIII

RECOLLECTIONS

SIGNOR FAGIANO stood in the beautiful parlor, and a malicious smile played about his lips.

The banker entered now. The scene in the painter's garden would not vanish from his mind. Fagiano had approached him then and triumphantly whispered:

"Monsieur de Larsagny, I know your past."

Larsagny had uttered a cry of terror.

"If I am to remain silent," Fagiano had added, "I must have money."

"But who are you?"

Whereupon the answer had come:

"Take care that you do not find out my name too soon."

With inward fear the banker approached the Italian to-day.

"Signor Fagiano, what brings you here to-day? This is the second time that you have crossed my path, and I hope it will be the last. I do not know you, you do not know me, and I cannot understand to what I am indebted for the honor of your visit. I am very patient, but everything has its limits, and only the position I occupy prevents me from throwing you out."

"Call your servants, Monsieur de Larsagny. I have no fear of publicity," said Fagiano, boldly.

The banker grasped the bell-rope, but let his hand fall again, and Fagiano, who noticed this, mockingly observed:

"Why do you hesitate? Would you prefer to finish our interview without witnesses?"

"Impudent puppy!" hissed Larsagny.

"Do not get excited! Let us come to the point."

"I have been waiting for that a long time," growled Larsagny; "tell me, first of all, who are you?"

Fagiano drew nearer to the banker, and, grinning, said:

"You really do not recognize me?"

"No."

The Italian laughed loudly.

"Then give me two hundred thousand francs," said Fagiano, "and I will disappear forever."

"I would be a fool to give an unknown person a single sou."

"You really do not know my name, then?"

"No."

"H'm; but I know yours."

"That isn't a great thing. My name is known on the street and at Court."

"Yes, the name of Larsagny; as Monsieur Danglars you are also known, though in a different way."

Larsagny trembled and was about to fall.

"You lie!" he hissed.

"What would you say if I told your sovereign that the man he put at the head of the syndicate is only one of that crowd of unhanged thieves who roam about in the world?"

"Wretch, you will say nothing of the kind," cried Danglars (for it was really he); and putting his hand in his breast-pocket he drew forth a revolver and held it at the Italian's breast.

"Softly, softly," said Fagiano, as he took the weapon away from the banker and put it in his pocket. "A little while ago I asked for two hundred thousand francs; now I must increase my demand to half a million."

"You are a fool," said Danglars, pale with rage. "You will never get a sou from me."

"Have no fear about that; as soon as I threaten to expose you, you will submit; I have some piquant details *in petto*."

"What do you mean by that?"

"Well, I will announce your name at the same time as mine."

"What has that got to do with me?"

"More than you think. Don't you really know me?"

"No."

"So much the worse. But tell me, baron, is Carmen really your daughter?"

"But—who—gives—you—the right—" said Danglars, stammering.

"Next you will deny that you ever had a wife?"

"Leave my wife's name alone."

"Good. Then let us talk of your daughter who is much older and does not bear the name of Carmen."

Danglars hid his face in his hands.

"Baron, you are the friend of the emperor and are very rich, and no one suspects that Baron Larsagny is the former forger and swindler Danglars. One word from me and you sink deep in the mud. It depends on you whether I am to be your friend or your enemy."

"Ah, now I know who you are," said the banker, springing up. "You are Andrea Cavalcanti."

"Right," laughed Fagiano.

"Now I remember. You put a title to your name, played the heir of a great fortune, and entered into near relations with my family. An impudence which the avenging arm of the law punished."

"Yes, I am Benedetto the murderer—Benedetto the criminal. But do you know who my father was?"

"Yes, I heard about the scandalous trial; I was not in France at the time, but— Go on, you," urged Danglars.

"And do you also know the name of my mother, baron?"

"No."

"Well, then, my mother was—the Baroness Danglars."

"The miserable creature—the wretch!" cried Danglars, hoarsely. "But no—you lie, it cannot be so."

"She was my mother," said Benedetto, accenting the word *was*.

"She was? Is she dead?" asked Danglars, softly.

"Yes, I killed her."

"Horrible," groaned Danglars, wringing his hands.

"If you want proofs," continued Benedetto, coldly, "here they are."

He took Anselmo's writing out of his pocket and handed it to the banker.

"Read," he said, indifferently.

"What do you want from me?" murmured Danglars, hoarsely.

"First, money, and then let us talk further."

"You shall have what you want," replied Danglars.

"Good; now comes the second point."

"Do not torture me any longer," said Danglars.

"Have you forgotten who it was that humiliated you, trod you in the dust?" said Benedetto, laying his hand on the banker's shoulder. "That man is your bad genius as well as mine. It was the Count of Monte-Cristo who taught me the pleasures of life only to throw me back to the Bagnio again. Since I have been free I dream of revenge against him. I know the spot where he is mortal. Can I count on your support?"

"Yes; but I fear our attempts will be fruitless."

"Fruitless? I swear to you that we shall be successful."

"But he is a supernatural man. You might as well attack God."

"And yet he has an Achilles heel! Once more, will you help me?"

"Yes; but I do not understand you."

"The whole of the Count of Monte-Cristo's affection is centred in his son, and through this son we must strike him. He shall suffer all the tortures of hell, and in his son, whom he idolizes, we shall punish him."

"Now I understand you," said Danglars.

"In the first place, you must give me money, and then wait until I call you."

"And you guarantee that the grief will kill him?"

"Yes, I guarantee it."

"Then I am yours."

CHAPTER XXXIX

DISAPPEARED

LET us return to the Vicomte Spero.

Three days had passed since Jane Zild had been taken to the elegant house. She still lay motionless and pale, and Madame Caraman nev,er left her bedside.

A slight moan from the invalid caused Mamma Caraman to bend over her.

"Poor child," she sorrowfully murmured, "she looks as if she were going to die. God knows what way she got the wound—I always fear that she herself fired the shot."

Jane moaned louder and felt her heart with her hand.

"Be still, my dear," whispered Mamma, Caraman. She poured a few drops of liquor into a cup and told the girl to drink it.

"No, I will not drink!" said Jane, passionately. "Leave me, I do not want to live," she suddenly cried. "Oh, why did you take the weapon from me? I cannot live with this pressure on the breast. The horrible secret pulls me to the ground—I am sinking—I am sinking! Ah, and she was nevertheless my mother—I loved her so—I love her yet."

With tears in her eyes Mamma Caraman tried to quiet the excited girl, but she could not do so. She pressed lightly on a silver bell which stood near the bed.

In less than five minutes the vicomte appeared.

"Is she worse?" he anxiously asked.

"Yes, she is feverish again, and I thought it might be better to send for a physician."

Spero drew near to the invalid's couch and took her arm to feel her pulse. Strange to say, Jane became calmer as soon as he touched her. The wild-looking eyes lost their frightened look; the lips which had muttered disconnected words closed, and the small hands lay quietly on the silk cover.

"She is sleeping," said Mamma Caraman, "I am sorry now that I called you."

"On the contrary I am glad I came. I will take your place and you can sleep a little."

"Not for the world," cried Mamma Caraman. "I am not tired at all."

"That is very funny; for three days you haven't closed an eye," said the vicomte. "Lie down for an hour, Mamma Caraman. I promise to call you as soon as the invalid stirs."

Mamma Caraman thereupon laid herself upon a sofa, and the next minute she was fast asleep.

An hour later the young girl opened her eyes and locked about her.

"Where am I?" she murmured.

"With me—under my protection," replied Spero, and pressing Jane's hand to his lips he added, "Ah, Jane, why did you wish to die? Did you not know that your soul would take mine along?"

The young girl listened as if in a dream, and unconsciously looked at the vicomte with sparkling eyes.

"Jane, before I saw you I hadn't lived," continued Spero, 'but now I know that life is worth living for, and I thank God that he allowed me to find you."

A smile of pleasure flitted across Jane's lips. She did not speak, but Spero felt a warm pressure of the hand, and enthusiastically cried:

"Jane, I love you—love you dearly; Jane, my darling, tell me only once that you love me!"

Jane looked silently at him and then buried her face in her hands, faintly murmuring:

"Yes, Spero, I love you."

"Thanks, my darling, for that word, and now I will leave you. Good-night, Jane—my Jane—oh, how I love you!"

The vicomte left the room and Jane closed her tired eyes.

Suddenly the heavy drapery which covered the door leading to the corridor was thrown aside, a man's form issued therefrom, and his sparkling eyes gazed at the two women.

The man took a vial out of his pocket, and, dropping the contents on a piece of white cloth, he held it to Jane's lips. Jane breathed fainter and fainter—then her breathing ceased—her arms sank by her side—her cheeks became pale as death.

The man watched these terrible changes without the slightest sign of anxiety. Bending down he wrapped her tightly in the silk cover and carried her out of the room in his muscular arms, while Mamma Caraman slept tightly and Spero was dreaming.

The reader will remember that Firejaws, who has died in the meantime, once jokingly compared Fanfaro to a Newfoundland dog, as he found means everywhere to rescue some one.

Fanfaro's presence in Paris is soon explained. His wife and his two children could not stand the Algerian climate long, and so they all came to Paris. Monte-Cristo had begged him to keep an eye on Spero. Since the count's departure not a day had passed but that either Fanfaro or his faithful Bobichel watched every movement of the vicomte, and the night the young man and the painter were walking in the Champs-Elysées, the former clown had followed them as far as the Rue Montaigne. Bobichel then went home.

It was three o'clock when he silently opened the street door. To his surprise Fanfaro met him as he entered, and told him that as he could not work he thought he would take a walk. Bobichel immediately declared that he would accompany him. It was in this way that they had rescued Anselmo and the old woman. Fanfaro very soon found out that the old lady was crazy. Fanfaro believed that there was some connection between the two persons he had saved from a watery grave, and Bobichel thought so too.

The crazy woman sometimes became terribly excited. In such moments she sprang out of the bed, and hiding behind the door silently whined:

"Spare me—I am your mother!"

Irene in such moments tried in vain to quiet her. When the physician examined her, he found a blood-red scar on her bosom, which, no doubt, came from a knife stab.

On the night of the third day after the rescue, Fanfaro sat at Anselmo's bedside. Bobichel had disappeared since forty-eight hours to make inquiries about Spero. Fanfaro heard through him that Spero had not left the Monte-Cristo palace for three days, and could not imagine what was the cause of it.

Anselmo now began to groan. Fanfaro bent over the invalid, and thought he heard the words:

"My daughter—my poor child—ah, is she dead?"

"Who is dead?" asked Fanfaro.

"Ah, she plunged into the water—she is drowned," groaned Anselmo.

Fanfaro could not believe his ears. Did the sick man imagine that the gray-haired woman was his daughter?

"Have you a daughter?" he asked.

"Yes, my Jane—my darling."

Just then the door opened, and Bobichel entered.

"Well?" cried Fanfaro expectantly.

"Ah, Fanfaro, a great misfortune!"

"A misfortune? Does it concern the vicomte?"

"Yes; he has disappeared."

"But, Bobichel, why should that be a misfortune? Perhaps he went on a short journey."

"No, both Coucou and Madame Caraman maintain that his disappearance is a misfortune."

"Tell me all that has happened."

"Then listen. On the evening that the vicomte came back from the *soiree*, he did not go home directly, but first took an opportunity to rescue a wounded girl."

"A wounded girl?" repeated Fanfaro.

"Yes, a young girl who had been shot in the breast. She was brought by the vicomte to his house."

"I can hardly believe it," muttered Fanfaro.

"Madame Caraman and Coucou are in the corridor; they will confirm my statement."

"Bring them in."

The next minute the Zouave and Caraman were in the room.

"The fault is mine! Ah, I will never forgive myself," cried Mamma Caraman, wringing her hands; and then she went on and told how Spero and Gontram had brought the wounded girl into the house, the care that had been taken of her, and how, at the suggestion of the vicomte, she had lain down on the sofa to rest for an hour.

"When I awoke," she continued, "it was broad daylight. On going over to the bed where the young girl lay, I found, to my surprise, that it was empty. I went to the vicomte's room and told him the girl had disappeared. The vicomte, without saying a word, hurried out of the house in a state of great excitement. Twenty-four hours have passed since then, and he has not been back since, and—"

"What bothers me most," interrupted Coucou, "is the fact that the vicomte took his pistols along."

Fanfaro became pensive.

"Have you any idea how the young girl was wounded?" he asked after a pause, turning to Madame Caraman.

"No, but Monsieur Sabran knows."

"The painter? I shall go to him directly."

"We have been to his house already, but he has not been home since this morning."

"That is bad," murmured Fanfaro. "Do you know the lady's name?"

"No, but I found this note in her pocket. If it is addressed to the young girl, then her name is Jane," said Mamma Caraman, handing Fanfaro an elegant little note.

"Dear Mademoiselle Jane," Fanfaro read, and, penetrated by a recollection, he repeated aloud:

"Jane—Mademoiselle Jane—if it is—but no—it can't be possible—"

A loud cry from the invalid's couch made him pause. Anselmo had gotten up, and, gazing at Fanfaro, stammeringly repeated:

"Jane—my Jane."

"Do you know the young lady?" cried Fanfaro.

"Certainly. Then it wasn't she whom I rescued from the river?"

"No; but for God's sake calm yourself," said Fanfaro, as he saw Anselmo make a motion to spring out of bed.

"I could have imagined that the return of that scoundrel, Benedetto, would bring me misfortune!" cried Anselmo, with flaming eyes.

"Benedetto—who speaks of Benedetto?" asked a hoarse voice.

All turned in the direction from whence the words came. At the door stood the crazy woman. When Anselmo caught sight of her, he uttered a terrible cry.

"Merciful God, where does she come from?" he groaned in terror. "Has the grave given up its dead?"

The crazy woman drew near to him, and grazed his forehead with her bony hand. She laughed aloud, and in a heartrending voice exclaimed:

"The galley-slave—he—Toulon—the Bagnio—oh! 'tis he!"

Anselmo trembled, and could not turn his eyes away from the old lady, who now wildly called:

"Benedetto! Who mentioned his name? I want to know it!"

"What can this mean?" whispered Fanfaro, shuddering.

"I will acknowledge everything," stammered Anselmo, and hanging his head down he told how he had been a galley-slave at Toulon.

"Who wounded you?" he then asked, turning to the crazy woman.

"My son. He was called Benedetto! Ha! ha! ha! Who could have given him that name? I do not know, for I thought the child was dead, and his father buried him alive in the garden. Benedetto—Benedetto," she suddenly cried, "come and kill me. I cannot live with this bleeding wound in my heart!"

Fanfaro hurried out of the room in search of his wife, and Irene's entreaties had the effect of causing the invalid to follow her. They had already reached the threshold when the old lady paused, and, turning to Fanfaro, hastily said:

"He has forgiven me long ago, and will not punish me any more. God sent him to the earth to reward and punish, and he has punished them all—all with their own sins. Do you know him? It is the Count of Monte-Cristo!"

She left the room and those who had remained behind looked confusedly at one another.

"I do not understand everything," said Anselmo,

faintly; "but what I know I shall confess. Benedetto is a scoundrel and a murderer, and it was he who stabbed his own mother, this poor crazy woman. He is at present in Paris, where he came expressly to revenge himself upon the Count of Monte-Cristo."

"Do you know it positively?" asked Fanfaro uneasily.

Anselmo then related all he knew, and only kept silent with regard to the fact of his being Jane's father.

Fanfaro listened attentively to his words, and then said:

"I shall inform the Count of Monte-Cristo of this. In three days he will be here. You, Anselmo," he added, turning to the ex-convict, "are too weak and sick to take part in our work, but we shall keep you informed if anything important turns up, and—"

"For Heaven's sake," interrupted Anselmo, "do not leave me behind. Let us go at once, every minute is precious! O God, if she lives no more!"

"Let us hope for the best," said Fanfaro, earnestly; "forward then with God for Monte-Cristo and his son!"

"And for my Jane," muttered Anselmo to himself. "God in heaven take my life, but save hers!"

CHAPTER XL

A CONFESSION

GONTRAM was in love; night and day he only thought of Carmen.

"Either she or no one," he said to himself.

One morning, as he was returning home from a visit, the janitor addressed him.

"Monsieur Sabran," he said, "I have something to tell you."

"Well, what is it?" asked Gontram, expectantly.

"H'm, Monsieur Sabran, it is about a lady," murmured the man.

"A lady? Which lady?"

"I do not know her, and my discretion did not permit me to ask her."

Gontram, in spite of his impatience, laughed. He knew the janitor to be the most inquisitive person in the world, and judged his discretion accordingly.

"Monsieur Alain, won't you tell me what the lady wanted of me?" asked the painter.

"The lady was elegantly dressed, and asked me whether you were at home. When I told her you were not, she took a letter from her pocket and told me to give it to you at once."

"Where is the letter?"

"Here, Monsieur Sabran," said the janitor, taking a perfumed note from his pocket and handing it to the painter.

The latter hastily tore it from his hand and went back to his residence. In his study he threw his gloves and hat on the table, and looked at the note from all sides. It was signed "Carmen," and ran as follows:

"Monsieur Gontram—Or may I say, my dear friend —I would like to speak to you about a matter of some importance, and beg you to visit me this evening. I expect you at seven o'clock. Ring the garden bell. Be punctual. It concerns the fate of those you love.
"Carmen."

What did Carmen mean by the expression, "The fate of those you love?" What did she know of his connections? Why should he have to go to the back door? How came it that Carmen asked him to meet her in this peculiar manner?

Punctually at seven o'clock the painter was at the garden gate, and with a trembling hand Gontram pulled the bell-rope and was immediately let in by a maid.

"The lady is waiting," she said.

The maid opened the door of a charming boudoir and allowed Gontram to enter. With his hat in his hand the painter stood still in the centre of the room. The door was now opened, and Carmen, simply attired in black silk, entered. She was pale, but extremely handsome, and Gontram looked admiringly at her.

"Thank you," she said, offering her hand to the painter. "I hardly dared to hope you would come."

"You sent for me, and I have come," replied Gontram.

"Please sit down and listen to me."

Gontram took a seat next to Carmen.

"Monsieur Gontram, do you love me?" she suddenly asked.

Gontram trembled.

"Mademoiselle Carmen," he earnestly said, "I will answer your question candidly. Yes, I love you, love you warmly and tenderly, and if I have hesitated to tell you so, it was because I did not think myself worthy of you. I—"

"Oh, keep still—keep still!"

"But, Mademoiselle Carmen," said Gontram, "you know you can rely on me!"

For a time they were both silent.

"Listen to me," she finally said; "I hope you will not misunderstand me. Monsieur Gontram, I know that you are a brave, honest man. When you kissed me on the little balcony three days ago, I felt that you regarded it as a—silent engagement?"

"Yes!" cried Gontram.

"And yet," said Carmen, slowly, "you postponed asking Monsieur de Larsagny for my hand."

"I did not dare—"

"Thank God that you did not do it," cried Carmen, breathing more freely. "No, Gontram, I can never—never be your wife!"

Gontram sprang up.

"Impossible, Carmen!" he cried, passionately. "Tell me that you are joking!"

"No, Gontram, I am not joking," said Carmen, earnestly. "I can never become your wife. Only an honest girl has the right to put her hand in yours."

"Explain yourself more clearly," said Gontram, deadly pale.

"Gontram, I love you, love you tenderly, and if ever there was a pure love, it is mine for you. Before I made your acquaintance I went carelessly through life. Good and bad were unknown meanings to me, and I did not know what blushing was."

Carmen sank exhausted in a chair and burst into tears.

"Carmen, why do you cry?"

"Gontram, these tears are for me—for my lost youth —my tainted soul," whispered Carmen. "Oh, Gontram, I am not what I appear to be. I am not the daughter but the friend of Monsieur de Larsagny!"

Gontram uttered a wild cry, and, beating his face with his hands, he gasped for air; the shot had struck him to the heart.

"Yes, it is the truth," continued Carmen; "I am the friend of an old man. Ah, Gontram, how have I struggled with myself before I found courage enough to inform you of this."

Carmen had fallen to the floor. Clutching Gontram's knee she wept bitterly.

Gontram felt deep pity for her. He placed his hand on her hair, and gently said:

"Carmen, the confession I have just heard has shocked me very much; but, at the same time, it has also pleased me. That you did not wish to hear me, before you told me your story, raises you in my estimation, and let him who is without sin cast the first stone!"

"You do not curse me? Do not cast me off?" asked Carmen, in surprise.

"Carmen, God knows your confession tore my heart; but, the more painful the blow was, the more I comprehended the great extent of my love for you."

Carmen's tears still poured down. Gontram bent over her and tenderly raised her up.

"Carmen," he earnestly said, "tell me, what can I do for you?"

Carmen raised her eyes, which were still full of tears, and tenderly whispered to the young man:

"How good you are! Do you love the Vicomte of Monte-Cristo?" she suddenly asked.

"I love and esteem him. But what makes you speak of the vicomte?"

"Because danger threatens him, and I want you to warn him."

"What is the nature of the danger?" asked Gontram.

"Powerful enemies are united against him, and if we are not more prudent they will crush both him and us."

"Enemies! Who could be an enemy of Spero?"

"One of the enemies is Monsieur de Larsagny!"

"And the other?"

"Have you noticed the Count of Vellini's secretary?"

"Signor Fagiano? Yes, I know him."

"Fagiano is not his real name."

"Do you know it?"

"Not yet, but I hope to very soon. Signor Fagiano and Monsieur Larsagny have met before. When the Vicomte of Monte-Cristo was announced at your *soiree* the other evening, Monsieur de Larsagny became pale as death, his eyes stared at the young man as if he had been a spectre, and, under pretence of seeking a cooler spot, he hurriedly left the room.''

"Yes, I remember," said Gontram.

"As you know, shortly afterward we went out on the balcony and heard two voices quarrelling. One of the voices said: 'Monsieur de Larsagny, take care that you do not know my name too soon.' The next day I asked Monsieur de Larsagny about it, but he gave me evasive replies. Just then the visit of Signor Fagiano was announced and our conversation ended. That day I learned nothing; but two days later, when Signor Fagiano came again, I hid behind the drapery and listened. Don't think bad of me that I did such a thing, but there was no other choice. As soon as the two exchanged their first words, I saw at once they were partners in crime. I heard the Italian say:

" 'I have taken the preliminary steps, and guarantee the success of the plan. Revenge is assured for us, but I must have some more money.'

" 'Here is what I promised you,' replied Larsagny.

"I heard the crumpling of bank-notes. For a while all was still, and then Monsieur de Larsagny said:

" 'What do you intend to do now?'

" 'Oh, I have already struck the young fool a blow,' replied the Italian. 'She is in my power, and it will be easy for me to entrap him.'

" 'But be careful, the slightest haste might ruin us.'

" 'The Vicomte of Monte-Cristo shall suffer; he shall crawl and bend in tortures I shall prepare for him, and my plans are so made that the law cannot reach us.'

" 'Then I am satisfied. Ah, if he only suffers for one hour the tortures his father made me undergo,' hissed Larsagny.

" 'You shall be satisfied. I have also a debt to settle with him.'

"The conversation was now carried on in such a low tone that I could not understand what was being said. I hurried to my room and made up my mind to draw you into my confidence."

"I thank you, Carmen," cried Gontram; "Spero is a friend, a brother, and I would gladly offer up my life to save his."

"Of whom could Fagiano have spoken when he said: 'She is in my power?'" asked Carmen.

"I hardly know. God help the scoundrels if they touch a hair of his head!" Gontram had risen. He put his arm about the young girl's waist and gently drew her toward him.

"Carmen," he whispered, tenderly, "your confession was a bitter pill for me, but my love for you is the same as ever. Tell me once more that you love me, too!"

"Oh, Gontram, I do not deserve so much kindness," sobbed Carmen.

"Now good-by," said Gontram. "You shall soon hear from me."

A last kiss and they separated.

CHAPTER XLI

ON THE TRAIL

HALF dreaming, Gontram strode through the streets. It was ten o'clock when the painter reached the Monte-Cristo palace. To his surprise all was dark, and hesitatingly Gontram pulled the bell.

The footman opened it. When asked if the vicomte was at home, he said he had gone out.

"Gone out? Will he soon return?" asked Gontram.

"We do not know."

"H'm! Can I speak to Madame Caraman?"

"She is also out."

"And the Zouave Coucou?"

"He has gone out, too; and none of them has yet returned."

Just then a carriage rolled up, and Madame Caraman and Coucou got out, followed by Fanfaro and Anselmo.

"Ah, here is Monsieur Gontram," cried Madame Caraman, joyfully, as she caught sight of the painter.

"That is what I call luck," said Fanfaro. "Monsieur Gontram, allow me to introduce myself. My name is Fanfaro. I am an honest man, and devoted to the Count of

Monte-Cristo and his son. I fear all is not right with our friends."

"Why not? What has happened?" asked Gontram.

"You shall soon find out, but first let us go inside."

With these words Fanfaro preceded the others and entered the vestibule. The footman ran to him and anxiously cried:

"Monsieur Fanfaro, the vicomte is not at home."

"I know it."

Turning to Coucou, he said:

"Can you remember when the vicomte left the house?"

"Last night."

"About what time?"

"I do not know, I was asleep."

"And I too," sobbed Madame Caraman.

"Coucou, please tell the footman to come here."

The footman came immediately.

"When did Vicomte Spero leave the house?" asked Fanfaro, turning to the man.

"I—I—do not know," stammered the footman.

"You do not know when the vicomte went out?"

"I—that is—well, the vicomte did leave the house, but he returned within an hour."

"Then he must be in the house?" they all repeated.

"I do not know. He has not left it."

"How do you know?" asked Coucou. "The vicomte might have gone out by way of the garden."

"That is not possible," declared the footman. "I locked the gate myself yesterday while the vicomte was in his study."

"We must search every nook and corner," said Gontram.

"We shall do so," said Fanfaro. "Anselmo can remain under Madame Caraman's care, while Coucou can look in the garden and yard, and we in the house."

Coucou disappeared, but soon returned, accompanied by Bobichel.

"I am glad you've come, Bobichel," exclaimed Fanfaro. "We have some fine detective work to do here, and that was always your hobby."

"What is it?" asked Bobichel.

Fanfaro told him the whole story in a few words.

In the meantime Gontram had learned from Mamma Caraman that Jane Zild had disappeared, and the thought flashed through his mind like lightning that Signor Fagiano's remark, which Carmen had overheard, related to her. He told Fanfaro about it, and they both resolved to examine Jane's room.

"There must be a third exit," said Fanfaro; "both the vicomte and Jane have disappeared without the footman's knowing anything about it. We can begin our work now, and may God grant that we find some trail."

Thereupon Fanfaro, Gontram, and Bobichel went to the room Jane had occupied. Gontram walked in advance, and soon all three stood in the beautifully furnished apartment. Bobichel crawled into every corner, and raised the heavy carpet which covered the floor, to see if there were any secret stairs. Then he got on top of Fanfaro's shoulders and knocked at the ceiling. But all was in vain. Nothing could be discovered.

Suddenly Fanfaro's eye rested on a small white spot in the blue, decorated wall. Drawing near to the spot, he saw that a small piece of white silk had been pressed in an almost imperceptible crack.

"Bobichel, your knife," cried Fanfaro, breathlessly.

"Master," said Bobichel, modestly, "there is a secret door there, and they generally have a spring attached to them."

"You are right," replied Fanfaro, "but how discover the spring?"

"I think," remarked Gontram, "that the spring is under one of the small blue buttons with which the wall is decorated. Let us search."

All three began to finger the numerous buttons, and finally Bobichel uttered a cry of triumph. He had turned a button aside and a little iron door noiselessly swung itself on its hinges.

"There is the secret way in which Jane and Spero have disappeared," cried Gontram; "Jane has, no doubt, been abducted. The piece of white satin in the crack must have belonged to the bed-cover, for Madame Caraman told me the cover had disappeared at the same time as the girl. Spero knew of this exit and probably had reasons for leaving the house secretly. Let us go the same way, and perhaps we may find out where the vicomte is."

"So be it," cried Fanfaro, "and then, in Heaven's name, forward!"

Gontram had in the meanwhile sent a note with Coucou to Carmen.

Each one of the three carried a three-armed bronze lamp, and the light they gave forth illuminated the marble steps of a staircase.

Gontram was the first to reach the top stair. At the

same moment a hollow noise was heard, and when the comrades turned around to find out the cause of it, they saw that the iron door had closed behind them. They tried in vain to open it again. It did not budge.

"We cannot return," said Fanfaro finally, "therefore forward with God's help."

CHAPTER XLII

THE TRAP

MADAME CARAMAN and Coucou had not exaggerated when they said that the vicomte's condition after Jane's disappearance was terrible. He rushed about madly, and when he could not find the young girl a deep despair took hold of him.

The young man's love for Jane was very great, and when he saw the young girl lying wounded, almost dying, in his arms the world faded from the sight of his intoxicated eyes. Either he must rescue her or go under himself. There was no third road for him.

Madame Caraman's information that Jane had disappeared paralyzed him. She must be sought for and found at any price, even though the world be torn in pieces for it.

But the world did not tear, not an atom moved on his account; and deep night settled about Spero. One night as the vicomte was sitting in the room Jane had occupied, buried in thought, he saw the drapery move slowly and a part of the wall glide slowly back.

In a moment he had sprung up and gone to the spot. A dark opening yawned before him, and as he knew not what fear was, he walked into the corridor which opened before him. Without hesitating, he walked down the marble staircase; the door closed behind him, and he found himself on strange ground.

After Spero had gone down twenty steps he found himself on level ground. He went further and further, and finally stood at the foot of a staircase which led toward the left. Without taking time to consider he ascended it and soon stood before a door—he put his hand on the knob and it opened.

A room furnished in dark red silk lay before the vicomte.

On a black marble table Spero espied an open letter. The Count of Monte-Cristo had always seen to it that his house was connected in a mysterious way with other buildings. It was only in this way that he was enabled to play the part of a *deus ex machina*—as Edmond Dantes, Count of Monte-Cristo and Lord Wilmore.

Spero had never heard of this secret passage. Like a man in a dream he strode toward the table, and seizing the note read the following:

"If the son of the Count of Monte-Cristo is not a coward, and wishes to find her whom he has lost, let him go at once to Courberode and hunt up a man named Malvernet, who lives at the so-called Path of Thorns. Here he will find out what he wants to know, and perhaps a little more."

There was no signature to the letter, and Spero cared very little for that. Suddenly his glance happened to fall on a large mirror and he gave a cry of alarm.

Was the pale man with the deep blue rings about his eyes the twenty-one-year-old son of the great count?

"One would think that the few days I have been away from my father had aged me many years," he bitterly muttered. "But no," he added, flaming up; "the enemies of the great count shall not say that his son is not a worthy scion! I will crush them if they touch a hair of Jane's head. My father did not name me Spero for nothing. So long as I breathe I can hope. I will not despair, I will conquer!"

He pulled out his two pistols and examined them, and with a soft, tender "Father, help me," he left the secret chamber.

CHAPTER XLIII

THE PATH OF THORNS

TWENTY years ago the village of Courberode looked different from what it does to-day. It consisted of a few miserable fishermen's cabins. One hundred feet from the beach a path filled with thorns led far into the country. The thorns in the course of time had become impenetrable walls, and this gave rise to the name, "The Path of Thorns."

Just behind it stood an old tumble-down house. The basement of this house consisted of a smoky room furnished with one table, two chairs and a flickering oil lamp. A man was walking up and down the low apartment.

"I wonder whether he will come," he muttered to himself.

At this moment a slight noise was heard outside. A knock came at the door.

"Who's there?" asked the man roughly.

"Does a man named Malvernet live here?" came back in reply.

"Yes. Come right in."

Spero entered, his clothes dripping wet, and blue-black hair hanging over his forehead.

"My name is Malvernet," said the other sharply; "what do you wish?"

"Do you know me?" he asked in a firm tone.

"No, I was told to come here and await a man. I was to do as he said and ask no questions. So I came and await your orders."

"Then listen to me. My father is the Count of Monte-Cristo. I am rich, very rich, and I can reward every service rendered me in a princely manner."

A mocking laugh came from the man's lips.

"What do you mean by offering me money?" he gruffly asked. "I have not asked you for payment yet, and perhaps it will not be in cash. Tell me now what you want of me."

"Robbers entered my house last night and robbed me of the dearest jewel I possess—a young girl whom I love."

"What's her name?"

"Jane! You promised to obey my orders, and I only ask you to lead me to Jane."

"And if I refuse?"

"Then I will kill you."

"Ha! ha! ha!" laughed the man, "that is well said."

"Do you refuse to obey me?"

"I did not say that. You need me, while I can get along without you. The game is therefore unequal."

"You are right, and I beg you to forgive me."

"Well then, vicomte, what do you command?"

"Then you really wish to help me?"

"Follow me," said Benedetto (for he was the man), as he opened a door.

"Anywhere," cried Spero, "if I can only find Jane again."

"I will go on in advance, and follow me closely, for the night is pitch dark and we might lose each other."

Spero nodded, and they both walked out into the pouring rain. Oh, why was the Count of Monte-Cristo far away? Why had he spared the wretch, when the sea cast him up? Why had he prevented Bertuccio from crushing the head of the poisonous reptile?

For a time the criminal and his company walked on in silence.

Suddenly it appeared to Spero as if the end of the way had been reached, and, pausing, he asked:

"Where are we?"

"On the banks of the Seine; in a few minutes we will be at the place."

"My poor Jane," murmured Spero, "how terrible it is to look for you in this deserted quarter."

"Are you afraid?" asked Benedetto mockingly.

Spero did not answer the impudent question.

"Go on," he coldly said.

Benedetto turned into a narrow path. Suddenly he stopped short and said:

"Here we are!"

Spero looked about him! In front of him rose a tall, gloomy building, and it appeared to him as if rough singing were going on within.

"Is this really the house?" asked the vicomte, unconsciously shuddering.

"Yes."

"It looks like a low den, and who guarantees me that I am not being led into a trap?"

"Vicomte of Monte-Cristo," replied Benedetto, "if I desired to murder you I could have done so long ago."

"You are right."

Just then coarse laughter and the noise of a falling body came from the inside of the house.

"Let us go into the house," cried Spero excitedly. "God knows what may be going on there."

Benedetto shoved his arm under the vicomte's and opening the door said:

"You will find more here than will please you."

They both entered a dark corridor now, the door fell back in the lock and Spero asked:

"Where are we?"

"On the spot," mockingly said Benedetto.

At the same time Spero felt the arm of his companion slip from under his, and he was alone. The room in which he was had neither windows nor doors, and gritting his teeth the young man said:

"The wretch has ensnared me in a trap."

Something extraordinary happened now. The wall before him opened, and an open space came to view. The room lighted up, and Spero saw—Jane, but, merciful God, in what company!

She formed the centre of a wild orgy; glasses rang, coarse songs and oaths were heard from the lips of a crowd of shameless men and women who surrounded Jane, and uttering a loud cry Spero buried his face in his hands.

CHAPTER XLIV

THE PASHA

AS WE have stated, Gontram had given a note to Coucou to deliver to Carmen. When the Jackal reached the palace in the Rue Rivoli he stopped in amazement. The doors were wide open and the whole front of the house swam in light.

The Zouave entered a restaurant opposite, ordéred a bottle of wine, and began a conversation with the waiter.

"What is going on to-day in the Larsagny palace?" he asked.

"Oh, the banker is giving a great ball," said the waiter.

"He is very rich, I suppose."

"Enormously so."

At this moment a soldier entered the restaurant and, approaching the waiter, asked:

"Can you not tell me, good friend, where Monsieur de Larsagny lives?"

"About a hundred feet away in that brilliantly illuminated house—you cannot miss it."

"Thanks," said the soldier. As he was about to turn away, a well-known voice cried to him:

"Well, Galoret, what do the dear Bedouins do now?"

"Hello, Coucou—where do you hail from?" cried the soldier, joyously.

"Rather tell me where you come from?"

"Ah, I have been only three days in Paris."

"What business have you in the Larsagny palace?" he asked.

"Oh, I must deliver a letter."

"So must I; from whom, if I may ask?"

"Oh, it is no secret. I have a Bedouin prince for a friend who accompanied me to Paris. About two hours ago my pasha fell down the stairs of his hotel and broke his right leg. The doctor says that it will take six weeks for the leg to be cured. As he was invited to a ball at the Larsagny palace to-night—"

"Does he know the banker?" interrupted Coucou.

"No—Mohammed Ben Omar is in Paris for the first time. As the pasha is unable to attend the ball, I have to bring his letter of excuse, and now I must really go on my way."

Coucou pretended not to hear these last words. He gazed at a group of men who sat at a side table, and whispered to Galoret:

"Look at those fools. How they stare at you. One would think they had never seen a Chasseur d'Afrique."

"Impertinent scoundrels," growled Galoret, and, turning to the gentlemen, he cried in an angry tone of voice:

"You boobies, have you looked at my uniform long enough?"

The gentlemen answered in not very polite tones. Galoret couldn't stand this. One word led to another, and finally chairs were taken up to settle the discussion.

Policemen now interfered. Galoret and two others with bloody heads were locked up, and then only did the chasseur remember his errand.

Coucou was waiting for this moment. He introduced himself to the policemen and offered to carry the letter himself. The policemen offered no opposition, Galoret thanked him, and Coucou satisfied his conscience with the maxim of Loyola, that "the end justifies the means."

"Now I can enter the Larsagny palace," he said to himself; "as the pasha they will admit me."

Coucou jumped into a carriage and told the coachman to drive to the Rue de Pelletier.

A quarter of an hour later a Bedouin clad all in white, whose brown complexion and coal-black eyes betrayed his Oriental origin, left the store of an elegant place in the Rue de Pelletier and, stepping into the coach which stood at the door, he cried to the coachman:

"Rue de Rivoli, Palais Larsagny!"

The horses started off, the carriage rolled along, and the Bedouin, in whose turban a ruby glittered, muttered to himself:

"One can get through the world with cheek!"

CHAPTER XLV

HOW CARMEN KEEPS HER WORD

IF CARMEN had not hoped to serve Gontram and his friends she would have left the Larsagny palace at once, but under existing circumstances prudence prompted her to stay and not to repulse the banker entirely; for she suspected that Larsagny held in his hand the threads of the mystery which threatened the Vicomte of Monte-Cristo. Carmen did not have much time to think, for hardly an hour after Gontram had gone, the banker appeared in the boudoir, and looking with astonishment at her, he said:

"What does this mean, Carmen? Our guests will soon be here, and you are not yet dressed."

"Our guests?" repeated Carmen, in amazement.

"Yes. Have you forgotten that the ball for which you yourself sent out invitations ten days ago, takes place to-night?"

"Really, I had forgotten all about it," stammered Carmen. "It is all the same, though; I have a headache and shall remain in my room."

"But, Carmen, what shall we do if you do not appear?"

"That is not my affair," replied Carmen, laconically.

The banker ran his hands through his hair in despair.

"Carmen, be reasonable," he implored, as he tried to take her hand.

"Don't touch me," said Carmen.

Larsagny bit his lips.

"What have I done to you?" he groaned. "Think of the shame if the ladies appear and find out that my daughter has retired to her room."

Carmen became pensive. Perhaps it might be better if she took part in the ball; she might hear something of interest to Gontram.

"Well, if you desire it, I will appear, but under one condition," she said, coldly.

"Name it."

"I demand that you shall not present me to any one as your daughter."

"But what shall I say?"

"Anything else. And now go, I must make my toilet."

"Carmen, I have one more favor to ask of you."

"Well?"

"I must leave the house about twelve o'clock for one or more hours—"

"He lies," thought Carmen to herself.

"To do this," continued Larsagny, "I must pretend some sudden sickness. You will have me brought to my room, and then—"

"Since when are the bankers and the money-brokers at night in their offices?" asked Carmen.

"But—"

"Do you mean to tell me that you have business on the Bourse at midnight?"

"Carmen, I swear to you that—"

"If you imagine that you can make me your accomplice in some crime that you are planning, you are mistaken. I will be the first one to deliver you over to the law."

Larsagny trembled, but he tried to smile, and with a hasty *au revoir* he went away.

Carmen hastily dressed herself; she didn't pay much attention to her toilet, and went down to the parlors, where a number of guests were already assembled.

. . . .

The greatest names of the empire had been announced by the lackeys.

Suddenly a murmur ran through the assembly. "Mohammed Ben Omar," the lackey had called, and all crowded about the reception-room to see the pasha.

With genuine Oriental grandeur the pasha slowly walked toward the host. Larsagny bowed deeply; the Bedouin answered the greeting by placing his right hand over his heart. That ended the conversation for the present, for Mohammed made a sign that he did not understand a word of French. Only when he saw a remarkably handsome woman he would say:

"Pretty woman."

Carmen had been distinguished in this way, and Larsagny, who felt flattered by it, tried to make the pasha comprehend that she was his daughter.

"Ah, pretty, pretty," repeated the Mussulman, and the banker, his face lighted up with joy, said:

"May I introduce her?"

Mohammed nodded.

Carmen bowed politely when the introduction was

made, and said nothing. Omar offered her his arm, and murmured as he pointed to some pictures.

"Allah il Allah. I come from the painter Gontram. Mohammed resoul il Allah."

"The pasha evidently wishes you to show him the picture-gallery," said Larsagny.

"Then come," said the young girl to the Oriental.

As soon as Omar was alone with his companion, he whispered:

"Pardon me, I have to speak to you."

"Who are you?" asked Carmen.

"A friend, a former Zouave in the service of the Count of Monte-Cristo."

"Well, what have you?"

"A note from the painter Gontram."

"Give it to me—quickly."

Coucou drew the letter from the folds of his bernouse and gave it to the young girl. It read as follows:

"Carmen, my friends are in danger; Jane Zild has been abducted and Spero has disappeared. If every sign does not deceive, the banker must know something about it. Perhaps you may be able to find out the secret.

"In great haste,

"G. S."

Carmen breathed more freely after she had read the lines.

"Well?" said the Zouave, expectantly.

"Go back to Monsieur Sabran and tell him I will move heaven and earth to find out the secret. Gontram is still in the Monte-Cristo palace, is he not?"

"Yes."

"If I have occasion to go there will I be admitted?"

"Yes."

At this moment a servant rushed into the parlor and exclaimed:

"Mademoiselle, Monsieur de Larsagny has suddenly become ill."

"I shall come soon," said Carmen, coldly, and nodding to Coucou, she went away.

In the banker's room great confusion reigned. The master of the house lay motionless, with closed eyes, on a divan. A physician who happened to be present, suggested opening a vein, and Carmen stood at the bedside, not knowing what to do.

At length she consented, and while the operation was being performed, Carmen searched all of Monsieur de Larsagny's pockets. She soon discovered a letter, and hurried with it to her room. The note read as follows:

"Our revenge is assured. Fanfaro, Gontram, and a former clown determined to discover the vic.'s whereabout, and thanks to their curiosity they have fallen into a trap in the M. C. palace. The little one is in the house in Courb., and the son of the man against whom we have sworn eternal hate will come too late.   C."

Carmen at once understood the meaning of these lines. She knew the house in Courbevoie spoken about, and throwing a long black cloak over her shoulders she left the palace by the rear door.

CHAPTER XLVI

IN COURBEVOIE

WE LEFT Spero at the moment when the walls of the room he was in opened and presented the horrible spectacle which met his eyes. In what way had the poor child got in such company? Benedetto, of course, had done this dastardly act. He had drugged her after he had abducted her from Monte-Cristo's house, and the poor girl was unable to give utterance to a cry. She saw everything that went on about her, but was unable to say a word. And Spero had to gaze at these terrible scenes; he could not keep his eyes away. He tried in vain to find a means of entering the hall. The whole scene had been arranged by Benedetto and Larsagny in a satanic spirit. Larsagny owned the house in Courbevoie, and had often presided at its bacchanalian revels. Carmen had not called him a master of immorality for nothing. While Spero was beating the iron railing in despair, the light suddenly went out and all was still. The vicomte strained his eyes to see what was going on in the hall, and not seeing anything, waited in the agony of fear for what was coming.

In about ten minutes it became light again in the hall, and now the young man saw Jane again, but this time she was alone.

Spero breathed more freely, and, beside himself, he called:

"Jane! Jane! come to me!"

At the rear of the hall a door opened, and Spero recognized in a man who crossed the threshold—Monsieur de Larsagny.

Larsagny drew near to Jane, and, sinking upon his knees, he pressed his lips to the young girl's hand. Spero breathlessly followed Larsagny's movements, and when he saw that Jane made no resistance, he became violent. With all his strength, he threw himself against the iron railing; it gave way, and with a cry Spero rushed upon Monsieur de Larsagny. In a second the banker lay on the floor. Throwing his arms about Jane, Spero cried:

"Jane, my darling, do you not know me? I am—Monte-Cristo."

"Monte-Cristo!" cried Larsagny, in terror, and with a gasp he fell back dead—a stroke of apoplexy had put an end to his life.

Spero did not know that he was the living picture of his father. Edmond Dantes had just looked like that when he was arrested at Marseilles through the intrigues of Danglars, Fernand and Villefort, and Danglars-Larsagny had thought it was Monte-Cristo who stood before him.

Jane still lay motionless in Spero's arms. The vicomte called despairingly for help, but none came.

Suddenly it occurred to him that Jane's condition was due to some narcotic, and with a cry of joy he pulled a small crystal vial from his breast pocket. It contained a liquid the Abbé Faria had taught Edmond Dantes how to make. Putting the vial to Jane's lips, he poured a few drops down her throat.

The effect was instantaneous. Jane uttered a deep sigh, and looked at the young man with returning consciousness.

"Spero!" she cried. "You here in this terrible place? Oh, go—go away; you must not stay here."

"Jane, I have come to take you with me."

"No!—oh, no! I am accursed! I must not accompany you!" sobbed the young girl.

"What nonsense, child. You have been abducted from my house and brought here against your will. Come with me; I will bring you away, or else die with you!"

"Not for any price," groaned Jane. "Go—leave this place, and let me die! I cannot live any longer—the shame kills me."

"Jane, do not speak so. Jane, my Jane, do you really refuse to accompany me?"

"God forgive me if I do wrong; I cannot leave you," she murmured, as she threw herself into the young man's arms.

But at this moment the coarse songs sounded again, and a man entered the hall. It was Benedetto!

CHAPTER XLVII

THE DEVOTED

COUCOU had not taken time to change his clothes when he presented himself to Madame Caraman on his return home, and the worthy woman uttered a cry of astonishment.

"What is the meaning of this?" she asked. "I think that we have more serious things to think of than masquerading."

"Come, do not speak before you know everything," replied the Zouave; and in a few words he told her the story of his disguise.

"Where can Monsieur Sabran be?" asked Madame Caraman.

"What!" exclaimed Coucou, "where is he then?"

"I haven't seen him, nor Fanfaro, nor Bobichel since."

"Impossible! Are they still in Jane's room?"

"Perhaps."

"I cannot understand it, and—"

A hollow noise caused Coucou to keep silent. He and Madame Caraman looked at each other in terror.

"What can that be?" asked Madame Caraman.

Before Coucou could answer the question, the noise was repeated.

"The noise comes from the right side," said Coucou,

who had been listening; "let us hurry to Gontram and Fanfaro, and call their attention to it."

Mamma Caraman nodded, and they both went to Jane's room.

It was empty!

"This is getting worse and worse," cried Coucou, anxiously. "Do you know what I think? This room has a secret exit, and through it Jane, the vicomte, and Gontram and his comrades have disappeared."

"What are you going to do?"

"Break down the house if necessary," said Coucou, beginning to trample upon the floor.

"But you are ruining the carpet!" cried Mamma Caraman.

The sound of the door-bell at this minute prevented Coucou from replying. In front of the door stood Carmen.

"Thank Heaven you have come, mademoiselle."

"You haven't found Gontram yet?"

"No."

"Monsieur Gontram and his comrades are in subterranean chambers in this house."

"Knock at the walls, Coucou," said Madame Caraman, "and then we can wait for an answer."

Coucou knocked three times with a hammer against the wall. At the end of the second knock came back in answer twenty-five.

"What does that mean?" asked Coucou, in affright.

"I know," cried Carmen; "twenty-five knocks signify the letters of the alphabet!"

"Then we must answer to show that we understand the language," said Madame Caraman. "Coucou—quick—twenty-five knocks."

The Zouave did as he was told, and the answer came back in one knock which meant "yes."

Nine further knocks followed.

"I," said Carmen.

Nineteen knocks.

"S," whispered Carmen.

Seven knocks.

"G."

Ten knocks.

"J."

Two knocks.

"B."

Twenty knocks.

"T."

Carmen now read the meaning of this:

"There is an iron door under the wall decoration."

Coucou soon found the secret door.

At the end of five minutes Fanfaro, Bobichel and Gontram were again with their friends. In a few words Carmen related what had brought her there, and showed the letter she had taken from Larsagny.

"In Courbevoie!" cried Gontram. "How shall we find Spero there?"

"I know the house," said Carmen; "it belongs to the banker, and I believe we shall find the vicomte there."

"May God grant it."

Ten minutes later they were all on the road to Courbevoie.

CHAPTER XLVIII

UNITED IN DEATH

WHEN Benedetto entered the hall he was neither Malvernet, Cavalcanti or Fagiano. He was simply Benedetto.

"Whoever you are," cried the vicomte, "I implore you to help me bring this poor child out of here."

"Vicomte," replied Benedetto, coldly, "I will not help you, and you'll not bring this woman away from here."

"I will shoot you down like a dog," said Spero, contemptuously.

With these words he pulled out a pistol and held it toward Benedetto.

"You wish to commit murder, vicomte!"

"Do not speak of murder, wretch? You robbed me of my freedom, and this poor child, whose innocence ought to be sacred to you, you—"

"The poor innocent child," interrupted the ex-convict. "You told me it was brought here against its will!"

"Scoundrel, you lie!" cried Spero, angrily.

Benedetto laughed coarsely.

"Jane Zild," he then said, drawing back a step, "tell the Vicomte of Monte-Cristo that you are worthy of him. Don't you remember who your mother was, what your mother was, and where she died?"

"Mercy," cried Jane, throwing herself at Benedetto's feet. "Mercy!"

"Jane Zild, shall I tell the vicomte who your father was?"

"My father?" stammered Jane, confused.

"Yes, your father. Do you not remember a man who took care of you after your mother died? The man was formerly a galley-slave named Anselmo. Before that he wore the dress of a priest. Jane Zild is the daughter of the convict of Toulon and the woman of Lyons."

"Miserable scoundrel," cried Spero, "you lie! If you have weapons, let us fight. Only one of us dare leave this room alive."

"Just my idea," said Benedetto, as he took two swords from under his cloak. "Choose, and now *vogue ma galere*."

"The motto is no doubt derived from your past," said Spero.

"You shall pay for that, boy," hissed Benedetto as he placed himself in position.

A hot struggle ensued, and Benedetto was finally driven against the wall.

"Wretch!" exclaimed Spero, "your life is in my hands; beg for mercy, or I shall stab you through the heart."

"I beg for mercy? Fool, you do not know what you are speaking of! I hate you—I hate your father—take my life, or, as true as I stand here, I shall take yours!"

"Then die," replied Spero, and with a quick movement he knocked Benedetto's sword out of his hand and made a lunge at him!

But the lunge did not reach Benedetto's heart, but that of the young girl! At the same moment a shot rang through the hall, and Jane and Spero sank lifeless to the floor.

How had this horrible thing happened?

At the moment Benedetto saw Spero's sword turned toward his heart, he seized the pistol the vicomte had carelessly laid aside, and fired at his opponent. Jane saw the wretch seize the pistol. She threw herself into Spero's arms to save her lover, and received the death-blow from his hand!

.   .   .   .

The moment Spero breathed his last, loud cries were heard throughout the house, and many voices called Spero's name.

Benedetto grew pale. How could he save himself? Only one way was left to him, and he hesitated to carry it out.

Hasty steps were now heard coming along the corridor. Tearing the window open, Benedetto swung himself on the sill. He looked into the dark waters of the Seine, and firmly muttered: "Forward! Down there is hope; here, death!"

Fanfaro, Gontram, Carmen, Bobichel and Coucou now hurried into the hall. Benedetto looked at them with flaming eye, and mockingly cried:

"You are too late! I have killed Monte-Cristo's son!"

The next minute he had disappeared, and, while the waves rushed over him, Fanfaro and Gontram rushed toward Spero's body, and Fanfaro sobbingly exclaimed:

"Too late! Too late! Oh, poor, poor father!"

CHAPTER XLIX

THE SPECTRE

JUST as Benedetto had uttered the mocking words to the friends of Spero, the form of a man appeared in the doorway. He threw one horror-stricken look at the bodies, a second one at the ex-convict, swung himself also on the window-sill, and plunged in after Benedetto. It was Anselmo.

The water was ice-cold, but neither of them paid any attention to it. Benedetto only thought of saving himself, and Anselmo of his revenge. Benedetto did not know he was being pursued. Who would risk his own life to follow him? No, it was madness to imagine so. But now he heard some one swimming behind him. If he could reach the bushes of Nemilly he would be safe. He did not dare turn about—he felt frightened and his teeth chattered.

At length the long-looked-for bank was seen—a few more strokes and he would be saved. Now—now he pressed upon the sand. Dripping, trembling with cold, he swung himself upon dry land and looked back at the dark waters. He could see nothing: his pursuer had evidently given up the project.

Anselmo had really lost courage. He had the greatest

difficulty to keep himself afloat. Suddenly his almost paralyzed hand grasped a plank; he clambered on it, and reached the shore with its aid. He landed about one hundred feet away from Benedetto. Now he saw the hated wretch. But was it a vision, a play of his excited fancy? It seemed to him as if Benedetto were hurrying toward the water again! Behind him moved a white shadow; it seemed to be pursuing the scoundrel, and they were both flying toward the shore.

Benedetto did not turn around. Did he fear to see the white form? Both came toward Anselmo. Benedetto looked neither to the right nor to the left. Now his foot touched the water. Then came a soft, trembling voice on the still night air:

"Benedetto—my son! Benedetto—wait for me!"

With a cry of terror, Benedetto turned around. There stood his mother whom he had murdered. She pressed her hand to the breast her son's steel had penetrated. Now she stretched out her long, bony fingers toward him—she threw her lean arm around his neck, and he could not cry out. Slowly they both walked toward the river. They set foot on the dark space—they sank deeper and deeper, and now—now the waves rushed over them! Outraged nature was done penance to. The mother, whom Benedetto had stabbed in the breast, had drawn her son with her into a watery grave.

. . . .

The next morning fishermen found the body of an unknown man in the bushes—it was Anselmo. He had breathed his last as the sun just began to rise—his last word was:

"Jane!"

CHAPTER L

DEEP silence reigned in the Monte-Cristo palace—
the silence of death. Everything was draped in
mourning, and on a catafalque rested the bodies
of Spero and Jane.

They were all dead—Danglars, Villefort, Mondego,
Caderousse and Benedetto—but Monte-Cristo was alive
to close the eyes of his dearly beloved son.

Mockery of fate! The two men who watched the
corpses waited with anxiety for the moment when the
Count of Monte-Cristo should enter.

Before the vision of the older man rose the atrocious
scenes at Uargla. He saw Spero, a bold, brave boy,
scaling the towers—he heard his firm words, "Papa, let
us die"—and felt the soft, childish arms wind about his
neck. This was Fanfaro.

The other watcher was Gontram. Coucou, Bobichel
and Madame Caraman were paralyzed with grief. The
Zouave would willingly have died a thousand deaths if
he only could have saved the life of his young master.

The third day dawned, and Gontram and Fanfaro
looked anxiously at each other. To-day the count must
come.

Toward evening the door was suddenly opened.

Slowly, with a heavy tread, a tall man approached the catafalque, and, sinking on his knees beside it, hid his pale face in the folds of the burial cloth. The count looked neither to the right nor to the left; he saw only his son. Not a sound issued from his troubled breast; but with a cold shiver Fanfaro and Gontram noticed that the count's black hair was slowly becoming snow-white, and with profound pity the friends gazed upon the grief-stricken man, who had become old in an hour.

Monte-Cristo now bent over his son and clasped the dear corpse in his powerful arms. He went slowly and noiselessly to the door. Fanfaro and Gontram stood as if in a daze; and not until the door had closed behind the count did they recover their self-possession. They hurried after him, they tried to follow his track; but it was useless. The count had disappeared together with his son's body.

EPILOGUE

THE ABBE DANTES

FIFTY years ago a solitary man stood on a lonely rock.

The night was horrible! The storm drove the snow and rain into the face of the solitary man ,and whipped the black hair around his temples; but he paid no attention to this—he dug into the hard, rocky soil with pickaxe and spade.

Suddenly he uttered an ejaculation of joy. The brittle rock had revealed its secret to him. Unexpected treasures, incalculable fortunes, lay before his eager gaze.

Then the man stood erect; he glanced wildly around him toward all the four quarters of the globe, and cried aloud:

"All you, who have kept me imprisoned for fourteen long years in a subterranean vault into which neither sun nor moon could penetrate, who would have condemned my body to eternal decline, and enshrouded my mind with the night of insanity—you whose names I do not yet know, beware! I swear to be revenged—revenged! Edmond Dantes has risen from his grave, he has risen to chastise his torturers, and as sure as there is a God in heaven you shall learn to know me."

About whom was this solitary man speaking? He did not yet know, but he was soon to discover it.

Fourteen years before, Edmond Dantes, the young sailor, was joyously returning to the harbor of Marseilles on board the Pharaon, belonging to Monsieur Morrel. His captain had died on the trip and he was promised the vacant place. As soon as he had landed he hastened to his bride, the Catalan Mercedes, to announce to her that he could now lead her to the altar.

Then he was suddenly arrested. He was accused of transmitting letters to the Emperor Napoleon, then a prisoner on the Island of Elba.

He did not deny the fact. It was his captain's dying wish. He was ignorant of the contents of the missive, and of the one he had in his possession given him by the captive emperor to deliver to a Monsieur Noirtier in Paris.

Monsieur Noirtier's full name was Noirtier de Villefort, and his son Monsieur de Villefort was the deputy procureur du roi to whom Edmond Dantes handed the letter to prove his innocence.

The son suppressed the letter, in order not to be compromised by the acts of his father, and had the young man torn from the arms of his betrothed and incarcerated in the subterranean dungeon of the Chateau d'If.

Here he remained fourteen long years, his only companion the Abbé Faria, who was deemed to be insane. The abbé on his deathbed intrusted to him the secret that an enormous fortune was concealed in a grotto on the island of Monte-Cristo in the Mediterranean Sea. Edmond Dantes escaped from his dungeon and discovered the buried treasure.

He then left the island to accomplish the revenge he had sworn.

He found that his father had died of starvation and that Mercedes had married another. Who was this other one?

Fernand Mondego, now the Count de Morcerf, had become the husband of the beautiful Catalan. Formerly a simple fisherman, he had risen to become a member of the French Chamber of Deputies.

The second in whose way Edmond Dantes had stood was a man named Danglars. An officer on board the Pharaon, he had hoped to obtain the position of captain. Now he had become one of the principal bankers of the capital.

The third, Caderousse, an envious tailor, had allowed himself to be made a tool of to bring to the notice of the authorities the denunciation against the young sailor which Danglars had dictated and Mondego written down.

His worst enemy was Villefort, who had now become the procureur du roi at Paris.

Was Edmond Dantes to be blamed if he, after he had discovered all this, took the law in his own hands and began to execute his vengeance?

Danglars was his first victim. He ruined him and made him suffer the pangs of hunger which Edmond's father had suffered.

Fernand Mondego, Count de Morcerf, was the second. At first Dantes, who now called himself the Count of Monte-Cristo, wanted to kill Fernand's son, Albert de Morcerf, but he spared the young man for Mercedes' sake.

He looked up Mondego's past history. The latter had

risen to power through crime and treachery. He had betrayed Ali Tebelen, Pasha of Yanina, and sold the latter's wife Vassiliki and daughter Haydee into slavery. Haydee herself denounced De Morcerf's infamy in the Chamber of Deputies. De Morcerf, forever dishonored, and knowing the blow came from Monte-Cristo, sought to pick a quarrel with the latter. But the count, glancing him full in the face, said:

"Look at me well, Fernand, and you will understand it all. I am Edmond Dantes."

Then De Morcerf fled, and an hour afterward blew out his brains.

De Villefort's turn was next. Monte-Cristo discovered that he had buried alive a child of Madame Danglars and himself. Bertuccio the Corsican had saved the child and reared it to manhood. The boy had become the bandit Benedetto.

Monte-Cristo found him in the galleys at Toulon. He aided in his escape, and Benedetto assassinated Caderousse. Tried for this murder, Benedetto found himself confronted with his father, the procureur du roi. He boldly announced his relationship, and de Villefort fled from the courtroom only to find on reaching home that his wife had poisoned herself and her son. In that moment of agony Monte-Cristo appeared before him and told him that he was Edmond Dantes. The blow struck home. De Villefort went mad.

His work of vengeance was now accomplished. Monte-Cristo was rich and all-powerful. He married Haydee, and they had a son, Spero. Now, alas! Haydee was dead! Spero was dead!

It was ten years since Monte-Cristo, on that fearful night, bore off the corpse of his only son.

Again he stood alone on the rock on the island of Monte-Cristo. He had lived on this rock for ten years. He saw no one, heard no one, except when occasionally men came ashore for water. Then he concealed himself, watching them and hearing their gay laughter.

But the rumor that the island was haunted spread around, and the superstitious Italians claimed that it was inhabited by a spirit whom they called the Abbé of Monte-Cristo.

All these years Monte-Cristo had lived on herbs and roots. He had sworn never to touch money again while he lived.

One night Monte-Cristo entered the subterranean cave where the marble sarcophagus of his son was:

"Spero," he earnestly said, "is it time?"

A long silence ensued. Then—was it a reality?— Spero's lips appeared to move and utter the word: "Come."

"I thought so," muttered the Count. "I shall come, my child, as soon as my affairs are settled."

He took a package from his pocket, and unfolding it read it aloud:

"MY LAST WILL AND TESTAMENT

"The person who signed this paper, and who is about to die, has been more powerful than the greatest ruler on earth. He has loved and hated strongly. All is forgotten, all is dead to him except the souvenir of the son who was dear to him. This man possessed millions, but dies of hunger. He desired to domineer over every one, made a judge of himself and rewarded the just and punished the guilty. He has no heir, but he thinks it would be wrong for him to destroy the wealth he possesses. It is in existence, though hid away. He bequeaths it to Providence. It will bear this paper together with these mysterious signs.

"Will the money be found?

"Whoever reads this paper will do a wise act if he annihilates it. May he who finds this paper listen and heed to the words of a dying man.

"THE ABBE DANTES."

"February 25th, 1865."

Below this signature was a curious design. Monte-Cristo examined it.

"Ah, Faria!" he exclaimed, "may your money fall into better hands than mine!"

He felt singularly feeble and laid his hand on his heart. He entered the tomb of Spero and reclined beside him. His arms were crossed on his breast. His eyes shut. He was dead.

.   .   .   .

All those who ever knew him never speak of him or hear his name uttered without being deeply affected. One thing has remained a secret for them up to this day. Where did Edmond Dantes, Count of Monte-Cristo, perish?

THE END